Dorothea Sarah F.A. Phillips

Some South African Recollections

Dorothea Sarah F.A. Phillips

Some South African Recollections

ISBN/EAN: 9783744752008

Printed in Europe, USA, Canada, Australia, Japan

Cover: Foto ©Andreas Hilbeck / pixelio.de

More available books at **www.hansebooks.com**

Some South African
Recollections

A Transvaal. "Spruit."

Some South African Recollections

BY

MRS. LIONEL PHILLIPS

With 36 Illustrations

SECOND IMPRESSION

LONGMANS, GREEN, AND CO.
39 PATERNOSTER ROW, LONDON
NEW YORK AND BOMBAY
1899

I DEDICATE

PREFACE

THESE recollections of a page in South African history have been written as a record for my children of the part played by their father in the Reform movement in the Transvaal, as they were at the time too young to understand or appreciate all he did and suffered for the good cause. I have endeavoured to explain the origin of that movement, and why, for the moment, it failed. I venture to publish what I have written, as I am led to believe there are many people interested in the subject, but not sufficiently informed as to the true course of events, who would be glad to read the testimony of a South African.

FLORENCE PHILLIPS.

LONDON, *October* 1899.

LIST OF ILLUSTRATIONS

(Reproduced from Photographs by permission of Messrs. G. W. Wilson, *Aberdeen ;* Goch, Barnett, *Johannesburg, and others.)*

SOUTH AFRICAN
RECOLLECTIONS

CHAPTER I

In December 1895 I was with my children at Brighton,
and had been very ill for five months. It was then
arranged that I should go to Florence for a thorough
change instead of returning to Johannesburg as I had
intended, this alteration of plan being due to the fact
that my husband Lionel, and the members of his firm
in England, had informed me that my return was useless,
as he himself intended coming to England at the end
of January. When my arrangements were made and
I was simply waiting until the holidays were over, I
saw a telegram in the *Times* of 27th December which
completely altered my ideas as to visiting Italy. I
telegraphed to Lionel, asking him to let me know the
exact state of affairs at Johannesburg, and received from
him the reply that it was impossible for him to define
them until after the 6th January, but that I was not to
be anxious, as there was no danger of any kind. Nevertheless as I felt that grave events were impending, and

A

that my place was with him, I wrote to Mr. Wernher and asked him to take my passage by the steamer leaving for Cape Town on 11th January. He replied that he thought I was unnecessarily anxious, but that my husband would at any rate regard me in the light of a heroine, and advised me to take a costume *de vivandière*, as if it did not come in for the battle-field, it might for the ball-room. In spite of that, my passage was taken for the 11th, and we prepared for departure.

I was only acting on my own fears, for it was quite possible that nothing at all serious would take place, and was actuated by my own knowledge and by what I saw in the papers, viz., that trouble had been brewing for a long time, that after years of misgovernment gradually becoming more intolerable, certain men in Johannesburg had at last determined to give voice to their grievances, and intended publicly to demand redress from the Transvaal Government. The National Union there had convened a public meeting for 6th January, and had warned the Government that if on this occasion they were refused what for the last time they demanded in a constitutional manner, they would have to resort to force. Knowing the temper of the Boers, and knowing also that for the first time in its history many members of the Uitlander community were determined to stand together and risk everything to get justice, I felt very nervous as to the result.

I have mentioned my long illness at Brighton, and must now explain that I found myself without the necessary clothes. I debated with my maid as to where I could get the desired articles most quickly, and decided that in Paris I should find what I wanted.

We started *via* Dieppe (at night to save time) on New Year's Eve, she bewailing my recklessness in daring to travel during the first hours of the New Year, prophesying in dismal tones that we should travel much that year. And she proved right. I arrived in Paris more dead than alive, feeling very ill and disinclined for the affairs of life (not to mention dressmakers), and was still in bed when my sister-in-law came into my room waving a French newspaper and exclaiming—

" Have you seen the news ? Jameson has crossed the Transvaal border, fought the Boers, and surrendered."

"Jameson ? I don't know what you are talking of. What has Jameson to do with the Transvaal ? Nonsense."

" Well, I only tell you what I see in the papers."

Then my horrified senses took in the awful fiasco that had occurred, and I fell back in bed with a pain in my back which for many a weary month since then my doctor has known by the name of the "Jameson pain." I realised the horror of the situation, which was for the moment much increased in my case in that the cable service was out of order, and neither I nor any one I knew was able to get any news from Johannesburg. I sent many cables to Lionel and to Mr. Beit in Cape Town, begging for news, but most of these, as I after-

wards heard, were never received. For ten mortal days
we heard nothing. The most awful rumours filled the
air, and I pictured every horror—Lionel killed, our
house in flames ; in fact, everything that imagination
could conjure up. To make matters worse, and complete my perplexity and misery, I received a telegram
from Mr. Wernher, telling me that Mr. Dormer asserted
positively in London that Lionel had gone to Cape
Town. As soon as possible I returned to Brighton to
finish my preparations for departure. The wildest
assertions were printed in the newspapers at this time
—that Jameson not only had crossed the frontier to
aid Johannesburg, but that he had been basely left
in the lurch by the men of that town, which was
called "Judasberg," among other names ; Jameson and
his friends, Sir John Willoughby, the Whites, and
others, being extolled as heroes, and every imaginable
virtue was attributed to them. In fact, the English
public lost all reasoning power at this juncture, as all
publics are apt to do at critical moments, and knew no
moderation in its judgments of either side. The simple
expedient of waiting until they were sure of the facts
never occurred to the great mass, and blindly believing a few partial telegrams from Pretoria and Cape
Town, they fell down and worshipped Dr. Jameson
and his partners in military glory ; they did not
even wish to know that there might be another side
to the question. Enormous excitement was caused
by the telegram sent to President Kruger by His

Imperial Majesty the German Emperor, which ran as follows :—

"I express to you my sincere congratulations that without appealing to the help of friendly Powers you and your people have succeeded in repelling with your own forces the armed bands which had broken into your country, and in maintaining the independence of your country against foreign oppression."

But the climax was reached when the English Government ordered out the Flying Squadron. Then London literally went mad. People only talked and thought of one thing, and I have been told that such excitement had not prevailed since the days of the Crimean war—people rushing out bareheaded into the street at all hours of the night, eager to read any scrap of news that had come to hand. "'Tis an ill wind that blows nobody good," and surely the newspaper people must have been thankful for such a windfall.

Now, to make matters clear to the reader, I must go back a few years to explain how this state of affairs came about—how a sub-continent was plunged in misery; how an almost unknown country like the Transvaal could so suddenly spring into such prominence; how it was possible that by the rash and treacherous action of a few individuals a carefully-considered plan was wrecked, and how so many lives were lost or ruined.

CHAPTER II

WHEN the amalgamation of the diamond mines took place in 1889, we were living in Kimberley, and Lionel in consequence found himself without an occupation. He was very much in doubt as to what he should do, and hesitated between going up to Mashonaland, regarding which a Royal Charter had been recently granted, in connection with Mr. Rhodes, or to the newly-discovered gold-mines of the Witwatersrand, where Messrs. H. Eckstein & Co. had offered him a post. As the former course would have necessitated my return to the Colony or England with the children, few white women having yet ventured into that unsettled country, Lionel chose the other alternative; and accordingly in September 1889, as there was no railway, we started for Johannesburg by special coach from Kimberley. We took all servants with us, as the place being quite in its infancy, house-keeping was more difficult and the amenities of life scarcer than in most parts of South Africa. Coaching in South Africa is not the easy and pleasant pastime that it is in England. The very mention of a coach journey recalls the memory of much fatigue brought on by cramped positions, jolting roads, and the perpetual

A SOUTH AFRICAN COACH.

knowledge of over-tired, jaded horses or mules being thrashed and yelled at to keep them to their work. Ordinarily a passenger coach accommodated twelve people inside, and besides the driver and his assistant with a long whip, six or seven outside, in addition to luggage and the mail-bags. The more luxurious way of travel—that of hiring an entire coach—was too expensive to be indulged in by most people. Ten horses or mules is the number generally used. The vehicle itself is by no means uncomfortable, but the leather springs give a peculiar rocking motion that makes some people feel very ill, especially when one adds to its charms an early morning start at three o'clock, with all the curtains down to keep out the clouds of dust, and every man smoking!

Whole histories could be written by those who have travelled much by coach. Capsizes were numerous, sometimes in the middle of a swollen river, and lives were occasionally lost. A not uncommon and exciting experience was when the coach arrived at a river too swollen to be crossed, and the unhappy passengers had to be hoisted across in a box. I have often sailed above the Modder River in that inhuman fashion. A rope would be stretched across, and a small packing-case hung thereto, which was worked by pulleys. It is a very curious feeling to dangle a hundred and fifty feet up in the air, with a roaring torrent beneath, and the knowledge that if the rope broke one would not be left to tell the tale. On one occasion, when soaring thus, the pulley would not work, and for a long time I remained suspended in mid-air. But, as it chanced, it was a broiling day, and the cool breeze up the river proved so delightful that I did not mind the delay. Once I saw an English lady who was so terrified at this mode of transit that she fainted, and in this state had to be tied into the box.

Talking of coach journeys also brings to my mind that curious phenomenon, the mirage, which one sees so often in the boundless plains of the Free State and the Karoo on hot days. Going along wearily and painfully, with nothing to relieve the eye only the horizon on a vast unbroken plain, one would suddenly see a beautiful lake surrounded by trees, and so vivid would the scene be that, in spite of past experiences, only when the spot was reached could one realise that it was but a mirage. Even cattle are deceived by it, and I have seen them run towards it after a long and thirsty march as if possessed, only to meet with bitter disappointment.

But though one remembers the unpleasant side of these journeys, there is also a phase that leaves ineffaceable memories, and that is the sunrises. To see the whole limitless plain bathed in a golden glory, changing to every shade of scarlet, and to feel the peculiar exhilaration of the early morning air, often made up for too little sleep, and I think that only on the veld is one fully conscious of the peculiar sensation of being absolutely alone with Nature. Nowhere have I ever realised to the same degree the vastness,

ORANGE RIVER AT NORVAL'S POST.

the stillness that is almost frightening, as in South Africa. And this peculiar feeling is most vivid in the autumn, when nature is more still than at other times. "Veld fever" is a malady, a longing indescribable, which comes over many South Africans who have lived much on the veld, and about the month of April many people feel it in full force. I suppose it is the same kind of home-sickness that the Swiss feel for their mountains—"Heimweh."

When I was a child the principal means of locomotion were the Cape cart and the ox-waggon. Naturally a whole family could not go by the former, so the more tedious way was adopted. The coaches of course only followed fixed routes. These long journeys have their charm. Sometimes for days together we would not "outspan" near a house, and had to sleep either in the waggon or under it. On a bright starlit night in that climate, it is no punishment to wrap oneself in a kaross and sleep in the open. Even the melancholy cry of the jackal is not unpleasant, if not too near. The thunderstorms, however, are often very dangerous and terrifying, and many people never get over their nervous terror of the lightning and thunder, though a grander sight it is impossible to see—the whole heavens a mass of living flame, the darkness only relieved by the blue forked flashes! Still, I think most people prefer to be under more secure shelter than a waggon when an African thunderstorm bursts. Torrents of rain, accompanied by heavy gusts of wind, sweep the parched earth, and in the twinkling of an eye every little furrow becomes a miniature river.   I have known a flash of lightning to kill a whole team of oxen, the current being doubtless conveyed by the "trek" chain; and the thunder succeeds it instantaneously, crackling at first like pieces of stone in a fire, or the report of numberless muskets, and finishing with a terrific crash that seems to shake the very earth.   It is not at all unusual during such storms for hail suddenly to fall, many of the stones equalling pigeons' eggs in size, which causes the greatest havoc amongst fruit-trees and cultivated lands, and kills many sheep.

With constant relays of horses and mules, we made the journey very pleasantly in four days to Johannesburg, and settled down in the "mansion," as the newspapers called the house that Mr. Hermann Eckstein had built for himself.   He being in Europe, we succeeded to the mansion—a bungalow built of corrugated iron, containing four rooms, a verandah round three sides, and a kitchen.   We were delighted with the place. Coming from arid Kimberley, where everything was literally dried up and there was no rest for the eye, the fact that there was a little green grass on the side of the ridge facing our house, and that in the small garden surrounded by a reed fence, roses and carnations flourished, gave us infinite pleasure.   Kimberley lies in a desert where in summer the glare is intense, and the hot wind soon shrivels up everything.

In spite of the discomforts, those were the happy

JOHANNESBURG IN 1889.

days of Johannesburg, for most of the people who first established themselves there knew each other, and, the place being very primitive, they were mutually dependent; hence the opportunity for little acts of kindness which formed bonds of friendship. But everything was indeed very uncomfortable. There were not enough hotels, and as newcomers were daily rushing in, many and funny were their experiences. To sleep under a billiard-table while the game was still going on was a very common occurrence, and some friends of ours who came up there told me they were obliged to pass the night of their arrival in an unfinished house, with damp walls and no roof.

Water was very scarce, and, when the rains were at all delayed, regular famines often occurred. A lady friend of ours staying at one of the hotels saw a tin bath half-full of water standing outside her door, and thinking that it was intended for her use, took possession of it. When the angry host discovered what she had done, greatly to her dismay she learned that it was the only water in the hotel, and was meant for cooking; he added, "It would not have mattered so much, only you have used soap!" Many times since have people been reduced to washing in soda-water, but in those early days that commodity was often unobtainable.

Just across the road in front of our house was a deep cutting, which we found had been made for a railway, and completely spoilt the look of the town.

But the railway was not mentioned except with bated breath, as this line was called a *tram-line*, and the trains which ran on it trams. The reason for this was that President Kruger was determined to have no train into the country until the line from Delagoa Bay to Pretoria (opened in 1895) was finished. By that means neither the Cape Colony nor Natal would reap the benefit of the Customs duties. The President wished to force importers to bring in goods by the longer sea route *via* Delagoa Bay, which is in Portuguese territory. The line opposite our house ran between Johannesburg and Brakpan, about fourteen miles distant, and was used for bringing coal from the latter place. Later on it was extended to Krugersdorp and the Springs, a distance of about forty miles, and was on a line with what every one was praying for, a continuation of the railway from the Cape Colony. The need of a railway was terribly felt, as the sudden rush of hundreds of newcomers to a hitherto almost uninhabited country made life very uncomfortable for every one, and the necessaries of life were dreadfully scarce.

Although a most fertile country, market produce was obtainable only in very small quantities, for the few Boers living in the neighbourhood were too deeply sunk in laziness and ignorance to realise that a fortune lay under their hands if only they chose to cultivate some of the land they possessed in great tracts. Those in immediate proximity to the gold reefs found a much quicker way of making a fortune,

WITPOORTJE, NEAR KRUGERSDORP.

namely, by selling parts of their farms for large sums
—large to them, as they had hitherto lived in abject
poverty—and as a Boer has quite as keen a sense of the
value of money as a Scotchman is said to have, it is
quite certain that they obtained full value for their
lands. They very rarely saw any money at all, as most
of their transactions were done by barter.

The Boers in out of the way places usually do their
shopping at "Nachtmaal" (the Sacrament of the Lord's
Supper), which takes place every three months. It is
quite an event in their lonely lives. They come in from
the surrounding country in their ox-waggons, bringing
their entire families. The richer men have perhaps a
small town house which they keep for these visits, but
the majority draw up their waggons together on the
market-square or on the outside of the town. They
utilise this occasion for their marriages and baptisms
also, and these are almost the only social events of the
year. *A propos* of shopping, they generally go to one
of the large Boer stores in the town or village where
they can satisfy all their requirements, and run up long
accounts lasting over some years. They are not nice
in their perceptions of honesty. I remember a store-
keeper telling me that at Nachtmaal he always had
a large extra staff simply to watch what the customers
pocketed, the items being added to the account, without
remarks being made on either side. He also told me
that a store-keeper of his acquaintance had lost his
whole Boer connection for ever because he was not

so wise in his generation, but prosecuted one of these pilferers.

I remember going occasionally in those early days to a farm a few miles out of Johannesburg, on the Riet River, the house and garden most beautifully situated in a niche among the hills. Lionel's firm had bought some of the farmer's ground lying on the river. This homestead was very typical of the dwellings of the more ignorant class of Boer, who form the majority of the inhabitants of the Transvaal. The house consisted of the *voorkamer* or hall, from which the kitchen and bed-rooms, few in number, led. The walls were white-washed, and the floors smeared with liquid cow-dung. The furniture consisted of a large table in the middle of the room, and rude benches and chairs, with the seats made of *riem* (hide) instead of cane, ranged round the walls. The family comprised the farmer and his wife, several married sons and daughters and their numerous progeny, all in the most hopeless state of dirt and sto-lidity. On entering the visitor would shake hands with every one in turn down to the smallest child, and amidst a chilling silence and solemnity, ask them their news, which would be given in the fewest possible words. These interviews are usually of a terrifying character, and either entirely subdue one or produce a wild de-sire to laugh, which if indulged would be fatal, as one would never be forgiven. The Boers, living as they do such solitary lives, have a morbid fear of ridicule, and as those of this particular class speak no English, they are

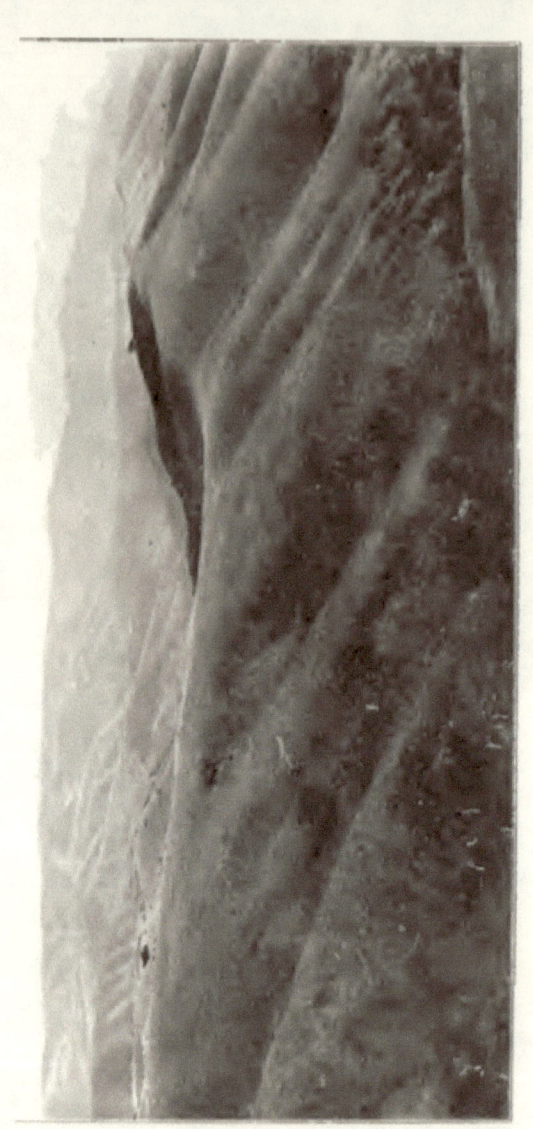

THE "LOW VELD" IN TRANSVAAL.

very suspicious of any one talking that language, and are prone to think they are being criticised.

The people whom I have in mind told me that they had come to the Transvaal in the great "trek" forty years before, that they had settled there, and dug the garden with spades until only the handles were left. The whole family had to dress in the skins of wild animals shot by the men, as in those days no shops existed within hundreds of miles, and even the wandering "Smouse" had not penetrated so far. Needless to say, having once planted the garden, made the wall of rough stones without mortar round it, built the house of unburnt brick, and made the kraal (also of stones), there was nothing more to be done for the rest of their lives except to sit smoking the pipe of peace and drinking bad coffee. Their fathers had done the same: why should they try to improve on their methods? And this in a land blessed by nature with a magnificent climate, fertile soil, and almost every natural advantage, which even without its extraordinary mineral wealth is one of the finest countries on earth.

To turn from this prospect to the many countries over-populated with men and women eager to work, but with no scope whatever, naturally gives rise to the question: Is it right or proper that a very small section of people should take possession of such a land and in their selfish conservatism rigorously exclude, the toiling crowd? The Boer's ideal of never seeing his neighbour's smoke is an Arcadian one, but in the natural order of things impossible of realisation. The contemplation of this handful of people, with their stolidity and laziness, trying to stem the inrushing tide of civilisation is pathetic as it is hopeless.

When one hears of people in England and elsewhere talking of the way in which the newcomers dispossessed the farmers of their land, and knows the reality of their sordid selfish existence, which, making no advance in thought of any kind, of necessity becomes retrograde, one wishes they could be transported for a few days to one of these many filthy hovels to see for themselves.

I wish it to be particularly understood that the Boers received substantial sums from the newcomers for everything they sold to them, and the assertion, often made abroad, that it was all very fine, but the strangers had gone there, deceived the innocent Boers, and taken their land from them for almost nothing, is emphatically untrue.

The older generation of Boers, those who came to the Transvaal in the great " trek " of 1835, are of much sterner stuff than those of to-day, and very interesting as a class that is fast dying out. The hard life they led, the struggles for existence, the constant warring with nature and wild animals and Kaffirs, brought out their many sterling good qualities—courage, faith in God, and marvellous endurance. But having once gained their object, which was to found a home away from all outside influences, these old *voortrekkers* relapsed into their lazy habits, and their descendants, not having the same incentives, lack many of their fine qualities. Doubtless these are latent, and circumstances might develop them, but the ordinary Transvaal Boer of to-day is not an attractive personality.

CHAPTER III

VERY soon after our arrival in Johannesburg occurred "the Famine," to which unpleasant event we owe the railway. The winter months in that part of the world are absolutely dry; no rain falls from the beginning of June until some time in October, and the veld consequently does not support many cattle. As everything, from the necessities of daily life, like flour to make bread, down to machinery, had to be brought to Johannesburg by ox-waggon, the rains were a very important consideration. That year they were unusually late, and as the daily-increasing population put an unusual strain on the transport drivers, the most ordinary necessaries were at a premium. Candles were quite unobtainable, and we burnt one lamp for fear it should soon be impossible to buy paraffin. I remember going to every shop in the place for white cotton in vain. Sugar rose to 4s. 6d. per pound. Every one thought they would prepare for the worst, and bought something in case of emergencies. I paid £5 for a bag of meal, the ordinary price being 25s. One lady in Cape Town sent her son by post a packet of sandwiches, saying she would do so every day while the famine lasted, not remembering that after nearly a week's journey they might not be

A BOER "OUTSPAN."

palatable even to a starving man. Fortunately, this state of things did not last long, as a bountiful Providence sent us rain, and very soon the much-needed provisions were to be had in plenty. But it was a lesson to be remembered, and people became more determined than ever to dissuade the President from his decision against the continuation of the railway, both from the Colony and the Natal border. Consequently, he listened to the petitions from all portions of the community, and condescended to come to Johannesburg to hear the demands of the people, he being on tour at the time.

Paul Kruger is so well known from the many portraits and caricatures that have appeared in recent years, as well as descriptions of him, that one from me seems superfluous. His clumsy features and small cunning eyes, set high in his face, with great puffy rings beneath them, his lank straight locks, worn longer than is usual, the fringe of beard framing his face, even his greasy frock coat and antiquated tall hat have been portrayed times without number. He is a man of quite 75 years of age now, and his big massive frame is much bent, but in his youth he possessed enormous strength, and many extraordinary feats are told of him. Once seen he is not easily forgotten. He has a certain natural dignity of bearing, and I think his character is clearly to be read on his face—strength of will and cunning, with the dulness of expression one sees in peasants' faces. "Manners none, and customs beastly" might have been a life-like description of Kruger. The habit of constantly expectorating, which so many Boers have, he has never lost. He is quite ignorant of conversation, in the ordinary acceptation of the word ; he is an auto- crat in all his ways, and has a habit of almost throwing short jerky sentences at you, generally allegorical in form, or partaking largely of Scriptural quotations—or misquotations quite as often. Like most of the Boers, the Bible is his only literature—that book he certainly studies a good deal, and his religion is a very large part of his being, but somehow he misses the true spirit of Christianity in that he leaves out the rudimentary qualities of Charity and Truth. As most of these people learn very imperfectly, they naturally do not always master the sense of what they read, but they nevertheless love to read aloud in sonorous and long drawn-out tones the parts of the Old Testament—the Kings and Chronicles for example—and dwell on the names of the old prophets and kings, pronouncing them in a way that is enough to make those hapless ones turn in their graves! The Transvaal Boers are fully persuaded that they are the chosen people of God, that their country is the Promised Land, and are constantly finding points of resemblance between themselves and the Israelites of old.

The Dopper persuasion, of which Kruger is a member, is not that to which the great mass of the Dutch population subscribes, but more resembles the Quakers, and to that sect as a rule only the very poor and ignorant class of Boer belongs. The Doppers are much more primitive in their way of life, and it is no uncommon thing for all the members of a family, representing three generations, to sleep in one room, and their uncleanness of body is only equalled by their dull immorality.

Thousands of people assembled at the Wanderers' Hall, and the President was to address them from the platform. I, among many others, was there, and the ludicrous affair is well graven on my memory. As it has since become historical, and much capital has been made of it, and as it is typical of all President Kruger's actions and his attitude to the people of Johannesburg, I relate it. I happened to have a seat just behind him. He advanced to the platform, surrounded by some officials and all the prominent men of the town. Just as he was beginning to speak in his ponderous manner, some youths in the crowd below began to sing " Rule Britannia." He glared stolidly into space for a moment, then roared out, as if speaking to a naughty child, " Blij stil." (Be quiet !) A burst of laughter was the natural response, as the ordinary untutored mind is not accustomed to the paternal methods he employs with his own people. Without a single word he turned his back, walked off, and all the protestations of the serious part of his audience were unavailing. He drove off to the Landdrost's house in Government Square, not having been five minutes in face of the thousands who were anxiously awaiting his decision on a vital question, thus ending one of the most childish exhibitions ever vouch-safed to a suffering community. That night the Trans-vaal flag flying over the Landdrost's house was pulled down, and two wretched men were caught, put into prison, and finally released six months after without ever having been tried. People said that they were not the offenders, which is quite possible, the town not being lighted. Certainly the police, usually conspicuous by their absence, were quite capable of anything, and even in those early days were notorious for their want of common honesty. However, this incident, always spoken of as "The Flag Incident," has been used by President Kruger as one of the main reasons for refusing the franchise to the Uitlanders, and he has given it over and over again. To those who were there at the time, and who saw the insignificance of the whole affair, it shed a strong light on his real character and his feelings towards the place, and everything he has done since has been equally unreasoning and blindly antago-nistic towards a people to whom his country owes its prosperity, and from whom he has exacted an enormous and ever-increasing revenue, without allowing them any voice in its expenditure. The oft-quoted rhyme of Canning,

> "In matters of commerce the fault of the Dutch
> Is giving too little and asking too much,"

applies to-day.

There is one aspect of the question which does not often strike people comfortably at home in England,

Rose Deep.

and that is the risks these newcomers took upon themselves, and the courage so often shown by pioneers. At
this day (1899), when the Witwatersrand mines have
been proved to be the richest ever known, one is apt to
forget that in the year 1889 all that was still unproved.
The few courageous men who then invested comparatively small amounts, though in many cases they risked
their all, in what are now fully-developed mines, deserve
much for their pluck. I well remember the dismal
tales in those early days of the mines giving out, and
now that the deep levels are a fully-established success
it is difficult to remember the heart-burnings and
doubts and fears expressed by many as to their future.
One may say now, "Oh yes, the greatest mining engineers gave their opinion as to the mines being quite
positively rich," but equally great mining engineers
held an adverse view, and obviously engineers of repute
hesitated to predict as to the future in regard to a gold-
bearing formation which was quite unique. Even such
men as these have been at fault, and it is a recognised
fact that however bold one may be in investing one's
own money, it is quite another matter when one has
to deal with exigent and never-satisfied shareholders.
Thus I say all honour to the plucky men of the early
days, and may no one begrudge them their hard-earned
success!

When we first went to Johannesburg the mining
industry was still in its infancy, many of the managers
being men who had simply taken to it through being

on the spot, and there were few who had any technical
education. Consequently much of the work was done
in a slipshod, unpractical, and extravagant manner, as
the training of a mine manager is a slow process, requir-
ing much energy, technical knowledge, and knowledge
of one's fellow-men. Owing to the want of a railway, the necessary mining machinery was not forthcoming, and there was much to contend with. Many
evenings do I remember Lionel coming home utterly
worn out and discouraged by the innumerable instances
of bad management and the hopeless material with
which he had to deal. The organisation of the work
was a very lengthy and often a very disheartening task;
and in addition to the many natural difficulties, there
was the continual opposition of the Government to
everything conducive to the good of the place or its
advancement, and its varied devices to hamper the
work already in progress. Many and many were the
journeys by Cape cart that Lionel and his partners took
to Pretoria in order to try and soften the obdurate heart
of the President and induce him to listen to reason.
But of no avail. He never did listen to reason; that is
to say, he listened, and apparently acquiesced, and made
many promises, but as a matter of fact his whole policy
was directed to trammelling the gold industry, and by
this means restricting the foreign population. Here is
a striking example of his ignorant policy: When asked
to throw open town lands of Pretoria to prospectors, he
urged the Raad not to do so, as another Witwatersrand

FERREIRA DEEP.

might be discovered, and then where would they find the police to manage the people? He never listened to the men who were honest, and of whom he might have made good friends. No. The men to whom he listened were of quite another type, and, unfortunately, they were the people who have always had his ear, and who worked upon his suspicious peasant nature with their vicious advice.

To be able to speak his language is a great lever with a Boer, still more to speak it in just the particular manner he affects — a kind of familiar tone, with a suspicion of deference in it. The wily Hollander and German have long ago found this out, but unfortunately the Englishman will not take the trouble to study sufficiently the peculiarities of the people among whom he goes; he always expects the other person to do as he does. The Boer is always on the lookout for ridicule; that is a crime he never forgives, for he is utterly lacking in the sense of humour, and his ignorance of English makes him very suspicious. Amongst themselves the Boers indulge in a coarse kind of horseplay, but a more refined sense of the ridiculous is quite denied them.

When—I forget in what year—some 5000 sovereigns and half-sovereigns were struck (every one had always used English money in the Transvaal), they were immediately withdrawn from circulation, for two reasons. On the one side the ox-waggon had been wrongly represented with shafts instead of a "disselboom" or pole,

and on the other side were the mystic initials "O. S."
—the name of the designer. The word "os" is the
Dutch for "ox," and nothing would persuade Kruger
that it was not meant as a personal reflection on
himself.

This is the secret of much of the extreme dislike
with which the English are regarded by the Boers in
South Africa. They come out there, and instead of
studying the idiosyncrasies of the Africander, they
assume a condescending and arrogant attitude towards
the people of the land, and expect them to act and
behave as if they were English. But as they are not
English, they naturally do not come up to the stranger's
expectations, and are consequently relegated into outer
darkness. This characteristic varies in intensity, of
course, according to the education and breeding of the
newcomer. Unfortunately, however, the hatred and
detestation felt towards the English by the Boers of
the Transvaal and out-of-the-way districts of the Cape
Colony is very real, and is in a great measure due to
the thoughtless way in which the former behave, especially in the face of the poor opinion in which they are
generally held by the Boers. Living very solitary lives,
without literature of any kind, every person with
whom they come in contact makes a deep impression
upon them, and those who lead a busier and more
varied existence are often unable to fathom the suspicious pride of these people. Extremely independent
and really hospitable in the truest sense of the word, I

have known many instances where these qualities have been ruthlessly trampled on through mere heedlessness.

Hospitality is ingrained in the nature of the people —they will share with you what they have, and it is only during late years that they will accept payment. On the lonely roads of South Africa travellers are often dependent for food and shelter on the dwellers in the few and scattered farms, and as a rule they are not disappointed in at least a hearty welcome; and any inconvenience you may put them to is looked on as a matter of course. If they have not a spare bed or kaross to offer, they will even go so far as to share theirs with you, not always to your gratification. The experience of the English bishop, travelling in an out-of-the-way up-country district, who was awakened in the night by the peaceful snores of his fat host and hostess, with whom he was sharing their bed, has often been repeated, with variations.

The Boer is a highly intelligent person. I do not think there is any class of person to be found in the world who more readily shows the advantages of education. He differs widely from the ordinary peasant of Europe in that he has always been independent, and has no feudal traditions whatever. Having had to contend with the forces of nature and to fight savages and wild beasts for many generations, he has always had to exercise his wits, and, moreover, his powers of observation have been developed and strengthened by the life he has led. When he inhabits a town he is no longer called a Boer (which is the Dutch for "farmer"), but an Africander of Dutch, German, or English extraction.

The early days of Johannesburg were the happy ones. As a rule the first immigrants were of a much more respectable class than many who have followed, and the majority were people from various parts of South Africa, more especially from other mining centres, anxious to try their luck in a new form of mining; men who brought their experience with them, who already knew that rich nuggets were not to be picked up at every turn, and who realised that to make a living hard work would be necessary. Consequently, they expected to make the place their home for some years to come, and Johannesburg did not remain so long as Kimberley in the tent or the iron-shanty stage. Very soon people built more settled habitations of brick with the inevitable iron roof, and made gardens and planted trees.

The mention of trees brings to my mind an interesting fact. The Witwatersrand is situated on what is known as the High Veld, and was formerly only inhabited during the summer by nomadic Boers, who trekked with their sheep and cattle to the Bush Veld before the inclement winter season. So there existed no settled homesteads, and the country was absolutely treeless. The newcomers very soon began tree-planting, and found that, unlike Kimberley, the soil and climate of this hitherto treeless tract of country was admirably adapted to their growth, which is more rapid than in any other part of the world. So every one who had a piece of ground immediately planted it, generally with some variety of Eucalyptus or Pine. Lionel's firm was interested in a farm situated about two miles out of town, called Braamfontein, a considerable portion of which they planted. Long before we left Johannesburg what had been veld, covered with tall grass, small bushes, and ant-heaps, and over which I had enjoyed many a pleasant canter in the early days, had become quite a pleasant, shady plantation, with numberless alleys in which to ride and drive.

That part of the country had been singularly devoid of animal life, and it was very curious to note how as the trees grew, hares and various other small animals, and even a few buck, were attracted to the district. I noticed many kinds of birds too, which were especially numerous in the Braamfontein forest, their gay notes making a very pleasant break in the curious silence that was so apparent at one time on the veld.

It is very strange to think that forty years ago this locality, which now struck every one as being so particularly lifeless, was swarming with every variety of game—elephant, rhinoceros, lion, all sorts of antelope, &c.

An old Boer woman, who lived on the Klip River not many miles from Johannesburg, told me that when they first went there the "Wild" (wild animals) were so numerous that they used to prowl round the house and come up to the very door, and that the river in front of the house was full of hippopotami.

An old Boer also related how once as they were trekking in an ox-waggon along the Crocodile River about twenty miles from where Johannesburg now stands, a rhinoceros charged the waggon, and his horn penetrating the sail, pierced the thigh of a woman of the party. He added that she recovered, much to every one's surprise.

THE CROCODILE RIVER, NEAR JOHANNESBURG.

CHAPTER IV

JOHANNESBURG was a most wonderful place. When it had been in existence only a very few years it presented quite a considerable appearance, and had a settled aspect different from that of any other mining camp either in South Africa or America. It was different also in that many people began to look on it as their established home, until the fatal day arrived when it was borne in upon their minds that this could never be under the existing laws or while they were described as Uitlanders, whether of South African or European birth, and treated as outcasts by the Transvaal Government.

Naturally there were a certain number of people who openly said their only aim was to make money, and that when they had enough they intended to go and spend it in countries where the comforts of life were greater and where a fuller intellectual life was possible; but this class of person, be it well understood, did not save and hoard while living there. There were many who felt a sense of duty towards the place, and who while living in it earnestly did all in their power to better it. Very large sums of money were spent by individuals to further the cause of education, and in charity of all kinds. In the establishment of philanthropic institutions small fortunes were disbursed. As the place grew and the population increased, both from within and without, naturally the wants of the inhabitants increased, as well as the necessity for laws suited to a larger community. The laws as they stood were not bad, but they were inefficiently applied.

The influx brought with it the scum of some of the large European towns, an element hitherto unknown in South Africa, and with whose undesirable habits and customs existing statutes were unable to cope. Unfortunately, a Transvaal Boer cannot distinguish between different classes of men; so long as they are white to him they are all the same, except perhaps that he would give the preference to those who did not speak English.

One of the most disastrous consequences of this inroad of the lowest class is the utter demoralisation of the Kaffirs, thousands of whom work in the mines, coming immense distances for that purpose. These are the despicable creatures who sell poison to the unfortunate native; they call it by various names, but in reality it is raw potato spirit rendered still more terrible by the addition of tobacco juice and other noxious ingredients. Even when we first went to Johannesburg, I noticed how very different was the attitude of the Kaffir towards the white person, especially the white woman, from that to which I had been accustomed in other mining centres.

To the Africander mind there is such a gulf between black and white that the Kaffir, whatever his private

KAFFIRS ON THEIR WAY TO THE MINES.

opinion may be, naturally keeps his distance, and the white person is treated with respect, or the semblance of it. Nowhere else, so far as I know, would a lady passing a group of Kaffirs be subjected to insolent looks and personal remarks. The Kaffir in his natural state is a happy-go-lucky, rather childish, person, and such a feeling as fear would never enter the ordinary Colonial woman's mind when among them; but in Johannesburg it has always been very different. To go on to one of the mines is a most unpleasant experience for a white woman, as she is openly stared at, criticised, and most objectionable remarks passed on her person, by Kaffirs who look in many instances more like demons than men, or the smiling, cheery creatures one had always been accustomed to see. This was one of my earliest impressions, and asking one day why there was that marked difference between the Kaffirs of the Rand and elsewhere, I was told that it was because the liquor laws were so badly administered; their provisions are good, but the police are most inadequate and corrupt, and allow the illicit traffic in liquor to be carried on under their eyes, it is even said to their profit.

This state of affairs constitutes one of the most crying evils of the Rand, because in its train so many others follow.

In South Africa, of course, people realise a little what the Kaffir problem is, and what it is likely to become, but it is almost impossible for those who

c

have never been in the country to understand it. With this difficult question looming in the future, there is, however, all the more reason that the less difficult one of the Dutch in South Africa should be once and for ever settled—that is to say, if England wishes to retain her supremacy there; and that supremacy is necessary for the retention of her interests in the far East.

The value of the Cape as a calling station to India has been a little lost sight of in England since the construction of the Suez Canal; but in the event of a war with Russia or any other European Power, were the Suez Canal blocked, the Cape would at once reassume its former importance.

And only to hold the Cape peninsula itself, which is all that is considered necessary by a very prominent politician in England, might fall short of the ideas of Englishmen, who consider that one of her claims to greatness consists in her colonial possessions. The "tight little island," with her overflowing population, would not fill quite so large a *rôle* in this world had she not her colonial outlets.

As a matter of fact, in South Africa England has always played rather a poor part, and the patience of the white population under misgovernment is in a great measure due to division amongst themselves. An Englishman will abuse his own Government as much as he likes, but let a foreigner dare! I am convinced this is the reason why the English in South Africa are amongst the most loyal of all

her Majesty's subjects; and by English I do not only
mean English-born men and women, for in the Cape
a great many who are not purely English call themselves so, from the fact that they speak the common
tongue. Indeed, it is the language of all educated people
there, Dutch being mainly spoken by the dwellers on
farms and in out-of-the-way places and by servants.
One hardly finds a colonial family of which the parents
are of the same extraction.

The Boer, like most people, admires pluck and
manliness, and those qualities he denies to the average
Englishman. He has never read history, and only
judges by what comes under his eyes. His experience
of the English in battle is a sad one for the latter.
The surrender in 1881 after defeat in their own territory, and the exhibition by Dr. Jameson at Doornkop,
have confirmed his opinion. Since the year 1848, when
Sir Harry Smith defeated the Boers at the battle of
Boomplaats, from one cause or another, the English have
invariably been worsted in every engagement. Even in
their encounters with the Kaffirs, victory has generally
been unnecessarily dearly bought. Naturally the Boers
do not analyse the cause: they only remember the result.
Being, as I said before, of a proud and independent
spirit, it galls them to be under a people to whom they
deny the quality of courage. Therefore the only solution of the South African problem is to establish the
reality of what at present in their eyes is only nominal,
and that is the supremacy of England.

The Boer is a fatalist, in every sense of the word —quite as much so as any Mohammedan—and if he is beaten, says, "It is God's will." He does not consider it any use to combat further. When the English were defeated at Majuba, the Boers on the whole took their victory in a religious and modest spirit. A schoolfellow of mine, whose father is a Dutch Reformed minister, and who went on a preaching mission through the Transvaal just after the war, told me at the time that they were not at all puffed up about their victory. They all said, "It was God's will that we should win. He is our General." I must say that since that time (1881) some of this modesty has disappeared, and they have come to think that perhaps they had a little more to do with their victory than they did at the moment. It is well known that the Boer method of warfare is a guerilla one. While he can sit behind a stone and "pot" men he is indefatigable, but the slightest reverse completely cowes him. It is generally allowed throughout South Africa that if once the English met the Boers on equal terms in pitched battle on a plain, as at Boomplaats, and proved themselves no such unworthy foes, it would do more to restore English prestige than all the despatches of years. The courage of the Boer is much impugned by some. Personally, I think the average Boer is much like the average free man of any other nation; but in a losing contest he gives in much sooner than another, not to my mind for want of courage, but on account

AMAJUBA.

of the inherent fatalism to which I have alluded. It must also be remembered that in a fight the loss of a man means much more to them than to any ordinary force of paid soldiers. They are all known personally to each other, and are frequently related, counting back as they do for many generations, and hence each man killed often means a double loss to his fellows.

The one great necessity for England in South Africa is to show that she is the paramount power in more than name. Many thoughtful South Africans consider that once the English prove their supremacy, the question will be solved. No one would feel more respect for his conqueror, or be a better and stauncher friend after defeat in fair fight than the Boer. Those who have really studied the question and know the country are well aware that the race war about which so much nonsense is talked, is merely a pretext—a fine bogey with which to frighten the conscientious.

It is the Little Englander in England and the ambitious Bondsman at the Cape, anxious to gain glory for himself, regardless of the fact that the country is not fit to stand alone, who have invented the idea. England's great safeguard in South Africa is that when it comes to a question of black *versus* white, in the face of a common danger there would be no subdivisions of Dutch and English. But from his point of view the Boer is right. How can he submit to be under a nation he despises? And during the last three years that feeling has been shared by many besides the Boer. The peculiar English characteristic of looking at the other side of the question to the neglect of his own is amply shown in the way they regard the treatment of English subjects in the South African Republic. When discussing the question the average Briton will begin with extolling the numerous virtues of President Kruger and the Boers, oblivious of the fact that in denying to his own countrymen some of the same good qualities he is damning himself. Why do English people think that the moment their fellow-countrymen go abroad they should become monsters of iniquity? I believe the quality arises from an exaggerated sense of justice in the nature of an Englishman, but in times of stress it is apt to become so exaggerated that all justice is left out of the question.

Mr. Gladstone, of course, is always blamed (and justly) for the absolute loss of English prestige in South Africa, but how many of his fellow-countrymen resemble him in the possession of the Nonconformist conscience? When, to salve that delicate organ, he gave up the Transvaal after Majuba, and ruined hundreds of innocent British families, not to mention the other innumerable ills that resulted, it was a pity he did not remember that "charity begins at home." But when that event occurred, excepting those immediately concerned, how many people realised all the disgrace? I remember when I first came to England many years ago talking to people who, I verily believe, laboured under the delusion that the English had won a glorious victory at Majuba. And at what a cost to South Africa are the English at last beginning to comprehend that there is another side to the question than that raised by Kruger, and that their suffering fellow-countrymen also have a right to be heard ?

So much has been said of the Uitlanders' grievances that at last the very phrase destroys belief in their reality, but that they are very substantial has been borne out by independent witnesses over and over again. One of the characteristics of the people of Johannesburg that always struck me as remarkable was their extraordinary patience. The cause of this, no doubt, was the fact that most of the men were married, with families, which naturally made them chary of running risks. It should also be borne in mind that the great majority of the leading men were the so-called capitalists, which, as Lionel once aptly remarked, "was not a criminal offence," and that meant the interests of thousands of shareholders to safeguard—no trifling responsibility, which he has since learned to his cost.

CHAPTER V

THE great curse of the Transvaal has been the pernicious influence of the Hollanders in the beginning, and certain Germans later. The two names that head the list of the internal influences are Leyds and Lippert. Kruger, had he had the good fortune to be advised by ordinarily honest men, who had the real interest of the country at heart, would never have found himself in his present entanglements. But unluckily both for the Transvaal and the neighbouring colonies, he was a splendid receptacle for the insidious and poisonous advice of these unscrupulous men. His ear was ready to listen to anything that could foster his suspiciousness of any English-speaking person. Kruger is a man who is quite illiterate, and though like many Boers he may understand English, he will not acknowledge it, and he certainly cannot speak it. It is easy, therefore, to understand that any one speaking Dutch at once has advantage over those who have to depend upon an interpreter. Kruger once made desperate attempts to learn English; it was on the occasion of his first voyage to England in 1878, I believe. A friend who was on the steamer told me he used to sit for hours poring over a Bible, one of the editions printed in Dutch and English, the one language divided from the other by a line drawn down the middle of the page.

As, of course, the business of the Government required men who could at least read and write, and as Dutch is the official language of the country, Kruger, following the example of the Orange Free State, imported Hollanders to do the work. I must, however, mention that in the Free State they have had for many years such an enlightened system of education that they are now able to employ their own countrymen to do the work of the Government. In the Free State the President has always been an educated man able to judge of events for himself, and many of the highest officials come from the Cape Colony as well as from their own Free State. But unhappily, in Pretoria, with very few exceptions, the Hollander is all-powerful. Now, the average Hollander who comes to South Africa dislikes the English, but for the Boer he has a most wholesome contempt in addition; he is careful to tell you that he does not understand their Dutch, and often leaves you to infer of what little account he considers them. However, the two languages are enough akin for him very soon to acquire sufficient to keep alive all the requisite dislike to the English. The Hollanders are well aware that the further the two are kept apart the better it is for their own purposes, which are to make as much money as they can while in the country, to keep in their hands the most lucrative posts, irrespective of the mischief they do, and then retire comfortably to Europe. These men are ideal mercenaries, and the pretended patriotism and friendship for the Boer is a well-known sham. And many of them have begun to realise this, but do not know the remedy. A Boer of the better class put the matter in a nutshell to me one day. Talking on the subject I said to him, "You abuse the Hollanders and blame them for much of your troubles, and still you employ them in the Government. Why does not President Kruger employ his own fellow-countrymen—men with education—from the Cape Colony, who understand the country and the people, instead of these imported Hollanders?" And he replied, "The fact is, if it came to a tussle with England, Kruger would not trust the Africander, and he knows he can always rely on the hate of the Hollander."

One of the earliest abuses from which the people of Johannesburg had to suffer was the granting of concessions. These same wily persons of whom I have just been writing, instilled into the old President's mind the idea that the gold-mines would very soon give out, and then all the revenue of the country would be gone, but if he established manufactories a more stable and lasting revenue would be the result. And there is great sense in the idea, but industries can only be established with success where the conditions and products of the land favour such enterprises. To render the population independent of the mines and to keep them distributed over the country is sound policy, but

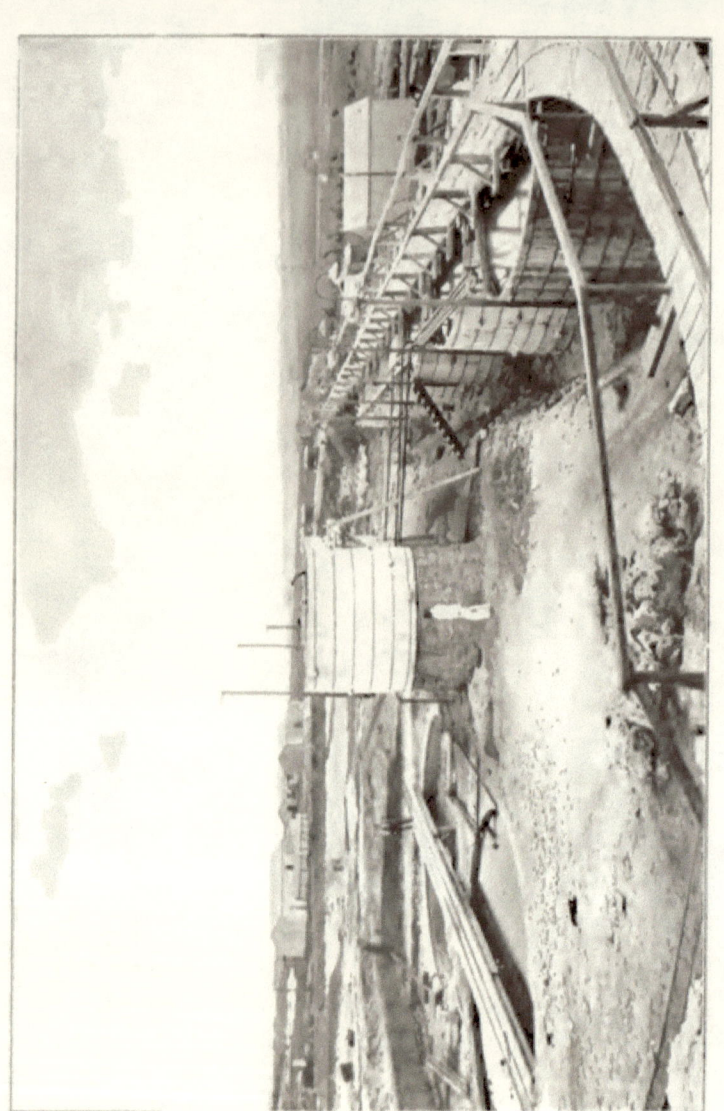

Cyanide Works on a Mine.

that was by no means the idea of these pernicious advisers. By their method of working the matter, they have amply shown that their only object was to benefit concessionaires at the expense of the wretched Uitlander. Once they had thoroughly imbued the President's mind with the idea they were safe, as nothing has ever been able to shake this conviction. How little he really understood the matter the following true tale will prove. Certain persons applied for a concession for the manufacture of cyanide of potassium. I must explain that this substance is a solvent of gold, and is therefore largely used, but to manufacture it in the Transvaal would have necessitated a greater expense than importing it. A well-known gentleman tried to represent this to Kruger, who replied, "Oh yes; but the gold will be finished some day, and then I shall still have my factory," not being at all aware that when the gold was finished there would be no use for cyanide of potassium.

His Hollander and German friends accordingly persuaded the President that by granting concessions to various people he was really serving his country. One of the first, and the greatest scandal of all the concessions, was the one made to Lippert to manufacture dynamite, which is so largely used in mines. I shall not go into that pitiful story; it is too well known. Suffice it to say, that the concessionaire amassed a huge fortune entirely out of the pockets of the Uitlanders, and when the political horizon began to look a little black, he who

has done more probably than any other man to injure
the country, betook himself to his native land, Germany.
The other great influence working on the President for
evil was Dr. Leyds, who had political ambitions, which
by now he also has no doubt attained in his native land,
Holland. Both these patriots, be it understood, have
always been far over the seas when danger threatened
their beloved adopted country.   Dr. Leyds was one of the
imported Hollanders, who rose to the position of State
Secretary in the Transvaal. Extremely clever and subtle,
these two men acting in concert moulded the poor,
ignorant, obstinate old Boer to their own way of thinking, so that to-day, when he is too old to learn wisdom,
it is a pitiable sight to see him struggling in his blind
and misguided way against the inevitable.

Since the reaction of opinion set in, people in England have often said to me, " But I suppose the Boers are
monsters, and Kruger the worst monster of all." These
very same people, not three years ago, said, " But of
course Kruger is a Christian saint, and his people are
very good and religious." Neither of these portraits
is true. Kruger is not a monster, but he is also not a
saint nor a Christian in my acceptation of the term.
Nor is he the great man he is taken to be. He is a
strong man with a strong personality, but has strict
limitations. His point of view is quite different to an
Englishman's, and his actions in consequence are different. For instance, he possesses one very characteristic
Boer trait, which in Europe is (or I should say *was*, as

everything has changed so) generally regarded as the height of genius, I mean the faculty of sitting still and letting things take their course. There are times when inaction has been described as "masterly." With the Boer it is habitual through constitutional indolence of mind and body. He does not live in the midst of railways and telegraphs. The ox-waggon is his ordinary method of locomotion, and just as slowly does his mind work in comparison with the European's. Nor can he read the newspapers except through an interpreter; hence he has not the usual outside influence of civilisation to keep his mind active. When in 1895 and at the beginning of 1896 he simply sat tight and let the world in general make mistakes all round him, Kruger was regarded as a great statesman. He was nothing of the kind. His mind could not keep pace with events, but luckily for him Fate played into his hands through the folly and mistakes of some people, and his greatest friend was the English public, who, as usual, only saw the other side of the question until too late.

When Mr. Hermann Eckstein left Johannesburg, Lionel was made President of the Chamber of Mines in his place. This institution was formed by the large firms in Johannesburg to supervise the general working of the mines and to guard their interests, and has done more to further the industry than any government rules and regulations; in fact, its history has been one long contention with the powers at Pretoria to obtain the merest justice. The history of all the shameful over-taxation and corruption has been written elsewhere, and this is obvious to any one who pays heed to statistics. It is easy to understand that, to a conscientious man, such a position presented many difficulties. I can only say that it is one which became more and more onerous as time went on, and the mines increased and the population with them. There arose the absurd anomaly that men representing millions of pounds and contributing nine-tenths of the taxes, who had given many proofs of friendship to their adopted country, had no voice in its government, not so much even as an uneducated peasant who could neither read nor write, and who exercised no influence on the country except a retrograde one. Kruger's great fear was that every one wanted to take his country from him, especially England, and this has been the key-note of all his actions.

In the early days of Johannesburg there was not, of course, the strong political feeling that came with time and growing misgovernment. The daily business of life took up quite enough of men's thoughts. They were there mainly for the purpose of making a living— possibly a fortune—and did not trouble themselves about political rights. I know that many of the first settlers, and they represent some of the best men of the place, did honestly strive in every way in their power to make friends with the Boers, and for a good many years themselves did for the place what they could not get the Government to do. Enormous

A Stamp Mill, Johannesburg.

sums were spent in private taxation, simply because some one had to do something, and the Government would not.

I believe that, if in the early days they could have foreseen even in a slight degree to what enormous proportions the mining industry would grow, the leading mining men would have acted more firmly and formulated their demands sooner, but not the most optimistic could fathom the riches of the Rand. And naturally they were a little timorous as to the future, and had to feel their way. Dismal prophecies as to the mines giving out were constantly being recited, and so for the first few years men's minds were more occupied with the daily task of money-making.

But as time went on and the population increased, and the town grew, the necessity arose for a little legislation, but none was forthcoming. The streets were left in a state of nature: for years one saw quite fine shops lining a dusty track, and no attempt made to improve it. With heavy ox-waggon as well as the usual traffic of a town, the state of dust in the dry season, and of mud and deep ruts in the wet, is more easily imagined than described. As Johannesburg is situated nearly 6000 feet above the sea, there is a constant breeze blowing, and when this breeze becomes stronger, and a good wind blew, the effects were awful. I have seen dust-storms so thick that one could not see one's hand before one's face. This red dust also was very unhealthy, for the sanitary arrangements being of a frightfully primitive kind, the place was very dirty, and fearful odours abounded. The dust flying about continually caused a great deal of illness of every kind. That no epidemic ever visited the town is due probably to the splendid dry temperate climate, and, I presume, to the constant breeze. In South Africa the dust-storms are known as "the doctor."

Johannesburg rejoices in a glorious climate. Although so near the Equator, it is very temperate owing to its altitude. During the winter, that is from June to October, there is rarely any rain. There is a cold, disagreeable wind, with rather a hot sun and plenty of frost, and the nights and mornings are bitter. Of course at that time of the year the dust is unsupportable, more especially in August and September. This is caused principally by local traffic, and does not sweep down, as in Kimberley, from a desert. Once the rains begin a more heavenly climate cannot be imagined. It has always gone to my heart to see a place so favoured by nature gradually becoming, through man's blind perversity, one of the most loathsome spots on earth. No place was ever started with fairer prospects or better chances.

The police were worse than useless; undisciplined, too few in numbers, notoriously dishonest and hostile, they were an element of disturbance rather than of order. Consequently in Johannesburg, unlike other colonial towns, it was customary for men to carry revolvers at night, and to have one very near at hand in their

THE MORNING MARKET, JOHANNESBURG.

bedrooms. Sir Drummond Dunbar, one of the pioneers, very soon formed a Ladies' Revolver Club, as it was felt to be necessary for women to know how to protect themselves a little. An amusing and almost tragic incident occurred at one of the first practices. Sir Drummond, holding up his hand as a signal, "Don't fire," a too eager learner, mistaking it, fired and shot off his little finger!

In Natal, where they have 581,000 idle blacks to 49,000 whites, there has long existed what the newspapers term "the social curse"; that is to say, the crime of rape by Kaffirs on white women and children. To the Kaffir a white woman is always an object of desire, but the crime is rampant in Natal because of the preponderance of the black and the often lonely position of the farms. The horror of it is of course apparent to all, and the punishment is death. Hence in most parts of South Africa it is kept in check to a certain extent. But in Johannesburg the thing assumed fearful proportions, becoming at one time quite an epidemic, and all women went in terror for their own and their children's lives. The punishment in the Transvaal is also death, but the sentence generally passed was six months' imprisonment. That was no check at all, and although I had faithful white servants, I remember many a time when dining out I have hardly been able to contain myself for fear of what might have happened in my absence. A poor little white girl of two, living not far from us, was violated one day by a coloured servant;

D

and dozens of instances occurred which never appeared in the papers through the horror and shame of it. I knew one poor woman with four little girls, who could not afford to keep white servants; she told me that when she was obliged to go away from home for shopping, &c., she used to lock them all in the house, and was in an agony of terror until she got home again.

We had moved away from our early home in the town on account of its unhealthiness, and had built ourselves a house about two miles out. I kept in the house a revolver for the women servants to take with them when they walked into the town, warning them if they went without it, and anything befell them, it would be their own fault; they were also forbidden to go alone. We kept some large dogs, which always accompanied us on our walks. One plucky woman in the town, happening to be in bed one night, and alone in the house when a Kaffir entered her room, shot him dead. But many instances occurred where women found themselves in positions where they could not defend themselves, and horrible tragedies occurred. In most of these cases the offender was never discovered. At times there were numbers of ghastly murders, and little apparent effort was made to discover the murderers. Verily, under such circumstances life was rendered needlessly hard, and the annoying part was that it was all so unnecessary. People did what they could to help themselves; to appeal to the English Government was a

"HOHENHEIM."

remedy that occurred to no one, as their utter indifference and ignorance of matters in South Africa had been so often displayed, that the fact of England being the suzerain power in the Transvaal had almost been lost sight of.

After making every available effort with the " powers that be " at Pretoria, and having signed numerous petitions for redress with absolutely no result—with everything, in fact, going from bad to worse, and life becoming intolerable—the conviction that it was high time to adopt more drastic methods began to take root in men's minds. Not only did they contribute practically all the revenue, but when the Government found themselves with more money than they were accustomed to, they began squandering it in the most extravagant way, and always to the detriment of the Uitlander. The Secret Service Fund was a perfect gulf for swallowing up money, for which no account was rendered.

The President, who receives a yearly pay of £7000, is well known to have amassed a huge fortune for himself and his numerous family. Also almost the entire staff of officials, down to the meanest policeman, and a great many of the members of the Volksraad, were notorious for their corrupt practices. There are a few exceptions to this rule, but very few. These are not wild statements, but can be proved over and over again. But as yet the people had not formulated any system of remedy, and their patience was wonderful. No organised body was in existence except the National Union, and as that was a political body, many of the leading men of the place, for obvious reasons, had not joined it. But people's eyes were opened suddenly, and men became alive to the fact that action was necessary.

CHAPTER VI

THE Boers had begun a war with Malaboch, a Kaffir chief on their northern border, and "commandeered" men to go and fight, as was their custom. Accordingly they not only commandeered their own men but a good many Uitlanders as well. Remember, these were men who under no conditions whatever could obtain political rights of any kind. So they very justly said to themselves, "If we are always to remain aliens, with no rights, why should we fight for the people who refuse them to us?" So all their protests being in vain, aided and abetted by some courageous Wesleyan ministers in Pretoria and Johannesburg, they refused outright to proceed to the front, and were accordingly cast into prison: a few men being sent up country by force to join the Boer Commando.

The result of this was that the British Government interfered, and sent Sir Henry (now Lord) Loch up to see into the matter. There was tremendous excitement in Pretoria. Kruger went to the station to meet the High Commissioner, and an incident occurred to embitter him still more against the British Uitlander, for he was too blind to see that it was entirely his own fault. There was a scene of the wildest enthusiasm, thousands

being there to welcome the Queen's representative, and
when he and Kruger got into the carriage (which also
contained Dr. Leyds) to proceed to the hotel, some
Englishmen took out the horses and dragged it, one irre-
pressible person jumping on the box seat and waving a
Union Jack over Kruger's head! When the carriage
arrived at its destination, Sir Henry, accompanied by
Dr. Leyds, entered the hotel, and the President was left
sitting in the horseless carriage. The yelling crowd
refused to drag the vehicle, and after some difficulty a
few of his faithful burghers were got together to draw
the irate President to his home. This was the more
significant, as it took place in Pretoria, which is well
known to be very matter of fact.

I shall never forget how frightened I was when
Lionel came home that night from Pretoria. I saw by
his face that something serious had occurred. His first
words were, "If I tell you to leave the place with the
children, if it is at an hour's notice, will you do it?"
He then told me of this ominous incident; also that
armed Boers had been parading the streets of Pretoria
that day, "looking as if they would willingly shoot down
any man, woman, or child." He also added that although the Turf Club in Johannesburg had invited Sir
Henry and his staff to come over to the races then
taking place, he sincerely hoped he would not do so,
as he was sure there would be a "row." Five hundred
armed Boers had also immediately been sent to remain
on the outskirts of Johannesburg, and they were vowing

vengeance on the *rooineks*. Then for the first time
I realised that, except for the two or three revolvers in
the house, we had no means of self-protection; that,
indeed, the whole population of the Rand was in an
utterly defenceless state in what was daily becoming a
hostile country. I insisted on Lionel buying a rifle the
next day, and a few others did the same, but it struck
me then and many a day after, that we were living on
a volcano. But the strangest part was that hardly
any one in the place attached any importance to the
matter, and, except by a few, the incident and its lessons
were soon forgotten.

Lionel again went to Pretoria the next day and
had a conversation with Sir Henry about what steps
the English Government would take in the contingency
of the Boers following out their threats and firing on
Johannesburg. It appeared that it would require several
days to bring troops from the border, and at the time
the garrisons were quite inadequate to meet any emergency. Sir Henry did not come to the races, but went
back to Cape Town. From that day things marched
quickly. Kruger gave in about the commandeered
men, and apparently things were smoothed over. But
in the history of the Rand these events marked a
distinct epoch. Much seed for reflection had been
scattered, and with the more serious-minded remained
the thought that the town with its huge population
of women and children would be utterly defenceless in
the event of hostilities. The Boers now showed more

openly than ever their contempt and dislike for the
Uitlanders, who would be utterly at their mercy,
and remembering that chivalry is foreign to the Boer
nature, that was no pleasant prospect. The unhappy
arrangement with Jameson later is to be attributed to
the " Loch incident."

This sudden outburst of dislike had more in it than
appeared on the surface. The commandeering had also
been tentative, with a deep-rooted purpose. For some
time past the Germans had been showing great friendship for the Transvaal, to which the President responded.
There are a great many Germans in South Africa, and
notably in the Transvaal. As Kruger was so friendly to
that nation, it occurred to the more astute among them
that here was a splendid opportunity for an outlet for
that overflowing country. The German Emperor is well
known to encourage colonisation, and so by degrees a
continually-increasing number of Germans had been
coming into the Transvaal, and were always most favourably treated by the Government. I do not, of course,
include the Germans with English associations, but those
who came direct from Germany.

There was a great fuss when the Delagoa Bay Railway was opened just before the Loch incident, when
the German Emperor sent Kruger a personal telegram
of congratulation, and at the banquet given in Pretoria
many assurances of friendship and amity were ex-
changed. Kruger took this occasion to emphasise his
contempt for Johannesburg. He had invited a great

many prominent people from all parts of South Africa
—the Orange Free State, Natal, Cape Colony, and the
Portuguese possessions. From Johannesburg he selected
one man, and that was Lionel. He, as well as most of
the prominent men in Johannesburg, resented this open
slight, considering that that town had practically paid
for the railway. Naturally he did not accept the invitation.

All this time Lionel with the rest of his firm had been
doing the best they could for the mining interest ; they
would not acknowledge themselves beaten, but continued
their futile and heartrending struggle with the Government. But of no avail. There was a weekly journal at
Johannesburg called *The Critic*, whose criticisms on men
in general were often more scurrilous than true, and
among others who were the constant target for their
envenomed shafts were the partners in Messrs. H. Eckstein & Co. Being capitalists, they could do nothing
right. *The Critic* was also a violent opponent of the
Government. About this time the editor wrote " An
Open Letter " to Lionel, which, to my mind, contained
many truths, and urged him to make a stand against the
ruling powers. We were staying at East London at the
time, and I remember on reading this "open letter"
I was furious at the abusive terms employed, but on
second thoughts felt that there was much truth in some
of the suggestions. I then said to Lionel, and repeated
the question several times afterwards, "Why do you
not take up a stand on political grounds, and show

the Transvaal Government that it is no longer possible to endure this intolerable state of things?" And his answer was the same invariably. "Do not talk nonsense. I have to consider my firm, and we represent the interests of far too many people to dare to risk them." My argument was that the Boer, through generations of dealing with Kaffirs, had imbibed many of their characteristics, a marked one being that anything in the shape of generosity or fairness is always looked upon as a sign of weakness. A Boer, like a Kaffir, must feel that you are prepared to enforce what you demand, or he will bully you. "Magnanimity" has been the bane of South Africa, and to the Boer the word is synonymous with fear. Complaints also were made at this time by the workmen on the Rand, that the capitalists only thought of themselves, and ought to take a more prominent part in politics and uphold their interests. Poor men! they were afterwards blamed by this very class for trying to help them. About this time, too, the National Union lost its President, and many people looked to Lionel to fill his place. But he persisted in his refusal to take a prominent part in politics, always for the same reason. I relate this particularly, as he and many others have often been accused of working up an agitation for the sake of money.

The men who suffered most and dared all for the sake of right in Johannesburg were the men who had much to lose and very little to gain, at any rate in a material way; and remembering the futile endeavour of years, and in the cause of justice, it makes my blood boil to think how falsely and groundlessly they were accused of one of the most sordid and mean of crimes. When later on one was forced to hear and read all the vile imputations made against those who risked so much for their duty, when a paper called *The World*, published an article headed "Murder for Money," it seemed inconceivable that there could be persons who judged their fellows by so low a standard. I do not talk of all the daily annoyances we had to put up with, nor all the various "grievances" which have been so often described. But to people comfortably settled at home in England, who do not know how wretched life can be made by the deprivation of things they look on as their right—to people who like to know that when they write a letter and send it by post it will be delivered, the following tale will appeal. An old housemaid of mine, who married, told me in quite a casual way that her husband, who had been out of work, had got a job at Christmas to help in sorting the letters, which were too many for the usual clerks at the post-office. And, she added, "when they were tired of sorting them, they had a trap-door in the floor to an underground place, through which they dropped those that were left!"

Having got their railway line finished from Delagoa Bay, the Transvaal tried to force the merchants to use it in preference to the more convenient and quicker route from the Cape Colony, and to this end they made the rates prohibitive from Vereeniging, on the frontier, to Johannesburg, which is only about forty miles. The merchants found it much cheaper to bring their goods by ox-waggon or mule-waggon from the border, so then the Government, determined to have their way, closed the drifts, and put armed men there to enforce the order. I must explain this. In a new country, of course, the rivers are not bridged, this being the case particularly in the Transvaal. With all their immense revenues they have never attempted a single public work except under extreme coercion, and then always with a view to the enrichment of some Dutch or German concessionaire.

On most of the South African rivers there are certain places called "drifts" (fords), which can be crossed by waggons. In cases where that is impossible there are ponts or bridges. The Vaal and Orange rivers being deep, are generally crossed by the latter methods. A propos of this, I remember being very much exasperated one day. After I had laboriously tried to explain to a London journalist the enormity of the action of the Transvaal Government in closing the drifts, he turned to me in the most innocent manner and said, "But you have all these rich men on the Rand, and if they are so anxious to do well for their mines why don't they build bridges?" not appearing to understand that this was hardly the point, and that if the authorities could close a drift they could even more easily close a bridge. The English Government decided

OX WAGGON CROSSING A "DRIFT."

A "PONT," VAAL RIVER.

that the closing of the drifts was contrary to the Convention, and sent the Transvaal an ultimatum, upon which they gave way. The few instances I have given, however, will prove how very inimical they were to the newcomers, or rather the old residents of Johannesburg, for such many had now become.

I need not say that all this time no stone had been left unturned by Lionel and many other leading men to convince the Government of their folly—how those men were anxious to be their friends, and to help them to do what was in the interest of the mines, and that meant the country. Up to this time there were very few Boers in Johannesburg, but many Africanders from all parts of the colony, who felt even more deeply than the Europeans the disgraceful state of subjugation in which we were all living. It is unnecessary to go into the details of the numerous petitions addressed to the President and the Volksraad praying for redress. The simplest action was misconstrued, and the petitions were openly laughed to scorn in the Raad, one member even going so far as to express the real, if unconfessed, opinion of the Government, and inviting the Uitlanders, if they wanted any rights, to come and fight for them! The President, who is as cunning and untrustworthy as he is stubborn, now made promises, now entirely ignored what was represented to him. Certainly it is a noteworthy fact that he has never kept a single promise nor done anything for the good of the place except under pressure, and he never will do anything unless forced to. He knows too well how little reason South Africans have to expect anything from England, and this is the reason why so many loyal colonists, tired of her half-hearted support of her subjects in South Africa, have gone over to the party of the Africander Bond, which almost openly supports Kruger in his opposition to British subjects and British rule, and still pretends to be loyal. It is this pernicious influence, subtle and treacherous in that it fears the light of day—an influence always at work, which drew fresh energy from the Raid—that is most inimical to British interests in South Africa. Many of the Bondsmen are notorious turncoats, joining whichever party is uppermost, and knowing neither truth nor courage. It is this party at the Cape which, in England's vacillation and want of a fixed policy, see a chance of fulfilling their aspirations, and which find in Kruger a still further aid to their ambitions. Hence their cry of "Africa for the Africanders" is not entirely an illusory one. And hence the danger.

Men in Johannesburg, and Mr. Rhodes in Cape Town, began at last to see that unless the burning questions of the hour were settled once and for all, the whole country ran a risk of being embroiled, that the uncertainty was paralysing trade and commerce, and that the country could never prosper with this "festering sore," as some one has justly described the Transvaal, in their midst. So men's minds in Johannesburg were more and more drawn to the conviction that they would

JOHANNESBURG IN 1895.

have to work out their own salvation. Accordingly they determined upon a plan for securing their just rights, and this is how they went about it.

Remember that those who started the Reform movement in Johannesburg were, most of them, serious men with families—men who, when they pledged themselves to do their best for their adopted country, did not shut their eyes to the gravity of the undertaking. Up to this time Lionel, while doing all he could, had never taken an active part in politics, except in so far as that all business in the Transvaal is inseparable from politics. But towards the end of 1895 he identified himself with the Reform movement in conjunction with a good many of the principal business and professional men.

I must interrupt this to relate that about June in that year I left Johannesburg on a three months' visit to England with the children, was taken ill on the way, and for five months was practically on my back, being at death's door once or twice. I also nearly lost my little girl from inflammation of the lungs, the result of an attack of measles, which was really the cause of my own illness, besides having the two boys down with measles. Lionel saw us on board the steamer at Cape Town, and we came on to England alone, no one realising how ill I was. I mention this particularly, as afterwards when the fiasco came in January people on all sides accused him of having sent us away expressly to be out of danger; but that was not the case. It was an old plan, and I fully intended to return in three months, but Fate willed otherwise. Had I done so, the bitter suspense and agony of mind which I had to go through would have been spared me. Although I was not informed that any active movement was contemplated, I knew—as indeed the whole of South Africa knew—that the situation was very acute. When I reproached Lionel afterwards for not telling me of the preparations that were being made by the leading Uitlanders, he told me that all the Reform party had sworn themselves to secrecy. At one time, when I was very seriously ill, Lionel, with his portmanteau ready packed, only waited for a telegram from me to start for England. As I took a turn for the better, he did not come. He announced to his fellow Reformers that, as I was dangerously ill, he might possibly be obliged to leave at a moment's notice. One of them (I will not mention his name) said to him, "Phillips, you cannot do it; men would call you a coward. In fact, if you heard your wife was dead, you dare not leave now."

Lionel did not join the National Union, but he publicly announced his views in a speech he made in November at the opening of the new building of the Chamber of Mines. Being President, he invited a number of ladies and gentlemen to the ceremony, but the social gathering resolved itself into a much more serious function than was expected. In his speech announcing the building open, he took the opportunity of warning the Government. It is too long to reproduce, but he enumerated the burning grievances of the Uitlanders, and ended with these words:—

"All we want in this country is purity of administration and an equitable share and voice in its affairs. (Cheers.) I hope that wiser counsels may prevail, and that the Government of this country may be induced to see that the present policy will not do. Nothing is further from my heart than a desire to see an upheaval which would be disastrous from every point of view, and which would probably end in the most horrible of all endings—in bloodshed. But I should say this, that it is a mistake to imagine that this much-maligned community, which consists, anyhow, of a majority of men born of freemen, will consent indefinitely to remain subordinate to the minority in this country—(applause) —and that they will for ever allow their lives, property, and liberty to be subject to its arbitrary will. I hope that the Legislature of this country will recognise this fact in time, and not attempt to do that which is impossible. If the population of this country were only accepted in the spirit in which it has offered itself, it would be a strength to the others instead of a weakness. (Cheers.)"

I happened to go up to London from Brighton that day, and I saw Mr. Beit, who was very unwell. He showed me the Reuter's cable summary of the whole proceeding, and was very much agitated. He asked me what I thought of it, and I told him I was delighted. I thought it quite the right thing to do, and I cabled

E

out to Lionel to congratulate him on the course he had taken. The speech created quite a sensation. In South Africa it was universally applauded; it was commented on in most flattering terms, in many cases under the headings, "The Writing on the Wall," "Mene Mene Tekel," &c., and warnings were addressed to Kruger on all sides. The English papers also noticed it favourably, but there was much agitation on the Stock Exchange, where I believe South African shares went down. I met a man the same day, who said to me, "Every one is going for your husband, and I believe if you appeared on the Stock Exchange, even you would be mobbed." That was one way of looking at the matter!

CHAPTER VII

I SHALL now continue my tale. The excitement in London and everywhere else was intense, and every scrap of news was eagerly read, but it took a long time for the facts to reach us, and to this day many people have but a hazy idea of what actually happened. It appeared that the Johannesburg men had called on Dr. Jameson to help them, and had then basely deserted him, that in consequence he had surrendered to the Boers, and with his men had been taken prisoner to Pretoria. At the first blush it was indeed a fearful tale of shame and treachery, and it was only natural that one side should be extolled and the other side abused. In fact, words were inadequate to describe the behaviour of either side. Kruger was lauded to the skies as possessing every Christian virtue. The Poet Laureate distinguished himself by a pitiful effusion in praise of Jameson's exploit, which did untold harm to innocent people. I suppose the poor man felt that his new official position necessitated a poem, so before he or any one else in England was aware of the truth, he rushed into print. This wretched jingle was nightly recited at the Alhambra by a person dressed as one of the Chartered Company's police, on a stage

decorated with tropical palms and intended to represent Krugersdorp, which place, by the way, is arid to a
degree. But the audience liked it, and nightly went
mad, and nightly cursed Johannesburg. They criticised
neither the style nor the material of the Laureate's
poem : they had found a real live hero to applaud, and
so they were not critical but happy.

Meantime for days no news came, only the most
awful rumours poured in on all sides. No one received
any cable messages, and one moment it was said that
the cable was cut, the next that the Government had
monopolised it. Messrs. Wernher, Beit, & Co. were without information for many days. When at last news
did come, it was but a succession of horrors. We heard
that Jameson, in response to a letter from some of the
leading Johannesburg men, had crossed the border
with 400 men to rescue the women and children. He
had been encamped on the borders of Bechuanaland
and the Transvaal for some time past, and on receiving
this letter had come helter-skelter. On hearing this
the Boers sent a grandson of the President to warn
Jameson not to proceed. The Government of the Cape
also tried to stop him, but without success. They took
no heed, and on January 1, 1896, were met by an armed
force of Boers, who, pursuing their usual tactics of
guerilla warfare, entrenched themselves behind rocks,
and after enormous bravery on all sides, Jameson, who
had expected the men of Johannesburg to reinforce
him, not seeing any sign of them, surrendered. I can-

not recount all the wild tales that were circulated:
that hundreds of Boers had been shot; how eye-
witnesses had seen waggon-loads of dead bodies being
carted off, and the theme was only varied by the accounts of heroism on the one side and the cowardice
and treachery on the other. I was in despair. No
words can picture the agonies of mind I went through,
and the suspense grew daily more and more terrible.
No explanation reached any one, and the wildest conjectures were heard on every side. Lionel and his
friends were accused of having worked the whole thing
up to make money out of it. It was alleged that they
wanted to make shares fall so as to buy in again, and
so make huge sums. The Government vouchsafed no
information, and gave no details, even if they knew any.
Then we heard of terrified women and children leaving
the place, of their sufferings, of the exodus of numbers
of miners, of the disaster to the Natal train, in which
many women and children—also flying from the place—
were killed. Still there was no definite news of any
kind, and I thought I should have gone mad. Mr.
Rhodes, of course, was also accused of every crime
under the sun. Sir Hercules Robinson, then Governor
of Cape Colony, went to Pretoria to try and settle the
differences on behalf of the English Government, and
to do all in his power for the redress of the Uitlanders'
grievances, on condition that they not only gave up
their arms themselves, but persuaded the whole of
Johannesburg to do the same, as Jameson and his men

were in danger of their lives. This was done, but with some little difficulty. We then read that Sir Hercules had left for Cape Town. The storm of abuse against the place increased, and sympathy for Jameson with it.

I did not know what to think. Remembering what fears men had entertained the year before when Sir Henry Loch was at Pretoria, and their many conjectures as to what would happen in case of any sudden need for outside help, I came to the conclusion that the men of Johannesburg must have made some arrangement with Dr. Jameson, and that he had come to their assistance in response to some treacherous call, and I for one gave him and his men all my sympathy. Naturally, I knew that a mistake had arisen, as it was not possible for the men in Johannesburg to have left them in the lurch, as it seemed they had done; but altogether it was an awful time. Mr. Wernher and his partners were staunch to their faith in Lionel and his friends, but too much paralysed by events to do anything. So for days the suspense dragged on, no one knowing what was happening. Mr. Wernher gave me stern orders to be careful as to what I said, as much now depended on every one concerned silently awaiting events. However, I am afraid I disobeyed him, and wrote the following letter to the *Times* :—

" To the Editor of the ' Times.'

"SIR,—It may be of interest to your readers to hear that I have to-day received the following message by cable from my husband, Mr. Lionel Phillips, at Johannesburg, dated this morning:—

"'Peace restored; expect amnesty all concerned on payment indemnity.'

"I may add that during the last ten most anxious days I have received no communications from my husband except a telegram giving me news of his personal safety. It is obvious to me, as it must be to every one else, that cable messages have been largely tampered with by the Transvaal authorities, as I am without reply to most urgent questions addressed to my husband by cable.

"In certain quarters it appears to be considered that the action of Johannesburg in not going to the assistance of Dr. Jameson is greatly to be blamed. But any one acquainted with the true feeling of the people of Johannesburg, and the very real grievances from which they suffer (not to mention the affection which all of us who know him bear Dr. Jameson), must feel certain that there lurks in the background some vile treachery which has not yet come to light.

"Let us first hear by whom the 'urgent appeal' was sent to Dr. Jameson. It is certain that an enormous sum has been spent in 'secret service' money during the last few months by the Transvaal Government, and is it not possible that a deliberate trap was planned and carried into effect by the Boer authorities? The declarations of a three days' armistice by General Joubert, just before the fight with Dr. Jameson's brave band, is, to say the least of it, a curious coincidence.

" To show that the grievances of the Uitlanders are indeed real, let me call your attention to a few facts. What would women residing in peaceful England say to the fact that one cannot take a walk out of sight of one's own house in the suburbs of Johannesburg with safety ? The Kaffirs, who in other parts of South Africa treat a white woman with almost servile respect, there make it a most unpleasant ordeal to pass them, and in a lonely part absolutely dangerous.

" Even little girls of the tenderest age are not safe from these monsters. This is, of course, owing to the utterly inadequate police protection afforded by the Government, the ridiculously lenient sentences passed on horrible crimes, and to the adulterated drink sold by licensed publicans to the Kaffirs on all sides. What would be said if, when insulted by a cab-driver, it was found that the nearest policeman was the owner of the cab in question, and refused to render any assistance or listen to any complaint ?

" The educational grievance has been so widely circulated that it is needless to mention it now; but what is to be expected of a Government composed of men barely able to write their own names ?

" Of course I, as a woman, do not wish to enter into the larger questions of franchise, monopolies, taxation, &c., but being myself an Africander, and well able to recognise the many good qualities of the Boers, you will quite understand that I do not take a prejudiced view of the situation, and I am in a position better than

that of most people to understand the grave reality of
the Uitlanders' grievances.—Yours faithfully,

"FLORENCE PHILLIPS.

"BURLINGTON HOTEL, W.,
    9th January."

It was printed, and I got into dreadful hot water
with Mr. Wernher and Mr. Michaelis, and that day, I
think, was one of the most miserable I ever spent. I
did not know what indiscretion I had committed. The
idea that I might have betrayed State secrets over-
whelmed me, and anguish is the only word to express
my feelings as I reflected that, although I had acted
with the best possible motives, I might perhaps have
done some terrible harm to those I had meant to help.

In my despair I did not know where to turn. I had for
the moment hopelessly offended all Lionel's colleagues,
and Mr. Beit having gone to the Cape in November, I
did not know any one who could advise me as to what
I ought to do. In this dilemma my thoughts turned
to Miss Shaw, of the *Times*, whom I had first met in
Johannesburg. She, I knew, was a true woman, kind
and understanding, and could give me sound advice.
So weeping bitterly, I was just getting into a hansom
to go and see her, when I met a friend in need on the
pavement, the Duke of Abercorn, who said he had come
to congratulate me on my letter! I told him my
trouble, and he reassured me considerably; and I pro-
ceeded to see Miss Shaw, who also did not fail me in

my need. All that kind womanly sympathy and a grasp of the situation could give she gave me, and in that she afforded more comfort and help than perhaps she was aware of. She also reassured me, and told me she thought I could not have done my husband any harm; in fact, she considered it a great pity that at that particular moment more exertions were not made to set the public right, as people were in the deepest ignorance of the whole question, and naturally went blindly by what they read in the papers. I blessed her, and she still has my warmest gratitude for her help when I was in such trouble. Miss Shaw then said to me, "You have of course seen the letter that was sent by the Johannesburg men to Jameson among the telegrams to the *Times?*" "No," I said, "I had not. I had missed it through travelling between Paris and London." "And," she said, in rather a grave voice, "the signatures of the men who sent it?" My heart sank when I read the names—Lionel Phillips, Charles Leonard, John Hays Hammond, Frank Rhodes, and George Farrar. I do not know how I had missed reading the letter some days before, and the ominous words sank like lead on my heart.

I returned to my hotel feeling crushed in body and mind and utterly perplexed. I found on the table of my sitting-room several telegrams, and among them the following one from Lionel: "The Transvaal Government arresting many men here, so have given myself up. Going to Pretoria prison to-day. Do not come

out on any account." My cup was full. My soul re-
belled at the idea of staying, but I did not feel justified
in disobeying. I felt that my only course was to do as
I was asked.

Most of our luggage had been sent on, as we were
leaving for South Africa the next day, and it had to
be brought back from Southampton. There were many
people who blamed me for not going out in spite of
Lionel's wishes, but to all I made the same answer,
"When any one is in deep trouble and wishes you expressly to do something for them, is it not a greater
proof of your desire to serve them to do as they wish
rather than the opposite?" At any rate, that was my
idea of the matter. I did not know what Lionel's
motives were in not wishing us to go out, for I knew
there could be no personal danger for us; but I thought
he probably had some private reason which he could
not divulge by cable, as the censorship was extremely
strict, and I did not know what means he would have
in prison for communication with any one.

I cannot describe the agony of mind I underwent
during those first weeks; my nights were made hideous
by the thought of his sufferings in prison, for I was
well acquainted with Pretoria and its primitive institutions, the filthy habits of its inhabitants, and its
almost tropical climate in January. I did not know
what to do for the best; and my utter helplessness
overcame me. Also, I was quite alive to the treacherous
character of the Transvaal Boer, and knew that of

Lionel in particular Kruger was very jealous, and that he would not be sorry to know that he was out of the way. I knew that Kruger was aware that there were people who, in writing or talking of Johannesburg, had dubbed Lionel "King of Johannesburg," and that it was gall to him. So knowing that he and his friends were in prison, I felt extremely uneasy as to their safety.

As a good Colonial, my thoughts naturally flew to the fountain-head, and I felt that if I could only see the Queen and put the true state of the case to her—set out the wrongs of Johannesburg in fact—all would be well. So I telegraphed to a kind friend, Lord Montagu of Beaulieu, to that effect, and he came up from Southampton on purpose to see me. He told me that under the circumstances he considered such a step would be useless, as her Majesty always acted in a constitutional manner, and it was a question for the Colonial Office. He added, "If it were a matter of life and death, I should think she might listen, but not otherwise." So I abandoned the idea, but was haunted by the knowledge that it *might* be a question of life or death.

The fact, however, remained that these men had given up their arms—with the result that they were now imprisoned—in obedience to Sir H. Robinson, who had acted under orders from the Colonial Office, and that consequently some one was responsible for their unjust treatment. So I went to Downing Street, determined to interview Mr. Chamberlain and find out a little of the truth.

I sent in my card and a note asking him to see me, and was left waiting in a little room for some time. It appears that there had been two very important meetings that very afternoon—one of the Cabinet and the other with the Chartered Company—but of this I was not aware. The Duke of Abercorn again came to my assistance, and took me off to see Mr. Fairfield, whom I found unnecessarily flippant on an occasion which to me was sufficiently grave, and who twitted me with the "nice mess that Messrs. Lionel Phillips & Co. had made of matters in Johannesburg." My reply, that they had shown more courage by remaining in Johannesburg than going out to meet Jameson, did not meet with his approval. So when I was told that Mr. Chamberlain could not see me, but that Mr. Fairfield would tell me anything I wanted to know, I did not feel inclined to pour my woes into that gentleman's ears, and insisted on seeing the Colonial Secretary himself. I thought that as he, through the High Commissioner, had been to a great extent responsible for the "nice mess" in which my husband found himself, the least he could do was to see me.

I was ushered into the huge room he occupied, and I must admit that if he was not conversational he was at least civil. He informed me that my husband's life was safe, which was somewhat reassuring. He declined to discuss the situation, which did not surprise me, but when I told him that we had been "groaning under Majuba Hill for fifteen years," I certainly was not aware that he had been in the Liberal Cabinet which was responsible for that "nice mess"—the retro-cession of the Transvaal.

Mr. Beit and Mr. Rhodes came over to England about this time, and I was at last able to get at a little of the truth, although even they, not having been farther north than Cape Town, could not tell me all or even half. Mr. Beit was a wreck, and utterly cast down about the hideous failure of everything. He told me that Jameson, in coming down to Johannesburg, had disobeyed Rhodes's orders, but probably felt that in doing so it would prevent the Boers from hearing of the preparations in Johannes-burg, and thought it was best to rush matters, "as," he added, "if the Transvaal Government had got wind of them (i.e. the preparations), and quietly imprisoned your husband and the others, the world would never have heeded the matter, the Colonial Office would not have bothered, and they might have lingered there for years." That, of course, is an extremely far-fetched argument, but, in his loyalty to his friends, Mr. Beit felt constrained to find a good reason for these unfortunate actions. He, I know, was suffering tortures at the thought of what some of his old friends were enduring in the loathsome Pretoria gaol, and I am sure would have been happy to change places with them. One night I remember reading in an evening paper the account of the sufferings of the "Reform" prisoners (for by that name they were known)—how the prison was filthy, infested by vermin, that no sanitary appliances were provided, that the men were herded together—and the whole hideousness of their case came over me anew. Hearing that Mr. Beit was with Mr. Rhodes in the same hotel as myself, I sent for him, and, I am afraid, imbued him with my own misery, as I never saw any one look so utterly, hopelessly wretched. I can honestly say that I believe the sufferers and victims in prison did not suffer as much for themselves as he did for them. I must also add that Mr. Beit absolutely relieved my mind of any lurking doubt I still felt as to the mischief my letter to the *Times* might have done my husband. His words, " Your motive was good, and you are not to reproach yourself," were balm to my soul.

By the way, this letter brought trouble on my devoted head in more ways than one, and I think I learnt a lesson on the danger of writing to the papers which will last me my lifetime. The fresh trouble took the form of reporters and professional interviewers. Having already got into trouble about my opinions, I was careful not to plunge deeper, and was warned, happily in time, under no circumstances to receive any one, for " so pertinacious are some of them that even the minute it would take to tell them you cannot be interviewed, would suffice to enable them to describe, with some degree of accuracy, your person, the colour of your eyes, or any trick of manner—which would be quite sufficient foundation for them to work on—opinions and conversations they supply themselves." Never under any circumstances, therefore, did I see any of the numerous people who came on behalf of their papers, and only once did a lady interviewer in a most perfidious manner get the better of me.

Naturally at a time of such excitement and general interest in South African affairs, the papers were anxious for anything to make "copy," and it amused me immensely to be asked for my photograph. I never could see how *my* photograph could throw any light on the situation, and so, of course, invariably refused. Apart from the horror of gaining a pitiful personal notoriety, I felt the real gravity and seriousness of the matter and of Lionel's position far too deeply to risk doing him any harm.

Another amusing experience at this time was the number of anonymous letters I received on the Uitlander question, signed by "Briton," "A Mother," "A Sympathiser," &c., from all parts of the British Isles.

But I had not much inclination to laugh at this juncture. The positive execration in which Johannesburg was held at that moment, and my ignorance of facts with which to refute the charges, made me very sensitive. I can remember carrying home parcels rather than give my name in a shop, and expose myself to the stares of the assistants. I also refrained from taking cabs or incurring unnecessary expenses, as I had been informed we were utterly ruined. That,

however, did not worry me very much, although, of
course, it did not tend to increase my happiness.

One of the things that took me out of my misery at
this time was the Pantomime. A kind friend used to
take me, and I saw "Cinderella" over and over again,
generally in a box behind a curtain, for fear of meeting
censorious acquaintances.

I tried several times to induce Lionel to allow us
to go to South Africa, but after receiving a cable
via Newcastle, in Natal, felt much easier in mind.
It was to the effect that he had positive private information that they were all coming out very soon, but
it was a dead secret, which I was not to breathe to any
one, and as he would leave for England immediately he
got out, I was to stay where I was. How many weary
times before they actually did come out was I to hear
this same tale, of the "positive private information from
some one in authority," and how many weary times was
I to realise that it was all part of the Boer game to keep
their prey on tenterhooks to their own profit!

But as time dragged on, and my passage had been
taken over and over again, and I was invariably stopped,
I began to realise that it was hopeless to wait, and so
finally one day in February I cabled to Lionel that I
was positively leaving with the children by the next
boat, and as this time he made no objections, we went.
Had I known then, what we all learned later to our
cost, that there would be eternal rumours of release,
eternal rumours of intervention by the British Govern-

F

ment to be invariably followed by disappointment, how
much unnecessary suspense and heart-burning we might
have spared ourselves!

Before I left England the British Government were
negotiating with Kruger, who had decided to keep the
Johannesburg men, numbering sixty-four in all, in order
to try them himself, and to send Dr. Jameson and his
fellow-raiders to England to be tried by their own
countrymen. The principals were Dr. Jameson, Sir
John Willoughby, the Hon. Henry White, his brother
Robert, Colonel Grey, and others. These were almost all
men in the employment of the Chartered Company. It
is not necessary for me to tell of all the thousand and
one attacks made on that Company. Suffice it to say
that most of its power was taken from it, and among
others Mr. Rhodes and Mr. Beit had to resign their
directorships.

Mr. Rhodes's exclamation when he heard of the
Jameson Raid, "Jameson has been my friend for twenty
years, and now he has ruined me!" ought to have convinced many people, if no other arguments did, that
whatever else they may lay at his door, the instigation
of the raid does not rest with him. Many people are
also convinced that Jameson did it, thinking to serve
Rhodes, and that the latter really wished him to dis-
obey orders. This argument is quite as far-fetched as
the various conjectures as to what would have happened
to the Uitlanders if he had not crossed the border.
If one is to be judged entirely on other people's inter-

CAPE TOWN, SHOWING TABLE BAY AND TABLE MOUNTAIN.

pretation of what we say, where is the use of truth-fulness?

In Pretoria the preliminary trial of the Reform prisoners was proceeding. Mr. Chamberlain in his negotiations with Mr. Kruger had not advanced very far. He sent a very fierce despatch to the latter, and published it in the English papers before it reached its destination. The Boer Government, advised by the astute Dr. Leyds, were not slow to take advantage of and make the most of this diplomatic mistake, principally by petty bullying of the Reform prisoners. This kind of thing continued the whole time they were in prison. Without reading the newspapers, they were made aware of any little differences of opinion between the two Governments by the way in which they were treated. Their treatment was a kind of barometer.

After our three weeks' voyage, which was a very anxious one, naturally I pined for news, but found on my arrival at Cape Town that there was no change whatever in the situation. The men were still under-going the long drawn-out preliminary examination. The majority had been let out on bail, but the four ringleaders and Mr. Fitzpatrick were in a cottage in Pretoria with a guard, on £20,000 recognisances. I found that the Cape Town people were much excited against Johannesburg—many men of the Ministry pub-licly decrying every one concerned in the whole move-ment, including Mr. Rhodes, who had long ere this resigned the Premiership of the Cape Colony. This is typical of the species, but it was a pitiful spectacle nevertheless, considering the way in which they had openly sympathised before the fiasco. Verily it was a time for the sifting of the tares from the wheat, a process of too painful a nature to make one wish for repetition.

There was great fun in Cape Town also over the escape of one of the Reformers, who, poor man, really did not deserve all the abuse he got. Being a Consul for a European country with Eastern ideas, it appears he was persuaded that, if he were found guilty, it might cause an international crisis, and that therefore he had better leave Johannesburg. So to avoid being seen, he hid himself, with a lady friend's connivance, under the seat of a railway carriage, and safely reached Cape Town; but alas for his well-laid plans—he was ruthlessly brought back, and played his part like a man during the rest of the time.

Lionel had asked our friend, Mr. Frank Robinow, to come down to the Cape to escort us up to Johannesburg, as people had been going through unpleasant experiences with the Customs officials at Vereeniging, which is on the border, and he dreaded lest, being the wife of a prisoner, I might be subjected to rather bad treatment. The officials, it appeared, were most zealous in their search for arms, and women were the victims of dreadful indignities in consequence. But our fears were groundless. They had evidently been warned of our presence in the train. On our arrival

HALL, "HODENHOLM."

at eleven at night, some one came up at once and asked if I was there, and on my declaring myself, in a most polite manner asked me to follow him. They were all perfectly civil, and, contrary to their habit, even went so far as to allow the poor tired children to sleep on, for which I felt sincerely grateful.

I had received one or two mysterious telegrams from Lionel *en route*, and then before arriving at our destination, I got one telling me that he and the three others had obtained a special permit for twenty-four hours, and that he would be at our home, "Hohenheim," to welcome us instead of in Pretoria. A mysterious action of the Government, which was as unexpected as it was pleasant! It appears that some of the prisoners' friends had asked for the privilege, and it was granted on condition that they did not enter the town of Johannesburg, and were back by Sunday night. By the way, in Pretoria they were escorted to and from the station by a troop of cavalry, while in Johannesburg they were left quite alone and unguarded. A childish performance, typical of all the doings of the Government! When we arrived at Johannesburg at two in the morning, after our three days' journey, it was very nice to find Lionel at Hohenheim. He looked very thin, but quite well and cheery. Colonel Rhodes was also there; the other three men had gone to their homes. They returned to their cottage in Pretoria next day.

CHAPTER VIII

AND now I must recapitulate and relate much that hitherto had been absolutely unknown to me or unexplained. I, in my turn, was able to explain many things to Lionel and his friends beyond what appeared in the papers, as they had heard very little news of the outer world. They had received very few letters, if any, from those who were cognisant of much that had occurred, for a very general fear of committing indiscretion prevailed everywhere. No one knew what facts the Transvaal Government were in possession of, so every one thought the less said and written the better. But that sort of thing can be carried a little too far, and I found these poor men, in spite of all their pluck, were growing a little uneasy at their prolonged detention, and to suspect more and more that they had got into a terrible mess through obeying the injunctions of Sir Hercules. The fact that their loyalty and obedience had cost them their liberty had not yet dawned on them in all its significance; it seemed impossible to be true. And many individuals also at this period were unaware apparently that to be in prison is a terrible thing—the utter helplessness and dependence of the prisoner make his plight one not to be laughed

at. Many people whom these men looked to and
thought their friends, had neither the moral nor the
physical courage to stand by them. Truly it was a
trying time for all. But, thank God, Lionel and the
majority of his fellow-sufferers showed themselves to be
men; whatever their mistakes, their credulity even, they
were honest, and all their actions bear the light of day.
Their loyalty to every one concerned, their patience
and pluck under the most trying circumstances, always
struck me very much. Hence, their failure in a good
cause, notwithstanding, these Reformers of Johannesburg may pride themselves on one thing, namely, that
they gained the respect of every one who had an opportunity of judging their conduct.

The Reform movement in Johannesburg failed because, as some one put it to me at the time, "they all
wanted to be a little too clever." They took too many
things into consideration; they wanted to provide for too
many contingencies; there were too many in the secret,
and too many divergent interests. And also the mass
of the people had not been sufficiently educated on the
subject; it was too much restricted to one class. It
was a conspiracy to get right done for the Uitlanders
and for the mines—and the mines are the life-blood
of Johannesburg—and Johannesburg directly and indirectly affects the whole of South Africa.

But the fact remains that there were three sets of
people concerned in this movement, each in their way
meritorious, no doubt, and having one end, but actu-

ated by different motives, and this constituted a great weakness to start with. This triangular movement consisted of, first, the men on the spot, afterwards called the Reform Committee of Johannesburg, who were working for the Uitlanders and their interests; Mr. Rhodes at Cape Town, who sympathised intensely with Johannesburg, but who was more interested in the whole of South Africa, and saw the necessity of settling this burning local question; and Dr. Jameson, Mr. Rhodes's right-hand man in Mashonaland, who had with him a number of irresponsible young men indifferent to either of the above-mentioned ideas, and possibly anxious for personal glory. The probabilities in a combination such as I have mentioned are, that at some one moment or another the main idea might be lost sight of, and the minor and personal one substituted; and that is what happened. But to use plain language.

When the men of Johannesburg eventually determined to make a stand against their oppressors and to demand their just rights, they knew perfectly well that in a town of 80,000 inhabitants, with a very large proportion of women and children, they, having no armed force of their own and not knowing how many arms they could smuggle in, would be utterly at the mercy of the Boer rifles. Consequently, outside aid of some sort was necessary, and aid that could be counted on in an emergency.

Although the Boers have no standing force to speak

of, every male Boer, from the age of sixteen and up-
wards, is in a sense a soldier. Every one can shoot,
and generally well. He says it takes fifteen Englishmen to beat one Boer, and certainly the ordinary
English Tommy Atkins usually sent out is not a
match for one Boer, of whom large numbers can be
mustered at short notice. As a rule, within an hour
after he has received a call to arms he is ready to
depart. He has no elaborate preparations to make.
He does not change his costume; standing in a corner
of the *voorhuis* (front room) his gun is ready for use.
During the short time it takes him to catch his horse
in the kraal, or to get him out of the stable and "up-
saddled," his *vrouw* (wife) can fill his saddle-bags with
biltong (dried meat), and off he goes. No long farewells
even keep him, as the life the Boers have led for
generations—ready for any emergency—does not admit
of much sentimentality. In fact, it is well known that
at Majuba, and in their numerous Kaffir wars, the
womenfolk loaded the rifles while the men fought.

Knowing that in the neighbouring country the
Chartered Company had a large force at their command, the leaders of the Reform movement made a
compact with Mr. Rhodes, who was the master-mind
there—the ruling spirit in every way—that he was to
help them. Accordingly Dr. Jameson, who had been
Administrator for the Chartered Company, came to
Johannesburg, and the Reform leaders informed him
that on a given date (probably the 28th December)

they intended to present an ultimatum to the Transvaal Government, stating that unless certain rights were accorded to them they would take them by force. In case of the latter alternative, Dr. Jameson, who would be on the border with 1200 to 1500 men and 1000 spare rifles and some ammunition, would, at the signal from Johannesburg, come to their aid. Remember he left Pitsani with less than 500 men! But as some justification in the eyes of his Directors, and in order not to implicate them, as well as to show to his men, the Reform leaders drew up and signed in Dr. Jameson's presence the so-called letter, which is here reproduced.

"To Dr. Jameson.

"Dear Sir,—The position of matters in this State has become so critical that we are assured that, at no distant period, there will be a conflict between the Government and the Uitlander population. It is scarcely necessary for us to recapitulate what is now a matter of history; suffice it to say that the position of thousands of Englishmen and others is rapidly becoming intolerable. Not satisfied with making the Uitlander population pay virtually the whole of the revenue of the country, while denying them representation, the policy of the Government has been steadily to encroach upon the liberty of the subject, and to undermine the security for property to such an extent as to cause a very deep-seated sense of discontent and danger. A

foreign corporation of Hollanders is to a considerable
extent controlling our destinies, and, in conjunction
with the Boer leaders, endeavouring to cast them in
a mould which is wholly foreign to the genius of the
people. Every public act betrays the most positive
hostility, not only to everything English, but to the
neighbouring States.

"Well, in short, the internal policy of the Government is such as to have roused into antagonism to
it, not only practically the whole body of Uitlanders,
but a large number of the Boers; while its external
policy has exasperated the neighbouring States, causing
the possibility of great danger to the peace and independence of this Republic. Public feeling is in a condition of smouldering discontent. All the petitions of
the people have been refused with a greater or less
degree of contempt; and in the debate on the franchise
petition, signed by nearly 40,000 people, one member
challenged the Uitlanders to fight for the rights they
asked for, and not a single member spoke against him.
Not to go into details, we may say that the Government
has called into existence all the elements necessary for
armed conflict. The one desire for the people here is
fair-play, the maintenance of their independence, and
the preservation of those public liberties without which
life is not worth living. The Government denies these
things, and violates the national sense of Englishmen
at every turn.

"What we have to consider is, What will be the

condition of things here in the event of a conflict ? Thousands of unarmed men, women, and children of our race will be at the mercy of well-armed Boers, while property of enormous value will be in the greatest peril. We cannot contemplate the future without the gravest apprehensions. All feel that we are justified in taking any steps to prevent the shedding of blood and to insure the protection of our rights.

"It is under these circumstances that we feel constrained to call upon you to come to our aid, should a disturbance arise here. The circumstances are so extreme that we cannot but believe that you and the men under you will not fail to come to the rescue of people so situated. We guarantee any expense that may reasonably be incurred by you in helping us, and ask you to believe that nothing but the sternest necessity has prompted this appeal.

> "CHARLES LEONARD.
> LIONEL PHILLIPS.
> FRANCIS RHODES.
> JOHN HAYES HAMMOND.
> GEORGE FARRAR."

This letter was undated, the understanding being that Dr. Jameson was to affix the date when authorised to do so. But what happened in reality ? Dr. Rutherford Harris, another Chartered employé, sent it from Cape Town to the *Times*, adding the date himself—28th December—the day Dr. Jameson started from Pitsani, no doubt with the idea of giving people in

England a reason for Dr. Jameson's action and to justify him. Let us hope that if the possibility of his surrendering had occurred to any one, Dr. Harris might have stayed his hand, as it was the publication of this letter which aroused the fury of all men against Johannesburg, and gained for it a reputation it was far from deserving, which has never been effaced. The Johannesburgers were the injured ones, the betrayed, but they were put in a very wrong light through the publication of this letter; and by fostering the impression that it had in reality been sent up post haste, Dr. Jameson and his friends made most treacherous use of it. The publication at the time is excusable, as no one in their wildest dreams could have thought of surrender, the inexcusable thing being that it had been in Dr. Jameson's possession for weeks, and that fact was never elicited until the British Parliamentary Inquiry months afterwards.

Most of the Reformers had known Dr. Jameson many years. One of them was his own brother. But they put him to too severe a test. Surrounded as he was by a number of young men who had come to South Africa fairly recently, to either try to make their fortunes or have some fun (most of them were soldiers), they became impatient at being kept on the border so many weeks, and talked themselves into believing that they could " walk through the Transvaal with 500 men." They were told part of the truth, and in London drawing-rooms weeks beforehand was discussed a subject that in Johannesburg itself was spoken of with bated breath by the few in the secret, and on which hung the destiny of a sub-continent. But one cannot blame these youths. One can quite sympathise with their military ardour: the pity is that they were not led by better men.

Colonel Rhodes was sent by his brother to Johannesburg, ostensibly to take a business position; arms were being smuggled in; and military men from Rhodesia were sent down to help in preparations which the Reform men, being civilians, were naturally not competent to arrange themselves. Then Lionel made his speech in November at the Chamber of Mines. So far so well.

The Reform Committee had expressly stipulated that the whole movement was to take place under the Transvaal flag, but it came to their ears, through a medium which they could not disregard, and of which they obtained confirmation, that when he reached Pretoria it was the intention of Jameson to raise the English flag. Now, there were many Africanders, Americans, Germans, and English interested in the movement who did not wish to see the Republic abolished, but merely its bad system of government. So this question of the flag was in reality a serious one. Mr. C. Leonard and Mr. Hamilton were despatched post haste by the Committee to Cape Town to confer with Mr. Rhodes, and the latter assured them he had no intention of changing the flag, but the day after they arrived there Dr. Jameson made his fatal start. Remember that in that large town of Johannesburg there were scarcely any rifles, that the population was comparatively unarmed, and every rifle to be used had to be smuggled in—a very tedious process. The arms were mostly concealed in oil-tanks, and all the precautions taken at the different mines to which they were sent caused great delay. The Reformers counted on getting about 2500 guns—not a very large number— but they were playing a desperate game, and relied on those they would get out of the arsenal.

The original project was that about 2500 rifles should be smuggled into Johannesburg, and that Jameson should have on the border a force of from 1200 to 1500 men, thoroughly trained and equipped, with about an equal number of extra rifles and a good supply of ammunition, ready to advance when called upon. An essential feature of the plan was the seizure of the arsenal at Pretoria, which at that time was defended by only ninety artillerymen (the standing army of the Transvaal), so that the task seemed easy of accomplishment. The arsenal consisted of a number of tin shanties enclosed in a square surrounded by sun-dried brick walls. In it were stored about 15,000 Martini-Henry rifles, a large supply of ammunition, and some Maxims. With a view to carrying out this project, 300 rifles were sent to a spot within ten miles of Pretoria, and mule-waggons were kept there in readiness. On the night of the outbreak the arsenal was to be seized, all rifles and ammunition were to be sent to Johannesburg, and any war material which could not be removed was to be destroyed.

Thus, according to the original plan, what with the smuggled rifles, those in private hands, the spare weapons to be brought by Jameson's men, and those men themselves, Johannesburg would have mustered a little army of not less than 5000 men, to say nothing of the guns which might possibly be captured in the arsenal. It was believed that with this force the town could be held against any attack that might be made by the Transvaal forces, and that, upon a failure in the first assault, the Boers would have adopted their well-known tactics of cutting off supplies, with a view to starving the town into submission. To meet this contingency the town was provisioned for two months, and it was supposed that the British Government would never sit still and allow the Uitlanders to be forced into capitulation in the face of the wrongs which they had suffered. In November, when Jameson came to Johannesburg, the supporting force had dwindled to 800. The telegrams apprising the Reformers of his advance spoke of 700, and in reality he started with less than 500 men.

In the midst of their preparations, the Reformers heard that Jameson was getting impatient on the border, but as he had agreed not to move without the signal arranged upon, they felt pretty safe. Conscious of the disastrous effect upon South African

sentiment, so far entirely in their favour, of Dr.
Jameson taking the initiative, fully aware of their un-
preparedness, but owing to the reports they received
of his restlessness, they despatched Major Heany and
Captain Holden (two of Jameson's officers who were
sent to aid them in organising, and who were fully
aware of the position) by different routes to warn him
not to start until called upon. Both these gentlemen
duly reached him and delivered their message before
he "took the bit between his teeth and bolted," to use
Mr. Rhodes' description of his mad action. Lionel had
also telegraphed to Cape Town predicting disaster if
Jameson moved. These facts were not known until
long afterwards—not, indeed, until the inquiry of the
Parliamentary Committee.

All the negotiations were made in cipher, and it is
an astonishing fact that the authorities in Pretoria
suspected nothing of the arrangements made with
Rhodes and Jameson, and the whole evidence against
the Reform Committee was contained in the tin despatch-
box brought in by Jameson's secretary, Major Robert
White.

But two unexpected delays took place towards the
end of the month. The most important was that the
majority of the expected rifles had not arrived, without
which nothing could be done; and, secondly, the usual
December race-meeting was being held, and it was
estimated that the population of Johannesburg was
increased by about 10,000 strangers. So for two very

G

good reasons it was decided to postpone the fateful meeting demanding their rights from the 28th December to the 6th January. The Government meanwhile had received notice from the National Union of its intentions, and for the first time in its existence found that it was to be treated with firmness. The Government got into a regular fright, and began making the most enticing promises; in fact, as a member of the Volksraad put it to me afterwards, "the Government was giving them what they asked with both hands," when the awful news reached Johannesburg that Jameson had crossed the northern border of the Transvaal and was marching to Johannesburg. Naturally, when they heard the disquieting rumours that reached them, the utmost confusion reigned, and these men realised the horror of having an unarmed population on their hands, with no protection for the women and children, and the knowledge that they were far outnumbered by the thousands of Kaffirs in the neighbourhood was an added anxiety.

But the internal question was all-absorbing. They felt sure that, whatever his motives for disregarding their wishes, Jameson, at any rate, was acting for the best, and loyal they were to him and loyal they remained many a month afterwards. The dreadful truth ultimately dawned on them that they had placed their trust in a very undeserving person.

They felt no particular uneasiness about Jameson. He had promised not to venture over the border with

MEN ASKING FOR ARMS AT THE REFORM OFFICE.

A Troop of the Australian Contingent raised for Protection of Johannesburg.

less than 800 men, and so they thought he was well qualified to take care of himself, especially as the most minute and careful preparations had been made beforehand for providing food for man and beast all along the road. So, working like slaves day and night, the Johannesburg men did their best to arrange for the safety of the town, and to provide shelter and food for the hundreds who crowded in from the neighbouring mines. The Government removed their wretched police immediately — the best thing they could do—the Reform Committee replacing them by volunteers, and I believe neither before nor since was such order maintained. Only one single instance of crime is recorded. They also immediately sent out and bought up all the liquor in the hundreds of canteens along the mines and destroyed it all. Companies of volunteers were posted in trenches round the town.

Whatever the Reform Committee did themselves was satisfactory, but it seemed as if the Fates were against everything connected with Jameson. He had undertaken to see upon starting that the telegraph wires were cut, but one of the men sent out by him failed to do this, with the result that the Boers received news of the invasion eight hours before the Reformers. In those precious hours Boers for many miles round flocked into Pretoria, and rendered the project| of taking the arsenal an impossible task. One of Dr. Jameson's trusted persons, sent especially for the occasion, was ordered to go and wrench up the railway line between Johannesburg and

Krugersdorp in order to interrupt communication from Pretoria in the direction of the Chartered forces. This man was discovered hours afterwards in the Rand Club, dead drunk, and the train that would have been prevented from coming was the one which brought the ammunition that was used against the invading force !

When the fearful news came that Jameson had encountered the Boers near Krugersdorp, that after the loss of some men he had surrendered, and that they had all been conveyed to Pretoria prison, a complete panic set in in the town. Many of the remaining women and children started off by the few trains for the Cape in the utmost terror. Some of them had good cause to know what it was to remain in a besieged town from their former Transvaal experiences. Many were too terror-stricken to care for appearances, and went off in the airiest attire—night-gowns and dressing-gowns. The scenes at the station were most heart-rending; women waited for hours in dense masses; and the climax was reached when those disgraceful cowards, that portion of the Cornish miners who left, "rushed" the trains and kept out the women. At all the stations down the line the same conduct was repeated. On hearing of the suffering of these poor refugees of their own sex, the colonial women assembled with food and other necessaries for them, but in every instance these brutes, unworthy of the name of men, used to rush them and snatch everything for themselves. And these were the creatures who, when they eventually arrived in England, were interviewed and their opinions upon the capitalists deemed worthy of record.

On these dreadful journeys in the heat of January, carriages and cattle-trucks were so overcrowded that children were suffocated and children were born. A friend of mine who, with her two delicate little children, was among the terrified runaways, told me that if a similar crisis ever occurred again she would sooner brave the horrors of a siege than endure the suffering she went through. She was four days in an open cattle-truck, in which they were packed like herrings. Many of those who first escaped got off at different stations, hoping that the next trains would be less crowded; but just the reverse was the case, and hence the frightful crush.

Then came the terrible accident on the newly-opened Natal line. The train, which was full of refugees, ran off the rails, and thirty-eight women and children were killed. I heard of one poor man who sent his wife and daughters away, and they were all killed. A friend who was in that train, but who escaped, tells me that the horror of it will never be effaced from her memory. She with her two children and nurse were in a carriage which capsized, but were unhurt, and she handed the children out of the window. The anxiety lest the boiler should burst was terrible, until happily the engine got detached and ran down the line. The sight of the many decapitated and injured people was one never to be forgotten. Verily the New Year of 1896

is one that many people in South Africa have cause
to remember!

Lionel told me that those few days were a terrible
experience. For five days and nights most of the
Reform Committee had very little sleep, and he said
that he was so wearied in mind and body that if he
had heard he was going to be shot he would scarcely
have minded. A friend of ours told me that he
happened to go into the goldfields offices, which were
used by the Reform Committee at this time, and found
him asleep on the floor with nothing but the cold oil-
cloth under him, and that he took off his coat and
put it under his head without awaking him.

Meanwhile they were all in a great suspense about
Jameson and his friends, not being aware that before
surrendering they had stipulated for their safety. That
was a little secret upon which much depended. Nor
were they informed that Major Robert White had
brought with him a despatch-box containing the key
to the cipher that had been used through most of the
negotiations, the copy of the so-called letter of invitation, the names of various people, &c. Therefore in
Johannesburg the only anxiety was for the personal
safety of Jameson and his friends. They thought that
for themselves there was no danger, the Government
having no evidence whatever against them, as every
scrap of writing had been destroyed. They felt that
they had been working for the good of the place, that
they had taken all possible precautions for the safety of

the women and children, and—the Government believed they had 20,000 rifles.

Even after Jameson's frightful blunder they had the game practically in their own hands, but lost it, for two reasons. The first and principal one was the interference of the High Commissioner, who, infected apparently by the air of Pretoria, made promises through the British Agent which were never kept; and the second and minor one, that the Reform Committee did not realise at the time their own strength. They knew that they had very few rifles and a hopelessly small supply of ammunition, and did not then realise that the Government was shaking in its shoes, convinced that they had 20,000.

Sir Hercules Robinson (late Lord Rosmead) offered his services to the Transvaal Government with a view to a peaceful settlement, and to show that the latter Government was most anxious for his intervention, it is well to emphasise the facts that Jameson surrendered on Thursday morning, that the telegraph line was in full working order, and that the Governor did not leave Cape Town until Thursday night. Having vanquished Jameson, clearly the Transvaal authorities, had they felt able to deal with the Reformers, would during that day have withdrawn their acceptance of his services. Sir Hercules came up to restore order and to do what he could for every one.

South Africa has been called "the Grave of Reputations," and when one thinks of the many good public servants of the Crown who have come to grief over its difficult problems, one sees much truth in the sweeping title. Here we see the sad spectacle of a careful Governor, a man beloved by all who knew him, but physically unfit for his work, undertaking a most difficult diplomatic mission, and making a dreadful mess of it. Sir Hercules was old and in indifferent health, and to make matters worse, the train he travelled by met with an accident before reaching its destination. The party arrived many hours late, much shaken, and what little nerve he may have had for his difficult task was quite gone. He stayed in Pretoria five days, and was seen by Kruger once. One little interview to settle the difficulties of years!

Anyhow, he sent the British Resident, Sir Jacobus de Wet, and Sir Sidney Shippard to Johannesburg, and they in turn addressed the thousands assembled. The gist of their speeches was that Sir Hercules had come as representing her Majesty's Government, and promised to see that the Uitlanders got their just rights, but first and foremost he must ask them to give up their arms, for the lives of Jameson and his men depended upon it, and without that preliminary no negotiations with the Transvaal Government could be conducted. There was strong opposition on all sides, but the leaders were persuaded to use their utmost influence, as Jameson's safety was absolutely at stake, and the matter urgent They were promised, however, that their grievances should be looked into and righted. So, naturally

believing what they were told, though in the teeth
of the most violent opposition from the mass of
the men, the disarmament was effected—every man
gave up his gun, no matter what the kind, at the
bidding of her Majesty's representative. The lives of
the Reformers were in greater danger at that moment
from their fellows than they had yet been from the
enemy.

When the guns were given up to the number of
2500 the Boers would not believe that was all. Even
the solemn word of the leaders would not convince
them, and for many months afterwards the vain search
for arms continued all over the town and in many of
the mines, naturally without result, as there were no
more. I remember some months afterwards when a
new recreation-room for the Robinson Mine had just
been finished, a search was ordered, and a square hole
was cut in the middle of the floor specially laid for
dancing, as somebody had made an affidavit that guns
were concealed underneath; also on another occasion
the water was pumped out of a mine at great expense
to try to find guns supposed to be concealed at the
bottom.

Having done his gruesome work, Sir Hercules returned to Cape Town, leaving Johannesburg absolutely
at the mercy of the Boers. He actually effected the disarmament of this large town without making one single
condition for its safety, and from that day the most
signal acts of tyranny and injustice were committed

over and over again by the Boer oligarchy, and there
was no one to say them nay. This was a critical event
for English supremacy in South Africa, this final act
of supreme weakness and folly! Many of her most
loyal subjects from that moment have wavered on the
brink, and some have gone over to the side of the
Africander Bond. It is such actions as these which
estrange the colonists, and which give a little reality to
the Bondsman's dream of a united South Africa under
a Republican flag.

The Colonial Secretary has been considerably criticised for this action and its consequences, but his
defenders say that through the action of the Governor,
who never found out the conditions of Jameson's surrender and hence effected the disarmament under false
promises, his hands were terribly tied, and that Sir
Hercules, losing a magnificent opportunity when the
game was still in his hands, completely handicapped
the Home Government. As some one graphically put
it, "Sir Hercules was the stick that broke in Chamberlain's hand."

BOER "COMMANDO."

CHAPTER IX

BEING now masters of the situation, one of the first acts of the Pretoria Government was to issue warrants against the principal Reformers, and consequently sixty-four of the leading men of the town were arrested and taken over to Pretoria prison. Remember that these men had been assured by the British Agent that "not a hair of their heads should be touched"! From the moment Sir Hercules left the place they were completely deserted by the English Government, and for some time to come we were to have, in all its naked hideousness, the painful spectacle of men who started with a firm belief in their country's justice and power, arriving by slow and heartrending degrees, and after months of agonised suspense, at the conclusion that unless they worked out their own salvation, they might spend the rest of their days in the prison where they had been cast through the false promises of their own countrymen. But that conviction had not yet forced itself on their minds—that was to come very slowly.

As to the redress of grievances promised by her Majesty's representative, except for feeble suggestions treated with contempt by Kruger, nothing was done, and at the moment of writing, more than three years after these events, Johannesburg is in a worse state than it was before. Kruger, finding he could do exactly as he liked, has made of the Transvaal a country absolutely impossible for free men to live in. If the men of Johannesburg could have foreseen that they were to be deserted, how much heartburning and bitterness of spirit they might have saved themselves !

The arrests were made very quietly and suddenly. One gentleman, as he was walking down the street, was informed by the Lieutenant of Police that he was arrested. He calmly went with the Lieutenant, but being a lawyer it dawned upon him that he had seen no warrant, and asked where it was. He was told there was no warrant out against him. " Very well," he said, " I refuse to be arrested without one." So he was left in peace, but lived for weeks under the disquieting impression that at any moment he might be dragged off to Pretoria, and I believe used to ask periodically when they were going to take him. But they would not have him at all, and he was never imprisoned.

Lionel, who was staying in Johannesburg at that time, gave himself up when he heard that arrests of the Reformers were being made. Mr. Rouliot, one of his partners, and others have told me since, that at the moment they were almost pleased at his detention in prison, for the mob in Johannesburg were so enraged with the Reform Leaders on account of the misery that had fallen upon the town, that they really feared for their safety. There were also people who whispered of

the danger of assassination—it would be so easy some
dark night on that lonely road to Hohenheim to get rid
of a man who was troublesome to more than one party.
Therefore, in spite of everything, the imprisonment of
these men was a great relief to their friends.

The names of the sixty-four members of the
Reform Committee are too well known for me to recapitulate them. Among these were mining men,
doctors, lawyers, and financiers—some very rich and
some very poor—but they were in the majority of cases
serious, earnest men, having the cause they had taken
up much at heart. In so large a number there were a
few whom one would scarcely expect to find amongst a
reforming body, but such elements are apt to creep into
any movement of the kind. Still they were a very representative body of men, and, as time proved, bore
their lot with patience and dignity. The prisoners
had a very uncomfortable journey to Pretoria, being
yelled at and threatened at all the stopping-places
en route, and on their way from the station to the
prison the escort rode on to them using every sort
of abusive epithet. An excited mob was there to yell
at and insult them, and Captain Mein, a man of nearly
sixty, was kicked and knocked down by a manly
bystander.

I must now describe the gaol, where so many weeks
and months were to be spent, and which was to become
so well known to us. The head gaoler, Du Plessis, a
coarse brute, filthy in mind and body, was an absolute

autocrat on his own premises; and as a connection and intimate personal friend of Kruger's one can imagine what were the prospects of the prisoners. Their one safeguard through the whole of their imprisonment was that the under-gaoler, Burgers, was a colonial Boer, a good-natured, simple sort of man, a great deal more humane than his superior officer, and that between the two existed bitter jealousy and dislike. To him the prisoners were indebted for many an act of kindness. When they reached the gaol, one of them remarked to Du Plessis, "Awful place, this gaol of yours." The latter responded with enthusiasm, "Yes, you are right! It is the only place the English built when they were in occupation here, and it is a disgrace to any town." So far the Boers had never had any white political prisoners, nor any but of the worst character, and the accommodation was of the most primitive order. The whole place was surrounded by a high quadrangular wall of sunburnt brick. Near the large gates stood, on the one side, a small guard-room, on the other the head-gaoler's house. Round the inside of the wall were the cells, few in number, and falling far short of the ordinary sanitary regulations. A little to the right, on entering, was what became known as "Jameson's cottage." Its two wretched little rooms were divided by a passage, and had windows, whereas the other cells only had oblong holes near the roof. As the building was not suited to receive such a large number of white men, who could not be left outside to brave all weathers, the way they were treated beggars description. On their reaching the gaol, they were thrust into whatever place they could be put, and were nearly stifled. The next day they were sorted.

Lionel, George Farrar, Colonel Rhodes, and J. H. Hammond were put into one cell, twelve feet square, without windows, and were locked up there the first three nights for thirteen hours. Then the prison doctor insisted on more space being allotted to them, and the door, which communicated with a courtyard twenty feet square, was left open at night. This was the space in which they were permitted to take exercise. They were not allowed to associate with their fellows at first. In January, in Pretoria, the heat is intense, quite semi-tropical indeed, the temperature varying from 90 to 105 degrees in the shade. As the weather happened to be at its hottest, the sufferings of these men were awful. The cells, hitherto devoted to the use of Kaffirs, swarmed with vermin and smelt horribly; while to increase their miseries, if that were possible, one of their number was suffering from dysentery, and no conveniences of any kind were supplied. With these facts in mind, any attempt to describe what the prisoners underwent would be superfluous. Add to all these hardships their mental sufferings, and then judge of their state.

The English Government, I think, is better aware than most people how very little these men's lives were worth at that moment. It would have given Kruger

and his satellites the liveliest satisfaction to have shot
most of them, but especially the four I have mentioned.
The fifth of the signatories to the letter was Mr. Charles
Leonard, but as he had not returned to Johannesburg
after being sent to the Cape on a mission to Mr. Rhodes
in the latter part of December, and as Mr. Fitzpatrick
had taken a very prominent part in the movement,
having been the secretary of the Reform Committee, the Boer Government thought later that he was
a useful person to complete the quintette.

After the first few days the prisoners were treated
a little more leniently, and were allowed to have their
food sent in. Their friends also were allowed to come
and see them. Then the preliminary examination
began, and nothing very incriminating was forthcoming. Jameson and his men were also imprisoned
in the same yard, although not in contact with the
others, but either did not, or could not, give the
Reform men sundry details which might have enlightened them as to their motives of action, nor
did they inform them of the capture of the famous
despatch - box. When the Reform prisoners heard
and read of the "Transvaal Government being in
possession of incriminating documents showing a
widespread conspiracy," they only laughed, knowing
that they had carefully destroyed all written evidence.
Hence their light-hearted attitude, which on my return
struck me, who had been undergoing agonies of mind
on their account, with dismay. Their physical dis-

PRESIDENT KRUGER LEAVING THE RAADZAAL.

comforts and daily humiliations they would not see; so, believing the Boers had not much evidence against them, and knowing that their own Government had promised to protect them, beyond bitter disappointment they felt very little uneasiness. Hence Lionel's unwillingness to allow me and the children to come out to him. He was convinced they would be set free for want of evidence against them, not suspecting for one moment the double betrayal they had suffered.

When I arrived at Johannesburg the lengthy preliminary trial was drawing to an unsatisfactory close. I went over to Pretoria next day and visited the Raadzaal, where it was being held, and was accommodated with a seat. It was so strange, knowing they were prisoners, to see these men come in in an indifferent manner, and take their seats, and then listen to the dragging examination, which was very slow and Boer-like in its methods, every sentence being interpreted from Dutch into English. It seemed also very strange to me, quite fresh to it all, to see that some of the prisoners even did their best to go to sleep; but, on second thoughts, it was not to be wondered at. They had been enduring an ineffable boredom for five weeks, and knowing what a hollow farce it all was, and hearing the perjury committed in the most barefaced way by many of the Boer officials, they had grown heart-sick, and strove to drown it all in slumber. Also, the heat was unbearable.

The majority of the men were then out on bail, but the principal offenders were in a little cottage on

H

the outskirts of Pretoria. Mr. Hammond, who was not very well, was in Cape Town on bail. He remained away most of the time, and, except towards the end, shared very little of the imprisonment of the others. He had to thank his ill-health, his clever wife, and the fact of being an American citizen for his immunity.

I went up to the cottage and found the four very cheery and trying to hide their anxiety, but it was nevertheless apparent. Their continued detention, the absence of news, either private or official, was beginning to take effect. I must say it struck me then, as it did many times afterwards, how loyal they were to all who had been concerned in the movement, and that they were positively optimistic in their reliance on Government protection. The doubts that kept creeping in were always overruled by one member or another of the party. They encouraged in each other an optimism they did not always feel, but had they not done so I am quite sure they could not have borne up so cheerily nor have come out of their troubles as unscathed as they apparently did.

The cottage they occupied was a little bungalow, consisting of four rooms—three bedrooms and a dining-room—with a verandah all round, and had a pleasant garden, full of roses and violets, as well as oleanders, moonflowers, and some trees. A faithful servant of ours cooked for them, and two of the men had their valets, so they were in Paradise compared with the gaol. They were watched by guards, who surrounded

Cottage at Sunnyside, Pretoria, where Lionel Phillips, Colonel Rhodes, Percy Fitzpatrick, and George Farrar were kept.

the Compound, twelve by day and six by night. They were nominally out on bail, but were kept under strict surveillance, and, in addition, had to pay for the guards at the rate of £1000 a month! The lieutenant, an ignorant, blustering young Boer, was a thorn in their side. Vulgar and omnipresent as he was, they had no privacy of any kind. He was very fond of their cigars and whisky, very often the worse for the latter, and used to bully them in petty ways that only his own mean little soul was capable of imagining. For instance, I remember one day Lionel and I, with a visitor from England, were sitting in the little dining-room, when the lieutenant, booted and spurred, with his hat on his head and his pipe in his mouth, came into the room. We were all talking, but he rudely interrupted us, standing in the middle of the room, with his legs astride, and saying to Lionel in a bully-ing tone, " What do you mean by looking at me like that ? " It appears that Lionel had lent him his bicycle that morning, which he had broken, being probably in his usual half-tipsy state, but the former had taken no notice whatever of the matter. On being questioned in this manner, Lionel replied, " I was not looking at you, I was talking to this gentle-man." " Oh," replied the lieutenant, " I know what it is. You are in a rage with me because I broke your bicycle, but I will make it hot for you if you dare to look at me in that manner again," and with these words he marched out of the room.

On another occasion the guards had been changed, and the one stationed at the gate did not notice that the prisoners had gone off on their bicycles before the escort was ready. Mrs. Fitzpatrick and I happened to be spending the day at the cottage. The lieutenant, when he saw the disappearing forms of the prisoners, got into a frightful rage, began using dreadful language to the terrified guard, and I really was afraid he would use personal violence. So adopting a bantering tone, I said to the lieutenant, "Don't get into such a state of mind. You know very well these men don't want to run away," and a few arguments of that kind. Then he burst out laughing, and said, "Oh, well, it doesn't matter if they do run away. We have two of the wives here, and we will take very good care to stick to them."

The four—Lionel, George Farrar, Colonel Rhodes, and Fitzpatrick—were a most united and happy quartette, and their constant companion and untiring errand runner was Percy Farrar, the brother of George, who had come out from England expressly to be with him. They were kept close prisoners, except for their one hour's bicycle ride every afternoon, which was always taken in one direction, away from the town. A very funny cortège they were too, when they went out. None of them indulged in a very correct toilet. The heat made them very thankful to patronise silk shirts, no coats, and the most varied of headgear. They used to start out in line on their "bikes" with the redoubtable lieutenant and two of his men on horse-back following them, and often this procession would be increased by some chance visitors from Johannesburg, following in little open flies, or also on bicycles. Their bicycles were a real godsend to the prisoners, and a good deal of their mornings used to be spent cleaning them, or practising wonderful feats in the garden. They were in too restless a frame of mind to read much, and passed many hours playing whist. Their lawyers, who appeared to be legion, also spent a good deal of time with them preparing their defence. They constantly had visitors from Johannesburg, who often stayed to lunch, and among the most frequent of these were their fellow-prisoners out on real bail.

So far, I had never told the children that their father was a prisoner. I thought the very word, at their age, might give them a shock never to be effaced. So I was most careful that they should not come in contact with any one who might tell them, thinking that, until the necessity arose, there was no need. Harold, especially, was then at an age—nine—to feel the horror of it without analysing it. But, of course, once we were back in Johannesburg the truth could no longer be entirely suppressed. But it was not in all its nakedness that they saw it—being in the cottage was not like being in a prison, and I was thankful. Soon after our arrival, they went over to Pretoria to see their father, and of course Harold's first question was, "What are those guards all doing here?" I then took the opportunity to explain to them that their father had been working for the good of Johannesburg, and of the people there, that the Boers, who were their wicked oppressors, had taken him prisoner in consequence, but that they had only cause to be proud of what he had done. This explanation sufficed, and a great load was lifted from my mind.

During the time these men were in prison Pretoria reaped a golden harvest. The constant stream of visitors from Johannesburg caused more activity on the wretched little railway than had ever been known before. (The journey of about forty miles, by the way, took two and a half hours.) The hotelkeepers and shopkeepers did not know themselves, and wished the miserable affair might drag on for ever, as at times it almost seemed that it would.

I must mention a very marked change which had taken place in Johannesburg during my eight months' absence. Formerly one saw very few Boers in the place—they had hitherto shunned the town—but now they seemed to abound, and also in the train and on the platforms they were to be seen on every side. There was a remarkable increase, too, in the number of Germans and Russian Jews. The place had indeed changed for the worse, and I could hardly realise I was in South Africa. I was warned on my arrival to be very careful in what I said, as spies were everywhere, and that also was such an un-colonial idea that I felt more than ever how the place had fallen on evil days. The waiters at all the hotels were credited with being in the pay of the Government, and from their conduct on occasions I was not surprised to hear it. We found out afterwards that even our own *chef*, a German, who had been with us for over two years, had played the spy on Lionel, and had given information of his movements to the Government before he was arrested. When one saw what a den of iniquity the town had become, and knowing that these methods, being entirely foreign to the simple ones of the Boers, were due to some of their German and Hollander instructors, it is no wonder that many of us were plunged in despondency to see this happening under our very eyes.

Once or twice, while the prisoners were living in the cottage, the relations between the English and Transvaal Governments became very strained, and they as usual were made aware of it by the methods already described. But at one time, as their trial approached, matters became quite serious, and we who were more intimately connected with them had fears for their personal safety. Negotiations between the two Governments were not progressing very favourably. It was at the moment when Mr. Chamberlain had invited Kruger over to England: the latter had refused, and a feeling of great irritation reigned. So much bad blood had been caused that the smallest thing gave rise to ill-feeling. We, on our side, were becoming more and more hopeless as to obtaining any assistance from England.

Sinister rumours were spread about, and we often heard the word " assassination." We also learned that the beam on which in 1816 the five rebels of Slachter's Nek in the Cape Colony had been hanged by the English Government of that date, had been unearthed from its resting-place in the house of one of their descendants in the Bedford district, and brought to Pretoria. The information reached Sir Hercules Robinson, and he wired from Cape Town to the British agent to make inquiries. Sir Jacobus de Wet happening to belong to the district referred to, speedily discovered that some Transvaal Boers had purchased this beam from the owner of the house into which it was built at Cookhouse Drift, paying the cost of its being replaced by a new one. He called on the President, who denied all knowledge of the matter. That night, however, two of his faithful burghers informed him that they had secured the historic beam to hang the leading Reformers upon. Meanwhile the Colonial Office had been made acquainted with the intention of some of the Boers to seize the chief prisoners one night and hang them before the trial. This drew forth a cable message to Kruger, holding him and his Executive personally liable for the lives of the prisoners. The English Government had awakened at last. Kruger, when again approached on the subject, admitted that the beam was in Pretoria, but declared that it had been purchased for the museum by his patriotic burghers !

I inquired of Lionel if precautions of any kind had

been taken in the event of their finding it necessary to make a dash for the frontier. He informed me that his partners in Johannesburg had made arrangements for getting them over the Natal border; but as I did not consider the details nearer home in case of a sudden flight very satisfactory, I took upon myself to make certain preparations in case of need, though with the exception of Lionel, who protested that in any case they would never use them, and Percy Farrar, I kept them to myself. I well knew the danger these men would be in were the word " flight " even hinted at. It was just what the Pretoria authorities were longing for—a good pretext to get rid of these troublesome prisoners. It would so exactly have suited their tactics, though not their protestations.

I made my preparations for the possible flight of the prisoners, and began by getting a woman whom I knew to be trustworthy to buy me four revolvers, as, since Sir Hercules' visit, no one possessed such a thing. I then sent for our doctor in Johannesburg, and had to tell him what I wanted. My plan was to have ready some drug to put into the whisky for the guards that would render them useless in case of an emergency; as they were much addicted to that liquid, and helped themselves freely to the prisoners', I hoped we might count on disposing of some of them. I also thought that if any of them should be seized with a fit of abstemious-ness, some chloroform might be useful. So, promising me his aid, the doctor departed. Next day he brought me a good supply of chloroform and a large bottle of solution of morphine, giving me directions how to use the latter. It was a sign of the times that, in a most matter-of-fact voice and manner, this extremely kind, quiet man should ask me, "Would you prefer something that would kill them outright, as this will only render them unconscious?" Not feeling inclined to commit murder, I refused a more powerful drug, and returned to Pretoria with my prizes. We kept them under the boards (which we lifted) of one of the rooms, but happily no occasion arose for the use of these desperate remedies.

It is well known that one of Jameson's troopers on the way down, falling ill, was taken prisoner by some Boers, and kept at their farmhouse some days. He was tied up, and forced to submit to all sorts of ill-treatment, being given dirty water to drink, for instance, when half dying of thirst. But his captor's wife had compassion on him, and at the end of several days, to his surprise, he was told that he was to be allowed to go free. The Boers gave him his horse, mounted him, and informed him the one condition they made was that he was to ride away as fast as he could. He naturally obeyed, and as he galloped off had several bullets put into him, poor fellow. That is a very favourite and well-known method of Transvaal Boer assassination. It gives them the pretext that a prisoner had been trying to escape.

A man who was concerned in the Reform movement and was put into Krugersdorp gaol and kept there some time, told me of a similar attempt they made on his life, only he, knowing their character well, saved himself. One morning in the prison yard one of the guards said to him, "You see that post," pointing to one a little way off, "try and see how fast you can run to it." Harrington turned to him and said, "Yes, so that you can shoot me in the back and say I was running away." The dumbfounded Boer saw that this joke was not to be practised on him.

I must here remark on a fact that is not always known in England and elsewhere, and that is that there is a considerable difference between the Boer of the Transvaal and the Colonial Boer. Though *au fond* their natures and character may be much alike, there is at this day a considerable difference in many of their ideas, owing to the different life they have led for several generations; and it must also be remembered that the Transvaal Boer is of a rebel stock, "his hand against every man, and every man's hand against him." In 1835, when the great "trek" from the colony took place, these men's ancestors were the men who defied the Government—with great good cause in many instances—and whose hearts were filled with bitterness and loathing, whose one idea was to get away from their oppressors. The difficulties and dangers they went through, fighting wild beasts as well as Kaffirs, although it gave them a rugged independence, at the same time developed some of the very qualities possessed by their new foes—viz., treachery and a callous cruelty.

Their treatment of the Kaffirs is barbarous in the extreme. Perhaps remembering what they suffered at their hands in their early struggles in Natal and the Transvaal, in course of time they have adopted some of their methods, and hence one has to distinguish between them and the Colonial Boer, who during the same period has gradually been enjoying the advantages of settled government and contact with a superior class of person. The Boer, living on his solitary farm, has been so exempt from laws, and has gone his own way for so many years, that now force is the only argument that appeals to him. The Kaffirs hate the Boers, and with reason. The latter have never credited them with a capacity for feeling in any form, describing them in their laws as "creatures," and, when they dare, rule them entirely by fear and cruelty. As a child, I remember being fascinated and horrified by a tale told at the Cape of a certain slave-owner there, who, being displeased one day at some action of a slave, put him into one of those huge outside ovens that one sees there, which was heated, and shut the door on him. Some time afterwards he looked in, saw the slave grinning the grin of an agonised death, and saying to the corpse, "Wat? lach gij noch?" (What? do you still laugh?) slammed the door to again. As cruelty is inherent in all human beings, and its eradication is purely a question of education, one can conceive that these men, who for several generations have worked their will without let or hindrance on the native of the Transvaal, partially exterminating tribes, would become more and more callous.

The Transvaal Boer has also imbibed another Kaffir characteristic, and that is his utter disregard of the truth. He only feels ashamed of a lie if he is found out, and so does a Kaffir.

I do not mean to say, however, that I consider the English treatment of the Kaffir the right one either. They go too far in the other direction, and treat a Kaffir as if he were a white man. A Kaffir is, of course, quite another creation, and must be treated as such. The mistake the English make is in forgetting the centuries which it has taken to make the white man what he is—centuries of religious and moral principle instilled into him. They fancy the Kaffir, with his limited brain development, must start from the point they themselves have reached. Naturally it does not succeed: the point of view is quite different. Ordinary kindness, unless accompanied by absolute unbending seriousness, is immediately construed by the native into weakness. But there is a great difference between the cruel callousness of the Boer and the indulgent kindness of the English, which almost acknowledges an equality of race. Rigid justice and firmness are essential in dealing with the Kaffir, and the full service for which he engages must be exacted. He utterly lacks any sense of gratitude. I remember a case where a "boy," who had been a long time in the service of an Englishman, became seriously ill with inflammation of the lungs. Eighty pounds were spent in doctoring and nursing him. When convalescent, he desired to visit his home, to which his employer consented. One day prior to his departure, he went to his master and said: "Baas, you owe me ten shillings for wages before I got ill." The master asked him how he could demand that ten shillings, knowing how much had been spent during his illness; and the native retorted: "Why did you spend so much; why did you not let me die? I did not ask you to!"

I forgot to mention that when the Reform men were taken prisoners, one of the first actions of the Government was to search everywhere for concealed arms or documents, and among other places our house in Johannesburg was not exempt. By some unaccountable oversight, a locked drawer in Lionel's study was allowed to be broken open, and his private letter-book was taken. It has always been a matter of bitter regret to me that I was not there, as I am sure my first impulse would have been to destroy any possibly incriminating documents. This famous book was a glorious find for the Transvaal authorities, out of which they made much capital, although it contained no reference to the projected revolt nor to any collusion with Jameson. There were copies of private business letters containing many allusions to the corruption and misgovernment at Pretoria, and it is to be regretted that a few of the home truths contained in them did not have more effect.

Lionel's private letters to his partners in England neces-
sarily included many unflattering comments on Boer
tactics and manners, but the Government made an un-
fair use of them by publishing extracts without the context, thus wilfully distorting the meaning to suit their
own purpose. For example, that phrase which has been
so useful to them as well as to certain Liberals in England, "There are many here who do not care a fig for
the franchise," assumes quite a different meaning when
the context is given. Then also the affairs of other
people mentioned in some of these letters were ruthlessly disclosed in the most dishonourable manner, one
of their own judges being ruined in consequence.

CHAPTER X

BUT the trial of the prisoners was approaching. I shall never forget the awful shock I received when, having gone over to see Lionel, he came out of the dining-room where they were all sitting in conclave with their lawyers, and taking me aside on the verandah, said in a solemn voice—

"You reproached me before because I had not told you everything, so now I wish to tell you something you ought to know. We have decided that the four principal prisoners are to plead Guilty—Guilty to High Treason! We have all along thought the Government had no evidence against us, but Dr. Coster (the State Attorney) has informed Wessels (their advocate) that the Jameson party brought in a despatch-box full of papers, which the Government has got, and the evidence against us is too great to make it worth while disputing the case."

It appeared that the despatch-box contained not only the key to the cipher used in all the negotiations, but a copy of the alleged letter of invitation which Major Robert White had sworn on affidavit was a true copy, and the signatures true ones—thereby putting another nail into the coffins of the Reformers, which to say the least was a peculiar proceeding. Very ugly reasons are given in Pretoria for this affidavit; but whatever Major Robert White's motives may have been, his action was most unjustifiable.

I thought I should never get over this fresh blow, and did everything in my power to persuade Lionel not to plead guilty upon such a charge. They had not committed high treason, and it seemed to me but one of the traps in which they had been caught so often. Lionel argued with me for some time and then got angry, saying to me, "You are most selfish."

I remember how I went away through the scented tropical garden that lovely evening, weeping bitterly, for my heart felt broken, and I was crushed with the hopelessness of it all. As I was going out of the gate, Percy Fitzpatrick ran after me and tried to comfort me, urging me not to lose my pluck.

Anyhow, my entreaties were of no avail, and there was nothing to be done. The whole thing was kept secret for a day or two, and then when it was finally determined on by the four principals, the rest were informed of the decision. The most plausible arguments were used, and all the lawyers were against me, but personally I shall always remain convinced that it was a mistake.

The four prisoners were told that if they pleaded guilty to high treason, a plea of guilty to quite a minor charge would be accepted from the rest, and everything would be much easier; and if, instead of irritating the

I

judges by a long defence, they consented to take this course, Mr. Wessels assured them that the State Attorney would come to a compromise, and they could rest assured that their own sentence would be a fine and banishment, in terms of the Statute Laws, while the remaining fifty-nine, some of whom were guilty of very little, would have a nominal fine—say about £100. So Mr. Wessels and the State Attorney arranged the matter, and the proposed compromise was considered a settled thing. Everybody then went about with light hearts, and the prisoners looked forward to a speedy end of their imprisonment. Of course we were told that the arrangement was not to be mentioned, for the sake of appearances, &c.; in fact, it was even suggested that the sending of the prisoners over the border might be delayed a week or two—also for the sake of appearances—and a nominal punishment, such as detention in a private house, insisted on at first, as of course the Government must not be made to look mercenary, and the feelings of the burghers must be considered.

In this large body of men certain among them were technically more guilty than others, although they were all included in one charge, and the four signatories of the letter thought that by taking the onus on their own shoulders they would spare the others; moreover, as Jameson and his fellows were still untried, they did not wish any evidence to be elicited which might have damaged them! All this happened one week before the trial.

There had been much discussion as to which judge should try the case, as the three judges in Pretoria were disqualified—two because they had given the Government advice at the time of the raid, and the third because he was a Scotchman, and known to be friendly to the prisoners. This matter was felt to be one of considerable importance. Just before the trial we were informed that Judge Gregorowski, from the Orange Free State, was coming, and the choice was looked upon as a bad one for the prisoners.

All this time I had been living at Hohenheim with my children, and Lionel's sister and her husband were also staying with me. I had made several trips a week to Pretoria to see him, but now we moved to that town, leaving the children at home, and I took up my residence at the Transvaal Hotel, where, from first to last, the proprietor, although a German and a friend of the other side, showed me the greatest kindness and consideration. I had a tiny bedroom leading on to a verandah, and all the rooms were equally small, but fortunately perfectly clean. The strain on the resources of Pretoria was great at this time owing to the unusual influx of strangers, and the two hotels of the place were crowded. I could not even get a sitting-room, and the whole time I was there Mr. Jahn lent me his own private room. It was real acts of kindness such as this which softened much of the suffering we had to endure.

Just before the trial, Mr. Hammond came up from

Cape Town to be present. The British Government sent Mr. Rose-Innes, a barrister from Cape Town, to watch the case for them. As there was no building in Pretoria large enough for the purpose, the market-house was turned into a court for the occasion. The acoustic properties were so bad that the prisoners never heard one word of the proceedings, and could not even catch the voices of the counsel or judges. I must here mention that all this time—more than three months—all business had been at a complete standstill in Johannesburg. To begin with, so many mine managers and directors of companies were among the prisoners that their continual trips to Pretoria sadly interfered with work, and the absence of so many important professional men was felt in various ways. Then the spirit of unrest which was continually spreading was a great deterrent to work, and caused incalculable harm to trade. A feeling of absolute distrust of the Government prevailed, and it is not to be wondered at that everybody was on tenterhooks, and that from day to day one never knew what might happen. The word "confiscation" was constantly whispered, but every one felt that this was too serious a matter for even the Transvaal Government to contemplate lightly, since by the ruin of these persons so many foreign shareholders would have indirectly suffered. It was always considered a great safeguard to the prisoners that among them were Americans and other foreigners.

Then one Friday the trial began, and the huge

MARKET BUILDINGS, PRETORIA.

market-house was packed. The judge, with his evil hawk-like face, seemed the very personification of cruelty and malice. He was seated in a sort of box; in front of him were the counsel for both sides; on the right, opposite the jury, but low down and far away, sat the prisoners. A small space in front of the barristers was reserved for ladies. My sister-in-law and I went early to get good seats, and found most of the other prisoners' wives and friends there, besides a number of the Pretoria ladies, the wives of some of the Hollander officials. Some of these latter looked on it as a most exciting exhibition of toilette, and I heard one remark, " Oh, I wish I had put on something else."

The first day was devoted to hearing the case for the prosecution. *A propos* of the Pretoria ladies, I must say that we poor " Reform ladies" were cordially detested by many of them, and a little incident which occurred the first day, miserable and trifling enough in itself, still helped to add its sting to my misery. When we returned to the Court, I found all the seats taken, quite half being occupied by Pretoria dames who were there out of pure curiosity; but I wanted most particularly to hear the speech for the prosecution, and not being very practised in Dutch, would not have been able to follow had I been far off. So seeing a vacant place in the front row, I requested the old usher to put two chairs there for us, which he did. Two women just behind (they were the daughter of the French Consul Aubert and the wife of the correspondent of the *Temps*) protested most vigorously, and the usher said to me in Cape Dutch, "Hulle is bije parmantige vrouwen" (They are very impertinent women). I assured him that did not signify in the least, but as I and my sister-in-law took our seats, the one lady remarked quite audibly, "Les femmes des accusés." She evidently thought the wife of the correspondent of a notoriously partisan paper had more right than the unfortunate wife of a prisoner to hear the argument on his life or death.

However, I scored my petty revenge through my knowledge of Cape Dutch, as I requested the usher to enforce their silence, which he did by standing guard over them for the rest of the afternoon.

Dr. Coster, as counsel for the State, presented the case against the prisoners in straightforward and moderate speech, without any evidence of *animus*, and appeared to conform to the understanding arrived at.

The next day was devoted to hearing the case for the prisoners. Mr. Wessels read a statement prepared by the four leaders, and then made a speech on behalf of the whole body. Here, according to legal etiquette, the matter should have rested until the sentence was given, but in spite of protests from Mr. Wessels and the barristers for the defence, the State Attorney got up and, as it were, repenting his previous attitude, made the most violent attack it is possible to imagine on the prisoners. He advised the judge, at least half-a-dozen times over, "to hang them by

THE REFORM TRIAL IN MARKET HALL, PRETORIA.

the neck until they were dead" and to confiscate their property. He did not stand in his place while making these cheerful suggestions, but ran up and down like one possessed, waving his arms in the air, and evincing a hatred towards the prisoners so passionate that it made me feel cold and hopeless. The prisoners themselves, however, not being able to hear his voice, sat on in the calmest manner, feeling quite safe in the promises that had been made them, and thinking that his frantic gestures were but a part of the old game of appearances. As, moreover, many of the listeners did not understand a word he said, his harangue did not produce much apparent effect. But the awful words, "hangen bij den nek," repeated many times with ferocious insistence, sank like lead on my heart, and I could not speak, being now quite certain what the sentence would be. He urged the judge to sentence the prisoners under the Roman Dutch Laws, ignoring the Transvaal local laws, and thus violating the understanding arrived at with Mr. Wessels. The sentence was to be delivered on the Monday. When we got back to the hotel, I told my sister-in-law the gist of the State Attorney's speech, and confided to her my opinion. I also added, "In one way, I rather hope that it will be the worst, awful as it seems, as it will make friends for the prisoners of many of the Johannesburg people who are now against them, and who have never appreciated all they tried to do on their behalf."

I do not like to remember the agony of mind I suffered during the next thirty-six hours. Being extremely unwell I spent the time in bed, and may I never again undergo such suffering and apprehension! The very cheerfulness of the prisoners seemed an added torture, and I lacked courage to tell Lionel what I feared. He had insisted that I should not be present in the Court on the Monday to hear the sentence, and I, feeling he was right, reluctantly consented. He said over and over again, "You might get a shock. They may give us a stiff sentence for form's sake, and it will be easier for me if I know you are not there to hear it." So on the Monday morning I drove up to the prisoners' cottage to see Lionel a moment before they left for the Court. He gave me all instructions about leaving the country in case they were conveyed over the border immediately. He told me he would then wait for me in Cape Town, where I was to join him with the children, after shutting up the house in Johannesburg and arranging about servants, horses, &c. He also said to me, "I am glad you are not coming into the Court, as they might give us a stiff sentence—they may give us five years' imprisonment; but let me beg of you not to mind. Remember it is arranged with Coster that we are to be put over the border, and that will in any case be done in about a fortnight's time at the latest." He also added how delighted he was to think the fifty-nine prisoners were going to be let off so easily, as it was a great relief to him. I could have laughed aloud, knowing my own thoughts. I remember seeing them all go off cheerily in their little hired flies to hear their sentence, and if any of them had any suspicion as to what it was to be they did not show it. Lionel was humming "Una Voce" as he drove off. An Irish friend of ours who was there said to me, as I went back to my little room at the Transvaal Hotel, "I will go to the Court, and as your husband will be the first to receive his sentence, I will run back as fast as possible and tell you what it is."

Mrs. Fitzpatrick was with me when, a very short time afterwards, he appeared. I hardly realised he had been to the Court at all, and said to him, "Oh, I thought you were going to listen to the sentence to tell me." Without speaking for a second he put his hand on my shoulder, and, with a great gulp in his voice, said, "You must be brave! you must be brave!" Of course I knew what he meant, but nevertheless the reality made me feel as though I were turned to stone. He stared at me when I said calmly, "You need not tell me; it is death." And his sobs were his answer. He then suggested I should write Lionel a few lines, which I did, and he ran back to the Court with the note. In a few minutes the verandah outside my room was full of agitated people, and I think the men on this occasion wept more than the women. We heard that the four principal offenders had received the same sentence; that the verdict on the fifty-nine was extremely severe—two years' imprisonment, £2000 fine, or in default an extra year's imprisonment and banishment for three years afterwards. We were proud to know that all, without exception, had received their sentences like men. We heard also they had all been sent from the Court back to the loathsome, evil-smelling prison, which had been carefully saturated with carbolic powder in an attempt to disguise the other awful odours.

When I look back on that fearful time, I sometimes wonder if it was not a hideous nightmare. I know that for the moment a feeling seized me that I no longer had any individual existence, that I had no right to feel or think anything, that something awful had happened which required all my immediate attention regardless of myself. I remember having but one distinct idea, that I would not allow anything to happen to Lionel, though I formulated no plan, and then the gruesome vision of a gallows would obtrude itself before my mind's eye. My sister-in-law came into my room weeping. I think I shook her and said, "This is not the time to cry. We want all our wits about us." I felt that if I once gave way I should have no powers of thinking left. How many times afterwards was I asked the question, "But you did not *really* think there was any danger for your husband; you did not really think they would hang him?" and my reply to it was, "No, I did not really think they would hang him, but the danger was a nearer, more real, more imminent one, and that was that some ill-advised sympathisers would try to rescue them or make some demonstration, and they would have instantly been shot in the prison." That was the real danger to these men, and the thought made my heart stand still.

However, others realised this also, and Percy Farrar, with a set and determined face, came to show me a telegram he was sending in the name of the prisoners, which was to be posted up all over the town and on the Stock Exchange of Johannesburg. It begged the inhabitants of that town, if they had any consideration whatever for their safety, not to move hand or foot in their interest—that the moment was critical, and that their lives depended upon the discretion of their friends. I also immediately sent a telegram to my butler in Johannesburg telling him to proceed with the three children and nurse by that night's train to Cape Town, which he did. I was afraid that in case of a riot or any disturbance in Johannesburg our house might be attacked, and if the children remained there I knew they would be a constant source of anxiety to me. Percy Farrar also left that night for Cape Town to see the Governor in the interest of the prisoners. Her Majesty's representative refused to see him, putting him off by sending his secretary to him, and he returned a week later from his fruitless mission, sick at heart.

How that awful day passed I scarcely remember. We were not granted permission to visit the prisoners.

As "my prophetic soul" had foretold, on all sides there was a complete revulsion of feeling in favour of the prisoners when the brutality of their sentence was made known. Some of the Boers themselves were horrified, and immediately initiated petitions on their behalf. The people of Johannesburg, who had hitherto stood aloof for fear of being compromised, made a stand against the sentence. The ordinary onlooker who waits to see how the wind blows before he decides, the many who fancied they had been ruined through the action of the Reformers, and the many who always must blame somebody for the sake of grumbling, all forgot their petty hesitations in the face of this wicked sentence, and with one accord went over to the side of the Reformers.

If the Transvaal Government had thought for years they could not have discovered a more signal way of making hundreds of enemies for themselves and friends for these prisoners than by their cowardly, treacherous sentence, and it is one of the few things we can thank them for. The sentence on the leaders—"to hang by the neck until you are dead"—dreadful as it was at the time, and dangerous trifling as it was with men's lives, did more to show the world in general, and Johannesburg and Pretoria in particular, the unscrupulous nature of the rulers of the Transvaal, and how little they are fitted for the responsibilities they assume. If the abortive revolution of 1896 was a fiasco, at least the workers of it did signal service to South Africa, and that was to expose one of the worst, most tyrannical, and criminal governments that has existed in modern times. And the good work begun by these devoted men will still bear fruit, although they personally may not benefit.

The manner in which the prisoners received their sentence also gained them many friends; every one who was present in the Court, without exception, said that this was so. Lionel being the first on the list was put to the severest test. He told me afterwards that it never once entered his head that the sentence would be death; the worst he feared was prolonged imprisonment. His suspicions were first aroused when he saw some men bringing forward a little dock and putting it near the judge; in this the four leaders were made to stand. The whole thing was very trying, and the torture was prolonged. When Lionel was told to stand forward, the judge first gave a long homily in Dutch, which was interpreted into English. Then he asked, " Do you know any reason why you should not suffer death?" and the reply was "No." He then put on his black cap and gave the sentence. Lionel told me that the only time when he felt as if he would break down was when they were coming out. At that point our friend Mrs. Spencer (whose husband was also a prisoner) came up to him with the tears pouring down her face, and shaking him by the hand, said, "Old friend, you are a brave fellow." I was truly thankful I was not there. The interpreter burst into tears,

women fainted in the Court, one man at the back had
a fit. Gregorowski was seen to smile; evidently the
gruesome spectacle gave pleasure to one of the par-
ticipators. *A propos* of this, I remember frequently
hearing at that time the remark, " He laughs best who
laughs last."

I was told by a Frenchman of our acquaintance
that after the sentence was pronounced, the two French
women I have already mentioned went up to him,
laughing heartily, and said, "They are going to be
hanged," whereupon he, utterly disgusted by their
frightful inhumanity, replied, " I am ashamed of you;
you are not worthy to be called women." I mention
these incidents, as the respective father and husband
of these women are the two men who have guided
French opinion as to events in the Transvaal, and
perhaps their womenkind, in expressing such inhuman
ideas, were only echoing the opinions of some members
of their family.

The whole trial was a monstrous farce, every scene
of which had been rehearsed beforehand. On arriving
in Pretoria, the first action of Gregorowski, the judge
imported from the Free State, had been to ask one of
the other judges if he had a black cap; this was before
he had heard or read one word of the evidence. Also
before receiving the coveted appointment he had remarked that he wished he could try the Reformers;
he would see that they got "what for." Doubtless
these sentiments publicly expressed gained him the

post. We had the poor satisfaction of knowing that when a little later he returned to Bloemfontein on a visit, he was hooted and howled at, and was forced to escape by a back street, and that for many a day afterwards he went in danger of being lynched by some of the more lawless spirits.

CHAPTER XI

WHEN the news of the sentences reached Johannesburg tremendous excitement prevailed. Even that "Sleepy Hollow," Pretoria, had been stirred out of its apathy for once, and Johannesburg observed the day as a day of mourning. Every shop and theatre was closed, as also the Stock Exchange, and such masses of people thronged the main parts of the town that all traffic was stopped. I believe Commissioner Street and the Market Square and all the streets in the neighbourhood were a surging mass of human beings. Nor was it due to the Pretoria authorities that desperate remedies were not applied at that moment. Many threats were made, and would have been carried out had it not been for the influence of Percy Farrar's telegram, and a few calm spirits who saw what frightful risks the prisoners ran. The departure that night of twenty thousand men armed with pickaxes and spades to effect the rescue of the prisoners was quite seriously contemplated, and that day and many a day afterwards quite respectable people might have been heard discussing the power of dynamite as an explosive, and suggesting that as they were disarmed the Uitlanders would have to resort to that material if they wished to obtain any redress. I am

THE MARKET SQUARE, JOHANNESBURG.

quite certain that the Volksraad buildings, the President's house, the State Secretary's house, and various other places, together with their occupants, would not have escaped at this period had it not been that the prisoners' lives would as certainly have paid for it.

Johannesburg, as I have before remarked, is a town not easily roused, and on this occasion the self-restraint shown was not due to want of feeling, but to a genuine consideration for the victims in prison, and once more Kruger and his satellites had to thank these men indirectly for much. It certainly was not due to fears of personal safety, nor yet to consideration for him, that Johannesburg stayed its hand. But the knowledge of the real helplessness of the place was a bitter fact to many. The guards in the Pretoria gaol were very numerous, and bristled with arms, and whenever they could make a display of their power, they were not slow to do so. Kruger took the precaution to surround himself with trusty burghers, and the side street in Pretoria in which he lived was closed up. No one dared to pass it—in fact, one day a man was arrested for walking on the public pavement in front of his house. Nor did Dr. Leyds lead a cheerful life at this time. He received so many threatening letters from various sources that he never moved without a guard, and his house and garden were always protected by men in plain clothes, who were concealed among the trees and bushes. But these were poor consolations to us, and from the moment the Reformers were put back into prison, they

K

and their wives were made to endure a life of positive
and systematic torture, which I am sure none of them
will ever forget.

The morning after the sentences had been passed,
the news was brought to us that the death penalty had
been commuted, but to what no one knew, and it was
not announced for a long time. Anyhow that was a
heavy load off our minds, and we could breathe again.
We also heard that if we went up to the Landdrost's
office and got a pass we would be allowed to see the
prisoners.

Just as I was going out for that purpose I was
told that some one wished to see me, and going into
the little sitting-room I saw an unknown, bearded
individual wearing new brown kid gloves. He in-
troduced himself to me, saying, "I am an Uitlander,
a Belgian, and I have numerous friends of different
nationalities, and we are going to rescue the prisoners.
But I thought I would come to tell you first." To
hear this crazy plan, to the danger of which we were
all so much alive, announced in this calm, matter-of-
fact manner, was too much for my brain, and I found
myself giggling inanely, not knowing how to deal with
the man. But a brilliant idea suddenly came to
me, and telling him to wait a moment, I fetched Mr.
Rose-Innes, to whom I made my visitor recount his
project. Mr. Innes did not deal very gently with him,
but used most forcible language as to his mad idea,
looking so fierce that the Belgian was glad to beat a

hasty retreat. That was the last of this hero, but it gave me a fright.

I went up to the Landdrost's office, and got a pass to go into the prison, and was told I could stay ten minutes. Never shall I forget the scene. The sight of that horrid, grey-looking prison-yard, filled with little groups of men one had known in happier circumstances, many of them personal friends, and the dreadful humiliation of their position, was almost too much for me. As I was led towards the condemned cell, where Lionel and his three partners in misery were, all the prisoners came up to me and shook hands silently. They also had not long known the news of the commutation of the original sentence, and I took this for a mark of their sympathy. Lionel, Colonel Rhodes, George Farrar, and Mr. Hammond were in an inner cell used for prisoners condemned to death, and guards were standing at the doors, rifle in hand. The indescribable sickening odour that pervades any place occupied by Kaffirs was here in all its vigour, and it went to my heart to see these men, honourable and upright, doomed to this humiliating captivity in these awful surroundings.

This was my first visit to the Pretoria gaol, and as I shut my eyes every detail comes home to me, the whole sordid scene—even the very odour I have mentioned which was so closely connected with all their sufferings. The cell was windowless; holes high up in the wall being the only means of ventilation;

and on the mud floor four wretched stretchers, covered with coloured Kaffir blankets, constituted the furniture. Our meeting naturally was one full of emotion. They were all very cheery, however, and full of pluck. Lionel tried to comfort me by saying, " Well, anyhow, it is not every man who has had the experience of being sentenced to death," but I am afraid the effort failed in its object. When I asked him how he had slept, he owned that he had had rather bad dreams, but I heard no complaints. They remarked that they could not eat the food, which was not to be wondered at. Even Du Plessis had said that it was not fit to give a dog, and that did not even mean an English dog, but a Boer's dog, whose life is not a pampered one. We were allowed but little opportunity for conversation, being ordered away before we could say much, as other ladies were awaiting their turn to come in, and only a few were admitted at a time. The food, I learned, was the same as that given to the Kaffir prisoners, and to judge by the living skeletons one saw on every side, it could not be tempting. It consisted of a tin pannikin of mealie meal pap (porridge), at six in the morning when their cell was unlocked, some dreadful-looking junks of beef, which had previously been used to make soup, and a tin pannikin of tea at twelve, and again in the evening before being locked up a pannikin of pap similar to that of the morning. These delectable meals used to be served in a manner worthy of the prison. Convicts

THE PRISON YARD, SHOWING CONDEMNED CELL AND LEAN-TO.

used to bring in the things on a huge tray, place them on the ground in the middle of the yard, and whoever wanted to regale himself had to fetch it. We felt that this meant starvation; but hearing that, as these were political prisoners, special regulations would be made, we tried to console ourselves with the idea.

The other prisoners, I learned, were distributed about the prison in batches. It appeared that so cut and dried was the whole thing that the authorities had built extra lean-to's of corrugated iron beforehand for the reception of these men, and the official idea of making the filthy places sanitary had been to strew about broadcast carbolic powder, which was not only very unpleasant to smell in such quantities, but very irritating to the olfactory nerves. I heard that the men were herded together in far too great numbers for it to be possible to be healthy, and that they were all locked up for thirteen hours every night with no ventilation, and scarcely any means of sanitation whatever.

We all came away from the prison most frightfully depressed with the feeling that the more immediate wants of poor humanity, like food and air, had for the moment assumed an importance that made all the greater evils fade into the background. I may remark here that during all the time these men were imprisoned no rules were made for their diet at all, notwithstanding the constant appeals made on all sides by their lawyers and friends; and when at last we were told that that came within the jurisdiction of the Land-drost, that functionary remarked, "Oh, I shall see to that question when I have time. So far I am so busy giving out passes for the prisoners' wives that I have no time for anything else." He never did find time all those weary weeks, and so no order was given; and a most hateful system of smuggling had to be resorted to by the womenkind, and all kinds of devices had to be invented, and bribery of the most barefaced order indulged in towards the rapacious jailers and guards. It was all part of the blackmail and torture to which we were subjected by these people, with the idea, on the one hand, I presume, of making us feel our helpless position, and in the hope, no doubt, of getting as much as they could from the prisoners in the end.

As to the famous passes for the prisoners' wives and friends, Mr. Schutte, the Landdrost, always had the excuse of hard work in making these out till the end. We petitioned to have one general pass made out for the wives, at least, but were refused; and so every day except Saturday and Sunday the ridiculous spectacle was seen of numerous women besieging the Landdrost's office for the pass into the prison, and generally two or three hours would be taken up each morning waiting for this little slip of paper, which at the most gave us five or ten minutes' admission to the prison. We were at any rate thankful to be able to get in to see them at all, and therefore tried not to heed the unnecessary trouble we were put to. The wives were allowed between two and four every day except Saturdays and Sundays, and the ordinary friends once a week. Saturday was the day taken for cleaning the prison (after a fashion), and Sunday, I presume, to give the officials a rest.

Pretoria always used to look very strange at the week end. It is a most sleepy, dull little place; but during the time the Reformers were in prison it became quite lively with the influx of the many strangers who took up their abode in the town in order to be near the prisoners. Most of the near relatives of the prisoners, if they did actually live in Pretoria, came over frequently to see them, but the two days debarred they mostly spent in Johannesburg. I had quite settled myself at the Transvaal Hotel, but used to run over to see how things were at home, though, as the children were absent, only necessity took me thither.

The second and third days after sentence was passed were very terrible ones, as we discovered to our dismay that no regulations were forthcoming for the feeding of the prisoners. The awful helplessness of their position struck us anew. There was no one to appeal to, no one to help. They were obviously deserted, to starve, unless we ourselves took some means of helping them. To appeal to the authorities at Pretoria was worse than useless. They had us in their power and meant to use it; and I here assert that no mediæval barbarities can ever again astonish me, when I remember how fiendishly, even in the nineteenth century, so-called civilised beings can behave to their fellows when their passions

are allowed unchecked play. There was a general look
of hopelessness on the faces of these men that day that
I shall never forget; and to hear strong robust men
saying, "For God's sake, try and get us in somehow
something to eat, some Liebig's essence, anything, we
are starving," was bad enough, and to contemplate the
older and more delicate members of the party was still
more heartrending.

This state of things went on for some days, although
the gaoler Du Plessis, being all-powerful here, could
easily have ameliorated their condition, but from the
first he showed his intention to wring as much money
as he could from these unfortunates. It was an aggra-
vation also, and one which he could not understand,
of course, that they must suffer in silence, for how
could they show an inferior such as he was what they
felt?—to be at his mercy was bad enough. I know I
went away from the prison that day feeling well-nigh
desperate. In addition to the starvation they were
suffering, the sanitary arrangements were so utterly inadequate that we really feared an outbreak of typhoid;
indeed, how it was avoided I cannot imagine. The
vermin and the general filth were indescribable. As
an example of petty tyranny, I may mention that
whenever the whim seized him, he ordered the Reformers to be stood up in line and searched.

So far, the men had been allowed to retain their own
clothes, but there were constant threats of their being
put into convict garb. I think that if this had been

CHARLESTOWN, WITH MAJUBA IN THE DISTANCE.

attempted there would have been a few corpses strewn about the prison yard. The authorities went so far as to have the clothes prepared I saw them—coarse dark-blue linen coats and trousers: but, for some inscrutable reason, in this matter the Government never went beyond threats.

On leaving the prison, I sent Mr. Beit a cable imploring him to inform the Colonial Office of the desperate condition of the prisoners, but although, as he told me afterwards, he did what he could, no results were apparent.[1] So we women, all filled with one idea, began devising every kind of plan for getting in food to the prisoners, and I should imagine that we must have emptied the few stores in Pretoria of their supply of meat juices, sardines, and other tinned provisions that did not take up space. I arranged with my friend, Burgers, the under-gaoler, who came to see me after dark, to take in as much as he could carry of what I had obtained, and from that time he used to pay me nocturnal visits, and go away laden with the most varied kind of provisions imaginable. Naturally our great desire was to avoid arousing the suspicion of the authorities, more especially of Du Plessis, who was very jealous of his subordinate, and did not wish him to participate in any of the gains. But this Burgers was

---

[1] To insure a telegram reaching its destination, one had to send a special messenger to Charlestown in Natal, twelve hours by train, as the Censor ruthlessly kept back everything he liked. As each word cost five shillings and sixpence by cable, the expense was immense.

a perfect godsend to us; without him I do not know how the prisoners could have existed at first. He told me that his method of getting the food to the four men was to go after dark, when Du Plessis had retired and the lights were out, to the side where the air-holes in the cell were, and tying a piece of string round whatever he wished to deliver, to let it down to them. It sounds too childish to believe, but this was one of the means by which these men existed for some time.

Then after a few days the gaol people got a fright. One of the prisoners became dangerously ill. He had been unable to obtain supplies from outside, and the prison food made him sick. The prisoners at first were rigorously watched, and could not give each other anything. To show how unprepared all these men had been to go to prison, none of them had made any preparations of any kind beforehand, and this particular gentleman had a very curious experience. It appears that he wore false teeth, which on the day of the trial were at his dentist's in Johannesburg, so he went to prison *minus* his teeth. They were sent to him there by parcel post, but Du Plessis naturally would not deliver them to him—it was a good opportunity for the infliction of a little extra torture. So not until the poor man was in danger of dying did they let him have his teeth, or grow less rigorous as to the smuggling of food. Had they allowed the prisoners openly to receive enough to support existence, it might have been possible to conform to the regulations, but this farce of smuggling in food was an unnecessary and humiliating hardship.

Every woman visiting the gaol used to secrete something eatable for one or more men, and it is one of the few occasions on record when we have been thankful to wear petticoats. One lady especially lost all vanity, and she used to look a very comical figure, but she was most barefaced over it, and generally succeeded in getting in what she wanted. She invented a kind of pocket that went quite round her skirt, and one can imagine her shape when she conveyed a bottle or two or any other bulky object. Occasionally, however, we were searched on entering, and everything sternly confiscated. Quite at the end of their imprisonment the idea struck some of us of openly sending in food in "three deckers" (tin or enamelled cans one above the other, used by workmen, in which the food kept hot), and to our surprise no objection was made by Du Plessis. The hot food was a great boon, as cold tinned food is very unhealthy even if one can take exercise and has fresh air.

The men used to take exercise by walking round and round the yard, but the close, fetid air of the place and the continual use of tinned and cold food was terribly trying, and only their determination to make the best of it kept them up; the one blessing they had was each other's companionship, and that they were allowed to see their friends. This latter privilege, however, was often turned to their torture, and in this wise. All kinds of persons in Pretoria—some well-meaning, no doubt, made a regular practice of coming to the anxious women to tell them "on the best authority" some piece of news about the prisoners' future disposition, for it was generally understood that things could not go on as they were, interminably. All business was stopped at Johannesburg owing to so many important business men being imprisoned; trade was at a complete standstill, and the tension every day became more dangerous, while in the Cape Colony and the whole of South Africa every one was awaiting the development of events with bated breath. Apparently the only people who took matters calmly were Kruger and the members of the Government. It must be remembered that we were waiting every day to hear to what the death sentences had been commuted. No one knew, and the fact was that the authorities did not dare to announce the monstrous decision at which they had arrived.

It was held over our heads continually also that the men were going to be distributed over the country, as they would be less dangerous when separated. One benighted village on the borders of Zululand even went so far as to petition the Government that some of the Reform prisoners might be sent to them—they had just done up the jail, and they thought the prisoners' wives would be so good for the trade of the place. We all shivered inwardly as the awful idea occurred to each of us that we might be the

REFORM PRISONERS AWAITING NEWS.

REFORM PRISONERS TAKING EXERCISE.

favoured benefactress of Vrijheid. As many of the
poor men said often afterwards, they would far rather
have supported a year's or even two years' imprisonment than go through the hourly and daily torture of
suspense in which they lived. What this was I cannot
describe—it was terrible to us all. For many weeks
no one knew what might happen from one hour to
another.

Once the men were thoroughly in the power of the
authorities, they invented every kind of petty tyranny
possible. The worst of all was the petition business.
To this day the very word "petition" recalls the most
hateful memories. They were informed that if they
wished anything done for them they must petition the
Government, but the mere idea was gall and wormwood.
Enormous pressure was brought to bear on these unfortunate men. Among their number were some who
indignantly refused, while others did not see any
indignity at all in the proceeding. Outside pressure
of every kind was put upon them also, and notably
indirectly through their wives and friends. It seemed
as if they were to be forced to drink to the dregs the
cup of humiliation. At last formal applications for the
revision of their sentences were sent to the Government
by the prisoners, as they were informed that this was
required by law. In the meantime thousands of signatures were obtained from every part of South Africa,
including the Transvaal, to a petition asking for the
release of the prisoners, Kruger giving out that it was

necessary for him to have many petitions "in order to strengthen his hand with his burghers"—the same old tale we had already heard so often, and which we knew was only said to cover the fact that he and he alone swayed the burghers. But they were and have always been a most useful tool to fall back upon. A man who went into one of the country districts near Pretoria told me that a great many of the farmers had never heard of the Jameson Raid, and were in complete ignorance of the political troubles of the moment.

And thus the days dragged on while matters seemed to become more hopeless, and we all felt we could put up with anything better than the continued uncertainty. One of the bitterest things we women had to bear on our own account was the daily wait at the prison gate when we paid our visit. The gate was controlled by a young Boer, generally half intoxicated, who was much after the pattern of the head gaoler, and a thorough bully. We always used to say that the hottest spot on earth was just outside the prison gates—the sun seemed to have a power there I cannot remember to have felt elsewhere. This place afforded a very strange sight each afternoon during visiting hours with its motley collection of cabs and carts, and waiting men and women who would come and go by a small gate in the large one; while sometimes the large gates would be opened wide, and gangs of convicts with their clanking irons would pass in or out.

On the whole the lady visitors were fairly well

OUTSIDE THE PRISON GATE.

treated. A limited number were allowed in for their brief visit, but we always felt it was a favour, and that its continuance depended upon our good behaviour. No matter whether the guards were insolent or complimentary after their clumsy fashion, one had to smile through it all, as any little exhibition of annoyance on our part would have been immediately visited on the prisoners we had come to see. But to the male visitors unbounded insolence was shown. They were kept waiting for hours outside the gates, although provided with the coveted pass, and although in many cases they had purposely made the journey from Johannesburg. One day when Sir Jacobus de Wet, the British resident, went to pay an official visit to the prisoners (armed with a pass, too) he was refused admission by this functionary, and had to submit. It was very important that the business men should see those connected with them, and the few minutes allowed to each visitor were very precious.

One day on going up to pay my daily visit I remember finding in the crowd Mr. Rouliot, one of Lionel's partners, who wanted to see him on some important business matter. In place of his usual amiable expression he looked hot and angry, and he told me he had been there for two hours in the baking sun, and that the gatekeeper had let in many others who had come after him. I was told to wait until some of the ladies came out, and some one kindly giving me a packing-case he had, I sat as near the gate as I could, saying to Mr. Rouliot, "Stand close to me. When the gate opens I will speak to the gatekeeper, and when he lets me in, you make a dash after me." He did so, but the irate gatekeeper, being determined that Mr. Rouliot should not come in, gave him a great push, and the latter rebounded like a ball; then fortunately descrying my friend Burgers in the distance, I ran to him and told him that Mr. Rouliot had come in on important business; otherwise, he would never have been admitted that day. Doubtless, it was a most comical encounter, at which we all laughed; but nevertheless the repetition of these scenes was not always comical to the actors in them. Every day in the prison there were new rules — one day the visitors were not allowed to go beyond the guard-room, and although this was filled to suffocation, even the privacy of the big open yard was denied to them. Another time chalk lines would be drawn across the yard, and one could not pass these imaginary barriers without a rifle being lifted by one of the guards to enforce obedience. The yard used to look very strange with numbers of straw mattresses strewn about. The prisoners were in the habit of bringing them out to air them, and also utilised them as seats in the daytime. We were allowed later on to take them books and papers, but as a rule they all felt too restless to read.

The lot of the men who were herded together in the iron lean-to's was terrible. The yard sloped down in that quarter, and consequently, as there were no foundations, the floor was at a lower level than the ground outside, and it was very damp. After some of the tropical rains, especially as there was no flooring, these mattresses were quite wet, and many of the prisoners became very unwell. It was very strange to see the interior of these cells, with their long row of mat-tresses placed on the ground as closely together as was possible. There was no ventilation at all except a few holes cut in the iron, and at night I believe it was suffocating. Another great discomfort to the prisoners was the difficulty of washing themselves: except for a very shallow furrow of most doubtful water which ran through one end of the yard, there were absolutely no means of ablution. That was not intentional cruelty, however; a Boer seldom washes, and does not expect any one else to do so. On the con-dition of strict secrecy—and £5—Burgers consented to take a small bath to Lionel.

CHAPTER XII

I HAVE mentioned that, except at night, these political prisoners were put with all kinds of criminals, black and white, and if the contact was a very unpleasant one, they at least gained an insight into Boer methods of treating their ordinary prisoners, which of itself alone is quite enough to prove how very far they are from following the precepts of Christianity. The cruelty witnessed on every side was revolting. On my visits to the prison I often noticed the forms of Kaffirs wrapped in a thin blanket, walking about, melancholy objects that made my heart bleed, for they were so attenuated that they were more like living skeletons than men. On inquiry I found that they were the chief Malaboch and a remnant of his followers, who had been taken prisoners in the very war which had occasioned the "commandeering" incident. The cruel treatment they received beggars description. They were forced to live out of doors in the yard, night and day, summer and winter, and in all weathers, their only protection being a thin Kaffir blanket. As the extremes of climate are great, and these wretched creatures, coming as they did from a much warmer one than that of Pretoria, were doubly susceptible, it is no wonder that an enormous proportion had died in a very short time. Through the burning heat of summer, the heavy tropical rains, and the cold winds and frosts of winter, on the most miserable diet imaginable, these unhappy Kaffirs dragged out an existence which fortunately for themselves was not a long one.

I also heard an instance of a "boy" who had been imprisoned for some minor offence, and who whilst in the gaol had been allowed to earn a little money by washing clothes for some of the Reformers. When his time expired, his convict garb was replaced by his own, and it appears that as he was going out of the prison, discharged, some of the guards told him he must be searched. He objected; they tried to do it by force. He resisted with all his might, and fought five guards like a wild animal. In the end he was worsted, his money was taken from him, he was hauled back with his clothes torn to some inner cell, and was never seen again. But the most awful sounds were heard proceeding from the place—one of my informants told me it sounded exactly as if he had been put between boards and was being flattened. The shameful scene at the gate was witnessed by many who felt anew their cruel helplessness.

All this time no intimation whatever had been given as to what steps were going to be taken as to the disposition of the prisoners, and the suspense increased. I remember some of them saying, one day, that all they asked was that they might hear no more news of their fate; they could bear anything except

the everlasting rumours, and announced that they had
resolved to throw brickbats at the next informant. The
uncertainty had preyed frightfully on some of the men's
minds, and in many cases their health began to give
way; a certain proportion were not too robust to begin
with, and in addition to their own trouble they were
oppressed by the knowledge that others had been
dragged into the mess. Some of them were not too
well off, so that sordid money troubles were added to
their misery. Very nearly all the Reform prisoners
were married, and the thought of the suffering brought
on their wives was galling. Among them, Mr. Gray
was one who took the whole thing very much to heart.
I had heard that he had lost all spirit, and was most
frightfully depressed; his fellow-prisoners were hoping
that the authorities would at any rate allow him to
go to a private house until he got better. But nothing
was done.

One Saturday morning we heard that he had committed suicide, and the awful news was a terrible shock
to us all. We were allowed to go into the prison that
morning although it was Saturday, and my heart bled
for all the men, as the ghastly deed had touched them
all very nearly, and the last sad offices were done with
their help. Mr. Gray was a young, strong-looking man,
over six feet in height. He had a wife and six children,
and was very well off. He looked one of the last persons to take his own life, but the constant uncertainty
was too much for his brain, and his poor wife had had

many anxious moments about him. Some of his fellow-prisoners had constituted themselves into a watch, and not only removed all dangerous implements, but took turns to be with him constantly. The prison surgeon was fully warned of his state, and reported upon it to the authorities, but no notice was taken, and hence the unhappy result.

It appears that early that morning on rising, Mr. Gray had asked one of his fellow-prisoners to lend him a razor to shave with. This was done, as he appeared quite rational. He retired to a place near, and as he did not reappear after a few minutes, some one went to look for him, and found him lying on the ground with his throat cut. The poor man who discovered him fainted away with horror, and one can quite well imagine what his comrades felt at his tragic end, as he had been liked by all.

It was a sad day in the prison. The bringing in of the coffin and the removal of the body deepened the gloom; but worst of all was the thought of the terrible shock to his poor wife, and her grief for his loss. That he was one of those who had been arrested without a warrant, was a circumstance that added to her sorrow. He was buried in Johannesburg. I believe the funeral was a most impressive one. Ten thousand men followed the body to its last resting-place, and Mr. Darragh, the Rector of St. Mary's there, made an oration over the grave, in which he dwelt upon what was recognised as a judicial murder.

The effect of this tragedy was very apparent in the prison. The Government realised that if they were not careful more such cases would follow. So several men who were ailing were released, and among them Captain Mein, who resisted to his utmost, saying he did not wish to desert the others. But he had no option, and a most affecting scene took place when he bade farewell to his fellows. They, however, were sincerely glad to see him quit the prison; he was not young, and had suffered very bad health there.

Poor Mr. Gray's death really gave the Transvaal authorities a fright, as it aroused afresh the indignation of Johannesburg and the whole of South Africa, and so at last they thought it time to give some little clue as to their intentions.

I remember that morning so well. Mrs. Morice, the judge's wife, who had been so kind and sympathetic to us all, sent in word that she had some news for me. I went out, and saw by her drawn and haggard face that it was not good. She said, "I wish to tell you so that when you hear it later it will not be such a shock. It is that the death sentence on the four principal prisoners, who include your husband, has been commuted to fifteen years' imprisonment."

Oh, merciful Heaven! it was almost worse than death, and the awful sentence had more reality in it than the first one. I thought of all those long years to be wasted in a prison, of men in their prime doomed to such a fate, and felt crushed indeed. Imprisonment is a terrible thing, and ever since that time in Pretoria, I have had great sympathy for even the most guilty criminals. The long-drawn out days, the hopeless monotony, the silence, the ugliness and sordidness of prison life! No words of mine can describe the horror. And to think of Lionel and his friends separated from every one, and after a time being gradually forgotten and probably relegated to some outlandish place in the Transvaal, where they would be at the mercy of their cruel and ignorant captors. I look back on that day as one of the worst we went through.

I went up to the prison feeling utterly cast down, and told Lionel what I had heard. While I was there an official came in and announced that the Government had determined to commute the sentences of all the men—some to three months', some to five, and some to a year's imprisonment—but at the time it was not announced that at the end of this term they would further reconsider their claim to clemency. So it was only a sham after all! The four leaders were not mentioned.

An incident took place which struck me very much. As I stood listening to all this, some one came up to me, the wife of one of the prisoners, her face blurred with weeping. She shook my arm, and said passionately, "Think of it, my husband has got three months' imprisonment!" Poor woman. She did not seem to realise that my husband's fate was too terrible even to mention. She was one of those who always declared her husband was innocent, as he had joined at the last moment, and thought he was ill-used by the others. She did not understand how much better for him it would have been had she tried to help him to remain true to his friends in distress.

To have arrived at some idea as to what the Transvaal authorities really intended to do, was at least an advance. Then a new theory was started, which was that any one having influence with the officials should do all in their power to persuade them how wrong it was to keep these men in prison, and how much harm was being done to the country by the continued agitation.

So all kinds of people came to Pretoria to do what they could. One case was rather funny. A certain lady and her daughter had gained much sympathy from the beginning of our troubles, when the latter's husband had been imprisoned as one of the Reformers, as they asserted that he had been induced to come out from England for the purpose, that he had relinquished a splendid military career, and had in consequence been ruined. But as I happened to know, the facts of the case were, that he had gone to Johannesburg to try and make a living, as his income did not permit of his remaining in the army, and that being connected with some of the Reform party, he joined the movement. He is a charming fellow, but up to the present time his military genius has remained unproved.

I heard this tale of woe on my arrival, and thinking that the Reformers were being blamed for a little more than they really deserved, I contradicted it, and Lionel and the husband of the lady told her she was labouring under a delusion. However, she had gained much sympathy on all sides, and there were plenty of people who were delighted to have something to add to the Reform leaders' crimes. The mother of this lady was one of those who had influence with the Dutch party, being herself of that nationality, and she accordingly went with her daughter to see what could be done with General Joubert. He was obdurate, and when she reproached him with the fact that her innocent son-in-law had received a year's imprisonment while some had only got three months, he turned to her and said, " But you know why he got a year?" "No," she said. "Why, because he came out from England expressly for the Revolution." Poor ladies; they swore by everything that was sacred that that was not the case—and what is more, told the story all over Pretoria themselves. So much for their sense of humour!

Even the old President received more lady visitors at this time than he is in the habit of doing, as many of the poor wives went up to "the Presidency" to see if they could soften his heart. He listened to their appeals, but I am afraid was not much influenced by them. Some of them also tried "Tante Sanne" (as Mrs. Kruger is called in Pretoria), and begged her to do what she could for their husbands. One lady told me the following story. After the Raid, when their respective husbands were imprisoned, some ladies went and begged Mrs. Kruger to use her influence with the

President in their behalf. She said, " Yes, I will do all I can for you. I am very sorry for you all, although I know that none of you thought of me that night when we heard that Jameson had crossed the border, and we were afraid the President would have to go out and fight, and when they went and caught his old white horse that he had not ridden for eight years. But all the same I am sorry for you all."

But now for once South Africa was at one on a question. Mr. Rose-Innes and Mr. Garrett of the *Cape Times* got up a public meeting in Cape Town, which was attended by thousands, and a general agitation was set on foot all over South Africa in favour of the release of the Reform prisoners.

Meetings were held everywhere. South African sentiment had undergone a complete change, and all the sympathy that Kruger had obtained at the beginning of the troubles was fast disappearing, as his fair promises of reform were unfulfilled, and everything that could conduce to the detriment of the Uitlander was done. Johannesburg was daily becoming more and more unsettled, no business was transacted, and every one was afraid of entering on new undertakings for fear of further trouble, while the helplessness of the prisoners alone protected the Government at this time. We heard and read that the Mayors or principal men of every town and village of any importance in South Africa were coming to Pretoria, and were bringing petitions to the President for the release of the Reformers.

One Saturday morning, when some of these delegates were actually on their way up, we were told that the great bulk of the men were coming out that day. All were to be released except the four principals and two others, Mr. Wools-Sampson, an Africander, and Mr. "Karri" Davies, an Australian. These two had persistently refused to sign any petition whatever. They said they had been cast into prison through obeying the Governor, the representative of their Queen, and this being the case, they considered it was but their due that he should obtain their release. So when the others were let out, it was announced to them that, as they had not petitioned, their case could not be considered. Their fellow-prisoners did their best to make them change their decision, but they stood firm. They said they were bachelors and had no one dependent upon them, and that therefore they were free to act on principle. They were quite right, but the others, from their own point of view, were equally so. Most of the prisoners were married and had children, and some were very poor, and it had been proved that unless they tried to help themselves they would remain in prison indefinitely, as the English Government either could not or would not do so. Having others to think of as well as themselves, they had felt it to be their duty under the circumstances to swallow their pride.[1]

[1] I may add that these two noble young Colonials, Sampson and Davies, remained in Pretoria prison until June 1897, when Kruger, not knowing what to do with them, and realising that their detention was a continual cause of unrest, released them on the Queen's Jubilee.

When the good news came it seemed almost impossible to believe, but it was true. They were released on condition of paying the £2000 fine, and signing a pledge not to interfere in politics for three years on pain of banishment. That there was great rejoicing goes without saying, and there was a general exodus from Pretoria by the two o'clock train that day. After so many false alarms, the release came at last quite unexpectedly, and the day being a Saturday, there were not very many visitors in Pretoria. The released prisoners had but one idea—to return to their homes as fast as they could, and to shake off their feet the dust of a town that had for them so many unpleasant associations.

That day was one of very mixed sensations for me and for the relatives of the men who were still imprisoned. Being June, the weather had become very wintry, with the peculiarly desolate effect produced by a cold wind stirring up the dust. That it was a day of this kind added perhaps to the depression which came over me when everybody had gone off, and Pretoria assumed an even more dull and deserted air than usual. Returning from the prison, where I missed so many familiar faces, my heart sank as I remembered its air of desolation, the forlorn appearance of the whole place and its remaining occupants. At this date my sister-in-law had been gone some time, my children were still at the Coast, even the hotel was almost empty, and I cannot describe the dreariness of my sensations. Mrs. Hammond was in Johannesburg ill, and Mrs. Farrar lived too far away for much intercourse.

One little gleam of brightness I found that day, but even this seemed to make everything else more dreary by contrast. One of our friends, instead of going back to Johannesburg with his fellow-prisoners, remained in Pretoria, and went straight from the prison to the house of a certain beloved young lady, proposed to her, was accepted, and came down late in the afternoon to tell me his good news, as I had already been let into the secret of his aspirations.

My friend, Mrs. Hennen Jennings was a good angel to me then, coming over to stay with me, and minding no trouble. She and her husband were among the most loyal of our friends, and we much appreciated their sympathy. As I said before, those troublous days estranged many. Friendships of years were broken, and much bitterness of spirit roused, and in many cases these sores have never been healed.

Once the fifty-six men were let out, the authorities at Pretoria seemed to think there was nothing more to be done. We heard also that there had been a tremendous quarrel amongst the members of the Executive, and that Kruger had entirely refused to mention the subject. For some little time before this I had been thinking of hiring a house in Pretoria and settling there, and had even taken certain steps towards that end. I had already sold our carriages and horses, and was seriously thinking of shutting up the house in

Johannesburg and selling all the furniture. I had given orders to my servants to begin dismantling the house, and was looking out for a place in Pretoria, but it was difficult to get one. Eventually I did succeed through an agent who had not divulged my name, for some of the townspeople had a pleasing habit of charging us double. This chanced to be another case in point, for as soon as the owners discovered who their would-be tenant was, they tried to tie me down to all kinds of ridiculous restrictions, and found various devices for adding to the rent originally asked. I was in too sore a frame of mind to put up with this blackmail, and refused outright to have the house at any price.

I had all this time been pining for the children, but feared to have them back, as in case of Lionel's release, they would be on the spot for departure to England, and I did not care for them again to make that long journey of 1000 miles each way. My superstitious maid had long been urging me to send for them, saying, " You will never have any luck until the children come back," but what her reasons were for this statement I cannot say. The prospect of release at this time looked more hopeless than ever, so I accordingly sent the order for them to return to me.

Lionel was obliged to go to the Pretoria Hospital just at this moment. The cold wind sweeping through the prison was very trying, and, weakened as he was by many weeks of bad food, he was seized with an attack of congestion of the lungs. There were no comforts of any kind to be obtained, and although to the last he resisted leaving his five companions, I insisted on the doctor giving an order for his removal to the hospital, which was done. After the release of the fifty-six men the remaining prisoners grew very depressed; their more fortunate companions, however, by no means deserted them—on the contrary, they were all doing everything in their power to obtain their release, and Mr. King and Mr. Hull took up their abode in Pretoria, declaring their intention of remaining there until their former fellow-prisoners came out.

I cannot remember all the tiresome negotiations that had been going on with the Government during this time. The way in which everything was managed was very funny. The authorities did not want it to appear that they were anxious to have the matter settled and to release the men, nor that it was a question of their buying freedom at the highest possible price. So all sorts and conditions of people were commissioned to convey to them suggestions as to what they should do to obtain their release. Of course Du Plessis, being entirely in Kruger's confidence, was a fine go-between, and another who must not be forgotten was a person who played, and may still do so, quite an important *rôle* in Pretoria—namely, Mr. Leo Weinthal, the editor of *The Press*, the Government organ, Reuter's agent, and Kruger's bosom friend. I should not like to guess what country lays claim to this gentleman—

whichever it may be it is not to be congratulated. I know that of all the many humiliations I had to suffer none was more difficult to bear than that of asking this individual into my sitting-room on one occasion when he was negotiating the question of release.

When it was suggested that the Reform leaders should buy their liberty, there was a great outcry. "No, it would never do: it would be Blood-money." But, with familiarity, the idea of blood-money apparently lost its terrors, and then the main endeavour was to get as much as possible.

This same Mr. Leo Weinthal was the President's great resource. He used to go and read the papers to him every evening and translate them. The President, not being able to read English, was quite dependent on those who would impart to him a little news from the outside world, and it can easily be imagined how tempting it must have been to any one not troubled with scruples to impart the news in the way he desired it to be received. I have often been amused, too, at the telegrams this individual used to send in his capacity as Reuter's agent. Being much in the President's confidence, he was able to represent matters exactly as the latter wanted and to give just the right colouring; indeed, to those behind the scenes it was very instructive to note how the telegrams from Pretoria would be worded, conciliatory or otherwise, according to the state of public feeling in England.

In the meantime all the various Mayors and representative men from all parts of the Cape Colony, Orange
Free State, and Natal had arrived in Pretoria with
petitions from their respective towns. There were some
two hundred in all, and as their coming had been
awaited for some time and the journey was in all cases
an expensive and lengthy one, they had a right to
expect a speedy audience of the President. But that
was "counting without their host." They arrived on
the Wednesday; the President announced that he could
not possibly see them until the Saturday. However,
there was nothing to be done, although the unexpected
delay was very tiresome to every one.

Lionel was now better, and had rejoined his companions in the prison, but was still far from well. Both
he and I were looking forward very much to seeing the
children, whom I expected by the midday train from
Cape Town on the Thursday. As the train was invariably late, and the prison was inaccessible to us
after four, I thought I would ask Du Plessis a favour
for the first time. The gaol-yard looked particularly
dreary that morning. A lady who had lately come
out from England and was paying her first visit to
the prisoners with her husband, was with me when I
made my request to Du Plessis. In the politest manner
I could command I said, "I am expecting my children
to-day, but the train is certain to be very late. In that
case will you allow me to bring them in for a few minutes
after hours, as Mr. Phillips is ill, and has not seen them

M

for so many weeks ? I should esteem it a great favour."
His answer quite silenced me. He swore at me in the
loudest of voices (I suppose it was to impress the
stranger), and asked me how I dared to make such a
request, that it was out of the question, &c. It was as
much as I could do to restrain my tears at this unnecessary rudeness, and the strange lady, whose name I have
forgotten, told me afterwards she could not have believed
such a scene possible had she not witnessed it herself.
But on various occasions many people made similar
remarks ; indeed, I generally found that many who were
most incredulous as to all we underwent for the sake of
our cause, ultimately became our staunchest partisans.

When the children eventually arrived, much too late
to go into the prison to see their father, I personally felt
a little happier, as I had missed them much all those
dreadful weeks. As soon as possible the next morning
I took them to the prison. (Visiting hours had been a
little enlarged since there were so many less passes to
occupy poor Mr. Schutte.) Lionel was overjoyed to see
them, and was in the act of embracing them when we
heard a voice calling to us from the gate.

It was Mrs. Leonard's voice, and she said, "I have
come to tell you that you are coming out to-day. I
have it on the highest authority."

This time there was no mistake, and they actually
did come out that day. My maid's prophecy came
to my mind, and it certainly was a curious coincidence.
Mr. Schutte came to announce the news officially. It

was to the effect that the President in his magnanimity was going to release them that day on the payment of £25,000 each, and banishment for fifteen years, this latter part of the commuted sentence being held in abeyance in consideration of a promise not to meddle in politics for that period on pain of its enforcement.

When he had fulfilled his official business, Mr. Schutte unbent very much, shook hands with Lionel cordially, informing him that he had come to the conclusion that he was an honest man, and had really had no intention of trying to take their country away from the Boers. He ended by remarking that he was on the point of going to the Warm Baths near Pretoria, but that on his return he hoped we would invite him to come and stay with us in Johannesburg, as he had heard we had a very nice house!

A great many legal formalities had to be gone through, but at five o'clock that afternoon, the 11th June 1896, Lionel and his three friends, Colonel Frank Rhodes, George Farrar, and John Hays Hammond were released, having been imprisoned five months. As Colonel Rhodes was an Imperial officer, he could not sign an undertaking not to meddle in the "internal or external" politics of the Transvaal, so he was taken to the train that night and escorted to the border of the Transvaal, proceeding thence to Mashonaland. The other three not deeming it advisable to sever their connection with the country entirely, signed the agreement.

Mr. Hammond, whose wife was ill, left for Johannes-burg at once; the two others followed early the next morning. They met with a reception which they are not likely to forget, and if I had regretted that the children should have come all that long way unneces-sarily, only to see their father a few minutes in prison, I changed my mind when they and I witnessed this never-to-be-forgotten scene. When the train drew up in the Park Station at Johannesburg, a dense mass of people was to be seen as far as the eye could reach. Lionel and George Farrar had no time to put foot to the ground, but were lifted on men's shoulders, and carried to waiting carriages, which were dragged up to the Stock Exchange, where they received a regular ovation and many congratulations on being once more free men.

And so ended one of the many painful episodes in a movement of which we have not yet seen the end.

The Mayors meanwhile had been awaiting the audi-ence with Kruger. It was accorded them—but not till the day after the prisoners were released. So instead of petitioning him for their release, they had to thank the President for what he had done, and received one of his characteristic allegorical homilies in return, which I believe did not conduce to allay their feelings of annoyance at his rudeness and want of common courtesy.

Two days later Lionel and Mr. Fitzpatrick left the Transvaal for England. They were in a hurry to get

ECKSTEIN'S OFFICES, JOHANNESBURG.

there. Dr. Jameson and his fellows were going to be tried, and they wished to be at hand to correct many misstatements which had got into the papers; also they felt sure that some misunderstanding still existed, and they relied on Dr. Jameson's sense of honour to do all he could to explain it away. Vain hope!

All they asked him to do was to get his counsel to state that he and his force had never expected the Johannesburg men to go out to meet them—that on the contrary he had disobeyed their explicit injunctions not to come down, and thus to clear them of the charge of cowardice still resting on them. They did not ask him to make humiliating concessions—only to say that instead of expecting their help he had come against their orders. He refused everything, and it was only later on, before the Parliamentary Select Committee, that the admission was dragged from him that he regretted having, prior to the disastrous raid, imputed motives of cowardice to them. So these men who from beginning to end had scrupulously kept their word to Dr. Jameson, who had almost sacrificed Johannesburg to save him and his fellows from a danger that seemed imminent, who even in their moments of confidence in the prison refrained from blaming him for the terrible ruin he had worked, always giving him credit for some noble motive, were disappointed.

Dr. Jameson was the popular idol, and had not the sense to see that at the moment of his trial there was still an opportunity of admitting the truth without

N

detriment to his own reputation. He did not comprehend that so convinced of his heroism and chivalry
was every one whose opinion he valued, that he could
well afford to allow that the Reformers were not what
he had led the world to believe, and that the undated
letter which he had carried about for weeks was no
urgent call of the moment. He thus lost an opportunity which will never come again, and time will but
prove the wisdom of the old adage, "Truth will out."

If the whole miserable affair had to be lived over
again fifty times, I would only wish Lionel and his friends
to take the course they did when things went wrong;
for whatever they or others had to suffer, they can feel
happy in one most vital matter—they endeavoured to be
true to themselves and their duty when they were sorely
tried; and, from my point of view, they succeeded.

About a year after the events related, Sir John
Willoughby attacked the Reform leaders of Johannesburg in an article in the *Nineteenth Century*. Lionel
replied to it in the same review, August 1897, defend-
ing himself and his comrades from the charges made.

In consequence of this action the Government of
the Transvaal enforced the sentence of banishment
from the country on him, notwithstanding the fact that
in the opinion of three of the first lawyers in England,
the article did not constitute any breach of the pledge.
By this act Kruger proved once more how short-sighted
is his policy, and how little he understands where the

true interests of his unfortunate country lie. It is not by alienating the men who have given the thought and hard work of years to the place, and who have honestly striven to do their duty to Johannesburg, that Kruger shows himself a serious statesman or a benefactor of his country.

THE END

Printed by BALLANTYNE, HANSON & Co.
Edinburgh & London

𝔄 Classified Catalogue

OF WORKS IN

GENERAL LITERATURE

PUBLISHED BY

LONGMANS, GREEN, & CO.

39 PATERNOSTER ROW, LONDON, E.C.

91 AND 93 FIFTH AVENUE NEW YORK, AND 32 HORNBY ROAD, BOMBAY.

CONTENTS.

INDEX OF AUTHORS AND EDITORS.

History, Politics, Polity, Political Memoirs, &c.

Abbott.—*A HISTORY OF GREECE.* By EVELYN ABBOTT, M.A., LL.D. Part I.—From the Earliest Times to the Ionian Revolt. Crown 8vo., 10s. 6d. Part II.—500-445 B.C. Crown 8vo., 10s. 6d.

Acland and Ransome.—*A HANDBOOK IN OUTLINE OF THE POLITICAL HISTORY OF ENGLAND TO* 1896. Chronologically Arranged. By the Right Hon. A. H. DYKE ACLAND, and CYRIL RANSOME, M.A. Crown 8vo., 6s.

Amos.—*PRIMER OF THE ENGLISH CONSTITUTION AND GOVERNMENT.* For the Use of Colleges, Schools, and Private Students. By SHELDON AMOS, M.A. Cr. 8vo., 6s.

ANNUAL REGISTER (THE). A Review of Public Events at Home and Abroad, for the year 1898. 8vo., 18s. Volumes of the *ANNUAL REGISTER* for the years 1863-1897 can still be had. 18s. each.

Arnold.—*INTRODUCTORY LECTURES ON MODERN HISTORY.* By THOMAS ARNOLD, D.D., formerly Head Master of Rugby School. 8vo., 7s. 6d.

Ashbourne.—*PITT: SOME CHAPTERS ON HIS LIFE AND TIMES.* By the Right Hon. EDWARD GIBSON, LORD ASHBOURNE, Lord Chancellor of Ireland. With 11 Portraits. 8vo., 21s.

Baden-Powell.—*THE INDIAN VILLAGE COMMUNITY.* Examined with Reference to the Physical, Ethnographic, and Historical Conditions of the Provinces; chiefly on the Basis of the Revenue-Settlement Records and District Manuals. By B. H. BADEN-POWELL, M.A., C.I.E. With Map. 8vo., 16s.

Bagwell.—*IRELAND UNDER THE TUDORS.* By RICHARD BAGWELL, LL.D. (3 vols.) Vols. I. and II. From the first invasion of the Northmen to the year 1578. 8vo., 32s. Vol. III. 1578-1603. 8vo., 18s.

Besant.—*THE HISTORY OF LONDON.* By Sir WALTER BESANT. With 74 Illustrations. Crown 8vo., 1s. 9d. Or bound as a School Prize Book, 2s. 6d.

Brassey (LORD).—PAPERS AND ADDRESSES.

NAVAL AND MARITIME. 1872-1893. 2 vols. Crown 8vo., 10s.

Brassey (LORD) PAPERS AND ADDRESSES—*continued.*

MERCANTILE MARINE AND NAVIGATION, from 1871-1894. Crown 8vo., 5s.

IMPERIAL FEDERATION AND COLONISATION FROM 1880-1894. Cr. 8vo., 5s.

POLITICAL AND MISCELLANEOUS. 1861-1894. Crown 8vo., 5s.

Bright.—*A HISTORY OF ENGLAND.* By the Rev. J. FRANCK BRIGHT, D.D. Period I. *MEDIÆVAL MONARCHY:* A.D. 449-1485. Crown 8vo., 4s. 6d. Period II. *PERSONAL MONARCHY.* 1485-1688. Crown 8vo., 5s. Period III. *CONSTITUTIONAL MONARCHY.* 1689-1837. Crown 8vo., 7s. 6d. Period IV. *THE GROWTH OF DEMOCRACY.* 1837-1880. Crown 8vo., 6s.

Buckle.—*HISTORY OF CIVILISATION IN ENGLAND, FRANCE, SPAIN, AND SCOTLAND.* By HENRY THOMAS BUCKLE. 3 vols. Crown 8vo., 24s.

Burke.—*A HISTORY OF SPAIN, FROM THE EARLIEST TIMES TO THE DEATH OF FERDINAND THE CATHOLIC.* By ULICK RALPH BURKE, M.A. Edited by Major MARTIN A. S. HUME. 2 vols. Crown 8vo., 16s. net.

Chesney.—*INDIAN POLITY:* a View of the System of Administration in India. By General Sir GEORGE CHESNEY, K.C.B. With Map showing all the Administrative Divisions of British India. 8vo., 21s.

Churchill.—*THE RIVER WAR:* an Historical Account of the Reconquest of the Soudan. By WINSTON SPENCER CHURCHILL. Edited by Colonel F. RHODES, D.S.O. With 34 Maps and 51 Illustrations from Drawings by ANGUS MCNEILL, also 7 Photogravure Portraits of Generals, etc. 2 vols. Medium 8vo., 36s.

Corbett.—*DRAKE AND THE TUDOR NAVY,* with a History of the Rise of England as a Maritime Power. By JULIAN S. CORBETT. With Portraits, Illustrations and Maps. 2 vols. Crown 8vo., 16s.

Creighton (M., D.D., Lord Bishop of London).

A HISTORY OF THE PAPACY FROM THE GREAT SCHISM TO THE SACK OF ROME, 1378-1527. 6 vols. Crown 8vo., 6s. each.

QUEEN ELIZABETH. With Portrait. Crown 8vo., 6s.

History, Politics, Polity, Political Memoirs, &c.—*continued.*

Curzon.—*PERSIA AND THE PERSIAN QUESTION.* By the Right Hon. LORD CURZON OF KEDLESTON. With 9 Maps, 96 Illustrations, Appendices, and an Index. 2 vols. 8vo., 42s.

De Tocqueville.—*DEMOCRACY IN AMERICA.* By ALEXIS DE TOCQUEVILLE. Translated by HENRY REEVE, C.B., D.C.L. 2 vols. Crown 8vo., 16s.

Dickinson.—*THE DEVELOPMENT OF PARLIAMENT DURING THE NINETEENTH CENTURY.* By G. LOWES DICKINSON, M.A. 8vo., 7s. 6d.

Froude (JAMES A.).

THE HISTORY OF ENGLAND, from the Fall of Wolsey to the Defeat of the Spanish Armada.

> *Popular Edition.* 12 vols. Crown 8vo., 3s. 6d. each.
> 'Silver Library' Edition. 12 vols. Crown 8vo., 3s. 6d. each.

THE DIVORCE OF CATHERINE OF ARAGON. Crown 8vo., 3s. 6d.

THE SPANISH STORY OF THE ARMADA, and other Essays. Cr. 8vo., 3s. 6d.

THE ENGLISH IN IRELAND IN THE EIGHTEENTH CENTURY. 3 vols. Cr. 8vo., 10s. 6d.

ENGLISH SEAMEN IN THE SIXTEENTH CENTURY. Cr. 8vo., 6s.

THE COUNCIL OF TRENT. Crown 8vo., 3s. 6d.

SHORT STUDIES ON GREAT SUBJECTS. 4 vols. Cr. 8vo., 3s. 6d. each.

CÆSAR : a Sketch. Cr. 8vo, 3s. 6d.

Gardiner (SAMUEL RAWSON, D.C.L., LL.D.).

HISTORY OF ENGLAND, from the Accession of James I. to the Outbreak of the Civil War, 1603-1642. 10 vols. Crown 8vo., 6s. each.

A HISTORY OF THE GREAT CIVIL WAR, 1642-1649. 4 vols. Cr. 8vo., 6s. each.

A HISTORY OF THE COMMONWEALTH AND THE PROTECTORATE. 1649-1660. Vol. I. 1649-1651. With 14 Maps. 8vo., 21s. Vol. II. 1651-1654. With 7 Maps. 8vo., 21s.

WHAT GUNPOWDER PLOT WAS. With 8 Illustrations. Crown 8vo., 5s.

CROMWELL'S PLACE IN HISTORY. Founded on Six Lectures delivered in the University of Oxford. Cr. 8vo., 3s. 6d.

Gardiner (SAMUEL RAWSON, D.C.L., LL.D.)—*continued.*

THE STUDENT'S HISTORY OF ENGLAND. With 378 Illustrations. Crown 8vo., 12s.

> Also in Three Volumes, price 4s. each.
> Vol. I. B.C. 55—A.D. 1509. 173 Illustrations.
> Vol. II. 1509-1689. 96 Illustrations.
> Vol. III. 1689-1885. 109 Illustrations.

Greville.—*A JOURNAL OF THE REIGNS OF KING GEORGE IV., KING WILLIAM IV., AND QUEEN VICTORIA.* By CHARLES C. F. GREVILLE, formerly Clerk of the Council. 8 vols. Crown 8vo., 3s. 6d. each.

HARVARD HISTORICAL STUDIES.

THE SUPPRESSION OF THE AFRICAN SLAVE TRADE TO THE UNITED STATES OF AMERICA, 1638-1870. By W. E. B. DU BOIS, Ph.D. Svo., 7s. 6d.

THE CONTEST OVER THE RATIFICATION OF THE FEDERAL CONSTITUTION IN MASSACHUSETTS. By S. B. HARDING, A.M. 8vo., 6s.

A CRITICAL STUDY OF NULLIFICATION IN SOUTH CAROLINA. By D. F. HOUSTON, A.M. 8vo., 6s.

NOMINATIONS FOR ELECTIVE OFFICE IN THE UNITED STATES. By FREDERICK W. DALLINGER, A.M. 8vo., 7s. 6d.

A BIBLIOGRAPHY OF BRITISH MUNICIPAL HISTORY, INCLUDING GILDS AND PARLIAMENTARY REPRESENTATION. By CHARLES GROSS, Ph.D. 8vo., 12s.

THE LIBERTY AND FREE SOIL PARTIES IN THE NORTH WEST. By THEODORE C. SMITH, Ph.D. 8vo, 7s. 6d.

THE PROVINCIAL GOVERNOR IN THE ENGLISH COLONIES OF NORTH AMERICA. By EVARTS BOUTELL GREENE. 8vo., 7s. 6d.

. Other Volumes are in preparation.

Hammond.—*A WOMAN'S PART IN A REVOLUTION.* By Mrs. JOHN HAYS HAMMOND. Crown 8vo., 2s. 6d.

Historic Towns.—Edited by E. A. FREEMAN, D.C.L., and Rev. WILLIAM HUNT, M.A. With Maps and Plans. Crown 8vo., 3s. 6d. each.

Bristol. By Rev. W. Hunt.
Carlisle. By Mandell Creighton, D.D.
Cinque Ports. By Montagu Burrows.
Colchester. By Rev. E. L. Cutts.
Exeter. By E. A. Freeman.
London. By Rev. W. J. Loftie.
Oxford. By Rev. C. W. Boase.
Winchester. By G. W. Kitchin, D.D.
York. By Rev. James Raine.
New York. By Theodore Roosevelt.
Boston (U.S.) By Henry Cabot Lodge.

History, Politics, Polity, Political Memoirs, &c.—*continued*.

Hunter.—*A HISTORY OF BRITISH INDIA.* By Sir WILLIAM WILSON HUNTER, K.C.S.I., M.A., LL.D.; a Vice-President of the Royal Asiatic Society. In 5 vols. Vol. I.—Introductory to the Overthrow of the English in the Spice Archipelago, 1623. With 4 Maps. 8vo., 18s.

Joyce (P. W., LL.D.).

A SHORT HISTORY OF IRELAND, from the Earliest Times to 1603. Crown 8vo., 10s. 6d.

A CHILD'S HISTORY OF IRELAND. From the Earliest Times to the Death of O'Connell. With specially constructed Map and 160 Illustrations, including Facsimile in full colours of an illuminated page of the Gospel Book of Mac-Durnan, A.D. 850. Fcp. 8vo., 3s. 6d.

Kaye and Malleson.—*HISTORY OF THE INDIAN MUTINY,* 1857-1858. By Sir JOHN W. KAYE and Colonel G. B. MALLESON. With Analytical Index and Maps and Plans. 6 vols. Crown 8vo., 3s. 6d. each.

Kent.—*THE ENGLISH RADICALS:* an Historical Sketch. By C. B. ROYLANCE-KENT. Crown 8vo., 7s. 6d.

Lang.—*THE COMPANIONS OF PICKLE:* Being a Sequel to 'Pickle the Spy'. By ANDREW LANG. With 4 Plates. 8vo., 16s.

Lecky (The Rt. Hon. WILLIAM E. H.)

HISTORY OF ENGLAND IN THE EIGHTEENTH CENTURY.
Library Edition. 8 vols. 8vo. Vols. I. and II., 1700-1760, 36s.; Vols. III. and IV., 1760-1784, 36s.; Vols. V. and VI., 1784-1793, 36s.; Vols. VII. and VIII., 1793-1800, 36s.
Cabinet Edition. ENGLAND. 7 vols. Crown 8vo., 6s. each. IRELAND. 5 vols. Crown 8vo., 6s. each.

HISTORY OF EUROPEAN MORALS FROM AUGUSTUS TO CHARLEMAGNE. 2 vols. Crown 8vo., 12s.

HISTORY OF THE RISE AND INFLUENCE OF THE SPIRIT OF RATIONALISM IN EUROPE. 2 vols. Crown 8vo., 12s.

DEMOCRACY AND LIBERTY.
Library Edition. 2 vols. 8vo., 36s.
Cabinet Edition. 2 vols. Cr. 8vo., 12s.

Lowell.—*GOVERNMENTS AND PARTIES IN CONTINENTAL EUROPE.* By A. LAWRENCE LOWELL. 2 vols. 8vo., 21s.

Lytton.—*THE HISTORY OF LORD LYTTON'S INDIAN ADMINISTRATION, FROM* 1876-1880. Compiled from Letters and Official Papers. Edited by Lady BETTY BALFOUR. With Portrait and Map. 8vo., 18s.

Macaulay (LORD).

THE LIFE AND WORKS OF LORD MACAULAY. 'Edinburgh' Edition. 10 vols. 8vo., 6s. each.

COMPLETE WORKS.
'Albany' Edition. With 12 Portraits. 12 vols. Large Crown 8vo., 3s. 6d. each.
Vols. I.-VI. HISTORY OF ENGLAND, FROM THE ACCESSION OF JAMES THE SECOND.
Vols. VII.-X. ESSAYS AND BIOGRAPHIES.
Vols. XI.-XII. SPEECHES, LAYS OF ANCIENT ROME, ETC., AND INDEX.

Library Edition. 8 vols. 8vo., £5 5s.
'Edinburgh' Edition. 8 vols. 8vo., 6s. each.
Cabinet Edition. 16 vols. Post 8vo., £4 16s.

HISTORY OF ENGLAND FROM THE ACCESSION OF JAMES THE SECOND.
Popular Edition. 2 vols. Cr. 8vo., 5s.
Student's Edition. 2 vols. Cr. 8vo., 12s.
People's Edition. 4 vols. Cr. 8vo., 16s.
'Albany' Edition. With 6 Portraits. 6 vols. Large Crown 8vo., 3s. 6d. each.
Cabinet Edition. 8 vols. Post 8vo., 48s.
'Edinburgh' Edition. 4 vols. 8vo., 6s. each.
Library Edition. 5 vols. 8vo., £4.

CRITICAL AND HISTORICAL ESSAYS, WITH LAYS OF ANCIENT ROME, etc., in 1 volume.
Popular Edition. Crown 8vo., 2s. 6d.
Authorised Edition. Crown 8vo., 2s. 6d., or gilt edges, 3s. 6d.
'Silver Library' Edition. With Portrait and 4 Illustrations to the 'Lays'. Cr. 8vo., 3s. 6d.

CRITICAL AND HISTORICAL ESSAYS.
Student's Edition. 1 vol. Cr. 8vo., 6s.
People's Edition. 2 vols. Cr. 8vo., 8s.
'Trevelyan' Edition. 2 vols. Cr. 8vo., 9s.
Cabinet Edition. 4 vols. Post 8vo., 24s.
'Edinburgh' Edition. 3 vols. 8vo., 6s. each.
Library Edition. 3 vols. 8vo., 36s.

ESSAYS, which may be had separately, sewed, 6d. each; cloth, 1s. each.

Addison and Walpole.	Ranke and Gladstone.
Croker's Boswell's Johnson.	Milton and Machiavelli.
Hallam's Constitutional History.	Lord Byron.
	Lord Clive.
Warren Hastings.	Lord Byron, and The Comic Dramatists of the Restoration.
The Earl of Chatham (Two Essays).	
Frederick the Great.	

MISCELLANEOUS WRITINGS
People's Edition. 1 vol. Cr. 8vo., 4s. 6d
Library Edition. 2 vols. 8vo., 21s.

History, Politics, Polity, Political Memoirs, &c.—*continued*.

Macaulay (LORD)—*continued.*
MISCELLANEOUS WRITINGS, SPEECHES AND POEMS.
Popular Edition. Crown 8vo., 2s. 6d.
Cabinet Edition. 4 vols. Post 8vo., 24s.
SELECTIONS FROM THE WRITINGS OF LORD MACAULAY. Edited, with Occasional Notes, by the Right Hon. Sir G. O. Trevelyan, Bart. Crown 8vo., 6s.

May.—THE CONSTITUTIONAL HISTORY OF ENGLAND since the Accession of George III. 1760-1870. By Sir THOMAS ERSKINE MAY, K.C.B. (Lord Farnborough). 3 vols. Cr. 8vo., 18s.

Merivale (CHARLES, D.D.).
HISTORY OF THE ROMANS UNDER THE EMPIRE. 8 vols. Crown 8vo., 3s. 6d. each.
THE FALL OF THE ROMAN REPUBLIC: a Short History of the Last Century of the Commonwealth. 12mo., 7s. 6d.
GENERAL HISTORY OF ROME, from the Foundation of the City to the Fall of Augustulus, B.C. 753-A.D. 476. With 5 Maps. Crown 8vo, 7s. 6d.

Montague.—THE ELEMENTS OF ENGLISH CONSTITUTIONAL HISTORY. By F. C. MONTAGUE, M.A. Crown 8vo., 3s. 6d.

Phillips.—SOUTH AFRICAN RECOLLE TIONS. By FLORENCE PHILLIPS (Mrs. Lionel Phillips). With 37 Illustrations from Photographs. 8vo., 7s. 6d.
. In this book Mrs. Lionel Phillips gives a record of her recent experiences of life in Johannesburg, and also her recollections of the events connected with the Jameson Raid.

Powell and Trevelyan. — THE PEASANTS' RISING AND THE LOLLARDS: a Collection of Unpublished Documents, forming an Appendix to 'England in the Age of Wycliffe'. Edited by EDGAR POWELL and G. M. TREVELYAN. 8vo., 6s. net.

Ransome.—THE RISE OF CONSTITUTIONAL GOVERNMENT IN ENGLAND. By CYRIL RANSOME, M.A. Crown 8vo., 6s.

Seebohm.—THE ENGLISH VILLAGE COMMUNITY Examined in its Relations to the Manorial and Tribal Systems, etc. By FREDERIC SEEBOHM, LL.D., F.S.A. With 13 Maps and Plates. 8vo., 16s.

Sharpe.—LONDON AND THE KINGDOM: a History derived mainly from the Archives at Guildhall in the custody of the Corporation of the City of London. By REGINALD R. SHARPE, D.C.L., Records Clerk in the Office of the Town Clerk of the City of London. 3 vols. 8vo. 10s. 6d. each.

Shaw.—THE CHURCH UNDER THE COMMONWEALTH. By W. A. SHAW. 2 vols. 8vo.

Smith.—CARTHAGE AND THE CARTHAGINIANS. By R. BOSWORTH SMITH, M.A., With Maps, Plans, etc. Cr. 8vo., 3s. 6d.

Statham.—THE HISTORY OF THE CASTLE, TOWN AND PORT OF DOVER. By the Rev. S. P. H. STATHAM. With 4 Plates and 13 Illustrations. Crown 8vo., 10s. 6d.

Stephens. — A HISTORY OF THE FRENCH REVOLUTION. By H. MORSE STEPHENS. 8vo. Vols. I. and II. 18s. each.

Stubbs.—HISTORY OF THE UNIVERSITY OF DUBLIN, from its Foundation to the End of the Eighteenth Century. By J. W. STUBBS. 8vo., 12s. 6d.

Sutherland.—THE HISTORY OF AUSTRALIA AND NEW ZEALAND, from 1606-1890. By ALEXANDER SUTHERLAND, M.A., and GEORGE SUTHERLAND, M.A. Crown 8vo., 2s. 6d.

Taylor.—A STUDENT'S MANUAL OF THE HISTORY OF INDIA. By Colonel MEADOWS TAYLOR, C.S.I., etc. Cr. 8vo., 7s. 6d.

Todd. — PARLIAMENTARY GOVERNMENT IN THE BRITISH COLONIES. By ALPHEUS TODD, LL.D. 8vo., 30s. net.

Trevelyan.—THE AMERICAN REVOLUTION. Part I. 1766-1776. By the Rt. Hon. Sir G. O. TREVELYAN, Bart. 8vo., 16s.

Trevelyan.—ENGLAND IN THE AGE OF WYCLIFFE. By GEORGE MACAULAY TREVELYAN. 8vo., 15s.

Wakeman and Hassall.—ESSAYS INTRODUCTORY TO THE STUDY OF ENGLISH CONSTITUTIONAL HISTORY. Edited by HENRY OFFLEY WAKEMAN, M.A., and ARTHUR HASSALL, M.A. Crown 8vo., 6s.

Walpole.—HISTORY OF ENGLAND FROM THE CONCLUSION OF THE GREAT WAR IN 1815 TO 1858. By Sir SPENCER WALPOLE, K.C.B. 6 vols. Cr. 8vo., 6s. each.

Wood-Martin.—PAGAN IRELAND: AN ARCHÆOLOGICAL SKETCH. A Handbook of Irish Pre-Christian Antiquities. By W. G. WOOD-MARTIN, M.R.I.A. With 512 Illustrations. Crown 8vo., 15s.

Wylie. — HISTORY OF ENGLAND UNDER HENRY IV. By JAMES HAMILTON WYLIE, M.A. 4 vols. Crown 8vo. Vol. I., 1399-1404, 10s. 6d. Vol. II., 1405-1406, 15s. Vol. III., 1407-1411, 15s. Vol. IV., 1411-1413, 21s.

Biography, Personal Memoirs, &c.

Armstrong.—*THE LIFE AND LETTERS OF EDMUND J. ARMSTRONG.* Edited by G. F. SAVAGE ARMSTRONG. Fcp. 8vo., 7s. 6d.

Bacon.—*THE LETTERS AND LIFE OF FRANCIS BACON, INCLUDING ALL HIS OCCASIONAL WORKS.* Edited by JAMES SPEDDING. 7 vols. 8vo., £4 4s.

Bagehot.—*BIOGRAPHICAL STUDIES.* By WALTER BAGEHOT. Crown 8vo., 3s. 6d.

Boevey.—'*THE PERVERSE WIDOW*': being passages from the Life of Catharina, wife of William Boevey, Esq., of Flaxley Abbey, in the County of Gloucester. Compiled by ARTHUR W. CRAWLEY-BOEVEY, M.A. With Portraits. 4to., 42s. net.

Carlyle.—*THOMAS CARLYLE*: A History of his Life. By JAMES ANTHONY FROUDE.
1795-1835. 2 vols. Crown 8vo., 7s.
1834-1881. 2 vols. Crown 8vo., 7s.

Cellini.—*CHISEL, PEN, AND POIGNARD*: or, Benvenuto Cellini, his Times and his Contemporaries. By the Author of 'The Life of Sir Kenelm Digby,' 'The Life of a Prig,' etc. With 19 Illustrations. Crown 8vo., 5s.

Crozier.—*MY INNER LIFE*: being a Chapter in Personal Evolution and Autobiography. By JOHN BEATTIE CROZIER, Author of 'Civilisation and Progress,' etc. 8vo., 14s.

Dante.—*THE LIFE AND WORKS OF DANTE ALLIGHIERI*: being an Introduction to the Study of the 'Divina Commedia'. By the Rev. J. F. HOGAN, D.D., Professor, St. Patrick's College, Maynooth. With Portrait. 8vo.

Danton.—*LIFE OF DANTON.* By A. H. BEESLY. With Portraits of Danton, his Mother, and an Illustration of the Home of his family at Arcis. Crown 8vo., 6s.

Duncan.—*ADMIRAL DUNCAN.* By THE EARL OF CAMPERDOWN. With 3 Portraits. 8vo., 16s.

Erasmus.—*LIFE AND LETTERS OF ERASMUS.* By JAMES ANTHONY FROUDE. Crown 8vo., 3s. 6d.

Faraday.—*FARADAY AS A DISCOVERER.* By JOHN TYNDALL. Crown 8vo, 3s. 6d.

FOREIGN COURTS AND FOREIGN HOMES. By A. M. F. Crown 8vo., 6s.

Fox.—*THE EARLY HISTORY OF CHARLES JAMES FOX.* By the Right Hon. Sir G. O. TREVELYAN, Bart.
Library Edition. 8vo., 18s.
Cheap Edition. Crown 8vo., 3s. 6d.

Halifax.—*THE LIFE AND LETTERS OF SIR GEORGE SAVILE, BARONET, FIRST MARQUIS OF HALIFAX.* By H. C. FOXCROFT. 2 vols. 8vo., 36s.

Hamilton.—*LIFE OF SIR WILLIAM HAMILTON.* By R. P. GRAVES. 8vo. 3 vols. 15s. each. ADDENDUM. 8vo., 6d. sewed.

Havelock.—*MEMOIRS OF SIR HENRY HAVELOCK, K.C.B.* By JOHN CLARK MARSHMAN. Crown 8vo., 3s. 6d.

Haweis.—*MY MUSICAL LIFE.* By the Rev. H. R. HAWEIS. With Portrait of Richard Wagner and 3 Illustrations. Crown 8vo., 7s. 6d.

Hiley.—*MEMORIES OF HALF A CENTURY.* By the Rev. R. W. HILEY, D.D., Vicar of Wighill, Tadcaster. With Portrait. 8vo., 15s.

Jackson.—*STONEWALL JACKSON AND THE AMERICAN CIVIL WAR.* By Lieut.-Col. G. F. R. HENDERSON. With 2 Portraits and 33 Maps and Plans. 2 vols. 8vo., 42s.

Leslie.—*THE LIFE AND CAMPAIGNS OF ALEXANDER LESLIE, FIRST EARL OF LEVEN.* By CHARLES SANFORD TERRY, M.A. With Maps and Plans. 8vo., 16s.

Luther.—*LIFE OF LUTHER.* By JULIUS KÖSTLIN. With 62 Illustrations and 4 Facsimilies of MSS. Cr. 8vo., 3s. 6d.

Macaulay.—*THE LIFE AND LETTERS OF LORD MACAULAY.* By the Right Hon. Sir G. O. TREVELYAN, Bart.
Popular Edition. 1 vol. Cr. 8vo., 2s. 6d.
Student's Edition. 1 vol. Cr. 8vo., 6s.
Cabinet Edition. 2 vols. Post 8vo., 12s.
'*Edinburgh' Edition.* 2 vols. 8vo., 6s. each.
Library Edition. 2 vols. 8vo., 36s.

Marbot.—*THE MEMOIRS OF THE BARON DE MARBOT.* Translated from the French. 2 vols. Crown 8vo., 7s.

Max Müller.—*AULD LANG SYNE.* By the Right Hon. F. MAX MÜLLER. First Series. With Portrait. 8vo., 10s. 6d.
CONTENTS.—Musical Recollections—Literary Recollections—Recollections of Royalties—Beggars.
Second Series. *MY INDIAN FRIENDS.* 8vo., 10s. 6d.

Biography, Personal Memoirs, &c.—*continued.*

Morris.—*THE LIFE OF WILLIAM MORRIS.* By J. W. MACKAIL. With 6 Portraits and 16 Illustrations by E. H. NEW, etc. 2 vols. 8vo., 32s.

Palgrave.—*FRANCIS TURNER PALGRAVE:* His Journals, and Memories of his Life. By GWENLLIAN F. PALGRAVE. With Portrait and Illustration. 8vo., 10s. 6d.

Place.—*THE LIFE OF FRANCIS PLACE,* 1771-1854. By GRAHAM WALLAS, M.A. With 2 Portraits. 8vo., 12s.

Powys.—*PASSAGES FROM THE DIARIES OF MRS. PHILIP LYBBE POWYS.* of Hardwick House, Oxon., 1756-1808. Edited by EMILY J. CLIMENSON, of Shiplake Vicarage, Oxon. With 2 Pedigrees (Lybbe and Powys) and Photogravure Portrait. 8vo., 16s.

RÂMAKRISHNA: HIS LIFE AND SAYINGS. By the Right Hon. F. MAX MÜLLER. Crown 8vo., 5s.

Reeve.—*MEMOIRS OF THE LIFE AND CORRESPONDENCE OF HENRY REEVE, C.B.,* late Editor of the 'Edinburgh Review,' and Registrar of the Privy Council. By JOHN KNOX LAUGHTON, M.A. With 2 Portraits. 2 vols. 8vo., 28s.

Romanes.—*THE LIFE AND LETTERS OF GEORGE JOHN ROMANES, M.A., LL.D., F.R.S.* Written and Edited by his WIFE. With Portrait and 2 Illustrations. Cr. 8vo., 6s.

Seebohm.—*THE OXFORD REFORMERS—JOHN COLET, ERASMUS AND THOMAS MORE:* a History of their Fellow-Work. By FREDERIC SEEBOHM. 8vo., 14s.

Shakespeare.—*OUTLINES OF THE LIFE OF SHAKESPEARE.* By J. O. HALLIWELL-PHILLIPPS. With Illustrations and Fac-similes. 2 vols. Royal 8vo., 21s.

Shakespeare's *TRUE LIFE.* By JAMES WALTER With 500 Illustrations by GERALD E. MOIRA. Imp. 8vo., 21s.

Stanley (Lady).

THE GIRLHOOD OF MARIA JOSEPHA HOLROYD (Lady Stanley of Alderley). Recorded in Letters of a Hundred Years Ago, from 1776-1796. Edited by J. H. ADEANE. With 6 Portraits. 8vo., 18s.

THE EARLY MARRIED LIFE OF MARIA JOSEPHA, LADY STANLEY, FROM 1796. Edited by J. H. ADEANE. With 10 Portraits and 3 Illustrations. 8vo., 18s.

Turgot—*THE LIFE AND WRITINGS OF TURGOT,* Comptroller-General of France, 1774-1776. Edited for English Readers by W. WALKER STEPHENS. With Portrait. 8vo, 7s. 6d.

Verney.—*MEMOIRS OF THE VERNEY FAMILY.* Compiled from the Letters and Illustrated by the Portraits at Clayden House.

Vols. I. & II., *DURING THE CIVIL WAR.* By FRANCES PARTHENOPE VERNEY. With 38 Portraits, Woodcuts and Fac-simile. Royal 8vo., 42s.

Vol. III., *DURING THE COMMONWEALTH.* 1650-1660. By MARGARET M. VERNEY. With 10 Portraits, etc. Royal 8vo., 21s.

Vol. IV., *FROM THE RESTORATION TO THE REVOLUTION.* 1660 to 1696. By MARGARET M. VERNEY. With Ports. Royal 8vo., 21s.

Wellington.—*LIFE OF THE DUKE OF WELLINGTON.* By the Rev. G. R. GLEIG, M.A. Crown 8vo., 3s. 6d.

Travel and Adventure, the Colonies, &c.

Arnold.—*SEAS AND LANDS.* By Sir EDWIN ARNOLD. With 71 Illustrations. Crown 8vo., 3s. 6d.

Ball (JOHN).

THE ALPINE GUIDE. Reconstructed and Revised on behalf of the Alpine Club, by W. A. B. COOLIDGE.

Vol. I., *THE WESTERN ALPS:* the Alpine Region, South of the Rhone Valley, from the Col de Tenda to the Simplon Pass. With 9 New and Revised Maps. Crown 8vo., 12s. net.

HINTS AND NOTES, PRACTICAL AND SCIENTIFIC, FOR TRAVELLERS IN THE ALPS: being a Revision of the General Introduction to the 'Alpine Guide'. Crown 8vo., 3s. net.

Baker (SIR S. W.).

EIGHT YEARS IN CEYLON. With 6 Illustrations. Crown 8vo., 3s. 6d.

THE RIFLE AND THE HOUND IN CEYLON. With 6 Illustrations. Crown 8vo., 3s. 6d.

Bent.—*THE RUINED CITIES OF MASHONALAND:* being a Record of Excavation and Exploration in 1891. By J. THEODORE BENT. With 117 Illustrations. Crown 8vo., 3s. 6d.

Bicknell.—*TRAVEL AND ADVENTURE IN NORTHERN QUEENSLAND.* By ARTHUR C. BICKNELL. With 24 Plates and 22 Illustrations in the Text. 8vo., 15s.

Brassey.—*VOYAGES AND TRAVELS OF LORD BRASSEY, K.C.B., D.C.L.,* 1862-1894. Arranged and Edited by Captain S. EARDLEY-WILMOT. 2 vols. Cr. 8vo., 10s.

Travel and Adventure, the Colonies, &c.—*continued.*

Brassey (THE LATE LADY).

A VOYAGE IN THE 'SUNBEAM'; OUR HOME ON THE OCEAN FOR ELEVEN MONTHS.
Cabinet Edition. With Map and 66 Illustrations. Crown 8vo., 7s. 6d.
'Silver Library' Edition. With 66 Illustrations. Crown 8vo., 3s. 6d.
Popular Edition. With 60 Illustrations. 4to., 6d. sewed, 1s. cloth.
School Edition. With 37 Illustrations. Fcp., 2s. cloth, or 3s. white parchment.

SUNSHINE AND STORM IN THE EAST.
Cabinet Edition. With 2 Maps and 114 Illustrations. Crown 8vo., 7s. 6d.
Popular Edition. With 103 Illustrations. 4to., 6d. sewed, 1s. cloth.

IN THE TRADES, THE TROPICS, AND THE 'ROARING FORTIES'.
Cabinet Edition. With Map and 220 Illustrations. Crown 8vo., 7s. 6d.

Browning.—*A GIRL'S WANDERINGS IN HUNGARY.* By H. ELLEN BROWNING. With Map and 20 Illustrations. Crown 8vo., 3s. 6d.

Churchill.—*THE STORY OF THE MALAKAND FIELD FORCE,* 1897. By WINSTON SPENCER CHURCHILL. With 6 Maps and Plans. Crown 8vo., 3s. 6d.

Froude (JAMES A.).

OCEANA: or England and her Colonies. With 9 Illustrations. Cr. 8vo., 3s. 6d.

THE ENGLISH IN THE WEST INDIES: or, the Bow of Ulysses. With 9 Illustrations. Crown 8vo., 2s. boards, 2s. 6d. cloth.

Howitt.—*VISITS TO REMARKABLE PLACES.* Old Halls, Battle-Fields, Scenes, illustrative of Striking Passages in English History and Poetry. By WILLIAM HOWITT. With 80 Illustrations. Crown 8vo., 3s. 6d.

Knight (E. F.).

THE CRUISE OF THE 'ALERTE': the Narrative of a Search for Treasure on the Desert Island of Trinidad. With 2 Maps and 23 Illustrations. Crown 8vo., 3s. 6d.

WHERE THREE EMPIRES MEET: a Narrative of Recent Travel in Kashmir, Western Tibet, Baltistan, Ladak, Gilgit, and the adjoining Countries. With a Map and 54 Illustrations. Cr. 8vo., 3s. 6d.

THE 'FALCON' ON THE BALTIC: a Voyage from London to Copenhagen in a Three-Tonner. With 10 Full-page Illustrations. Crown 8vo., 3s. 6d.

Lees.—*PEAKS AND PINES:* another Norway Book. By J. A. LEES. With 63 Illustrations and Photographs by the Author. Crown 8vo., 6s.

Lees and Clutterbuck.—B.C. 1887: *A RAMBLE IN BRITISH COLUMBIA.* By J. A. LEES and W. J. CLUTTERBUCK. With Map and 75 Illustrations. Crown 8vo., 3s. 6d.

Macdonald.—*THE GOLD COAST: PAST AND PRESENT.* By GEORGE MACDONALD, Director of Education and H.M. Inspector of Schools for the Gold Coast Colony and the Protectorate. With 32 Illustrations. Crown 8vo., 7s. 6d.

Nansen.—*THE FIRST CROSSING OF GREENLAND.* By FRIDTJOF NANSEN. With 143 Illustrations and a Map. Crown 8vo., 3s. 6d.

Smith.—*CLIMBING IN THE BRITISH ISLES.* By W. P. HASKETT SMITH. With Illustrations by ELLIS CARR, and Numerous Plans.
Part I. ENGLAND. 16mo., 3s. 6d.
Part II. WALES AND IRELAND. 16mo., 3s. 6d.

Stephen.—*THE PLAY-GROUND OF EUROPE* (The Alps). By LESLIE STEPHEN. With 4 Illustrations. Crown 8vo., 3s. 6d.

THREE IN NORWAY. By Two of Them. With a Map and 59 Illustrations. Crown 8vo., 2s. boards, 2s. 6d. cloth.

Tyndall.—(JOHN).

THE GLACIERS OF THE ALPS: being a Narrative of Excursions and Ascents. An Account of the Origin and Phenomena of Glaciers, and an Exposition of the Physical Principles to which they are related. With 61 Illustrations. Crown 8vo., 6s. 6d. net.

HOURS OF EXERCISE IN THE ALPS. With 7 Illustrations. Cr. 8vo., 6s. 6d. net.

Vivian.—*SERVIA:* the Poor Man's Paradise. By HERBERT VIVIAN, M.A., Officer of the Royal Order of Takovo. With Map and Portrait of King Alexander. 8vo., 15s.

Veterinary Medicine, &c.

Steel (JOHN HENRY, F.R.C.V.S., F.Z.S., A.V.D.), late Professor of Veterinary Science and Principal of Bombay Veterinary College.

A TREATISE ON THE DISEASES OF THE DOG; being a Manual of Canine Pathology. Especially adapted for the use of Veterinary Practitioners and Students. With 88 Illustrations. 8vo., 10s. 6d.

A TREATISE ON THE DISEASES OF THE OX; being a Manual of Bovine Pathology. Especially adapted for the use of Veterinary Practitioners and Students. With 2 Plates and 117 Woodcuts. 8vo., 15s.

A TREATISE ON THE DISEASES OF THE SHEEP; being a Manual of Ovine Pathology for the use of Veterinary Practitioners and Students. With Coloured Plate and 99 Woodcuts. 8vo., 12s.

OUTLINES OF EQUINE ANATOMY; a Manual for the use of Veterinary Students in the Dissecting Room. Cr. 8vo., 7s. 6d.

Fitzwygram. — *HORSES AND STABLES.* By Major-General Sir F. FITZWYGRAM, Bart. With 56 pages of Illustrations. 8vo., 2s. 6d. net.

Schreiner. — *THE ANGORA GOAT* (published under the auspices of the South African Angora Goat Breeders' Association), and a Paper on the Ostrich (reprinted from the *Zoologist* for March, 1897). With 26 Illustrations. By S. C. CRONWRIGHT SCHREINER. 8vo., 10s. 6d.

'Stonehenge.' — *THE DOG IN HEALTH AND DISEASE.* By 'STONEHENGE'. With 78 Wood Engravings. 8vo., 7s. 6d.

Youatt (WILLIAM).

THE HORSE. Revised and Enlarged by W. WATSON, M.R.C.V.S. With 52 Wood Engravings. 8vo., 7s. 6d.

THE DOG. Revised and Enlarged. With 33 Wood Engravings. 8vo., 6s.

Sport and Pastime.

THE BADMINTON LIBRARY.

Edited by HIS GRACE THE DUKE OF BEAUFORT, K.G., and A. E. T. WATSON.

Complete in 29 Volumes. Crown 8vo., Price 10s. 6d. each Volume, Cloth.

. *The Volumes are also issued half-bound in Leather, with gilt top. The price can be had from all Booksellers.*

ARCHERY. By C. J. LONGMAN and Col. H. WALROND. With Contributions by Miss LEGH, Viscount DILLON, etc. With 2 Maps, 23 Plates and 172 Illustrations in the Text. Crown 8vo., 10s. 6d.

ATHLETICS. By MONTAGUE SHEARMAN. With Chapters on Athletics at School by W. BEACHER THOMAS; Athletic Sports in America by C. H. SHERRILL; a Contribution on Paper-chasing by W. RYE, and an Introduction by Sir RICHARD WEBSTER, Q.C., M.P. With 12 Plates and 37 Illustrations in the Text. Cr. 8vo., 10s. 6d.

BIG GAME SHOOTING. By CLIVE PHILLIPPS-WOLLEY.

Vol. I. AFRICA AND AMERICA. With Contributions by Sir SAMUEL W. BAKER, W. C. OSWELL, F. C. SELOUS, etc. With 20 Plates and 57 Illustrations in the Text. Crown 8vo., 10s. 6d.

Vol. II. EUROPE, ASIA, AND THE ARCTIC REGIONS. With Contributions by Lieut.-Colonel R. HEBER PERCY, Major ALGERNON C. HEBER PERCY, etc. With 17 Plates and 56 Illustrations in the Text. Cr. 8vo., 10s. 6d.

BILLIARDS. By Major W. BROADFOOT, R.E. With Contributions by A. H. BOYD, SYDENHAM DIXON, W. J. FORD, etc. With 11 Plates, 19 Illustrations in the Text, and numerous Diagrams. Cr. 8vo., 10s. 6d.

COURSING AND FALCONRY. By HARDING COX, CHARLES RICHARDSON, and the Hon. GERALD LASCELLES. With 20 Plates and 55 Illustrations in the Text. Crown 8vo., 10s. 6d.

CRICKET. By A. G. STEEL and the Hon. R. H. LYTTELTON. With Contributions by ANDREW LANG, W. G. GRACE, F. GALE, etc. With 13 Plates and 52 Illustrations in the Text. Crown 8vo., 10s. 6d.

CYCLING. By the EARL OF ALBEMARLE and G. LACY HILLIER. With 19 Plates and 44 Illustrations in the Text. Crown 8vo., 10s. 6d.

DANCING. By Mrs. LILLY GROVE, F.R.G.S. With Contributions by Miss MIDDLETON, The Hon. Mrs. ARMYTAGE, etc. With Musical Examples, and 38 Full-page Plates and 93 Illustrations in the Text. Crown 8vo., 10s. 6d.

DRIVING. By His Grace the DUKE of BEAUFORT, K.G. With Contributions by A. E. T. WATSON the EARL OF ONSLOW, etc. With 12 Plates and 54 Illustrations in the Text. Crown 8vo., 10s. 6d.

Sport and Pastime—*continued.*
THE BADMINTON LIBRARY—*continued.*

FENCING, BOXING, AND WRESTLING. By WALTER H. POLLOCK, F. C. GROVE, C. PREVOST, E. B. MITCHELL, and WALTER ARMSTRONG. With 24 Illust. in the Text. Cr. 8vo., 10s. 6d.

FISHING. By H. CHOLMONDELEY-PENNELL.
Vol. I. SALMON AND TROUT. With Contributions by H. R. FRANCIS, Major JOHN P. TRAHERNE, etc. With 9 Plates and numerous Illustrations of Tackle, etc. Crown 8vo., 10s. 6d.
Vol. II. PIKE AND OTHER COARSE FISH. With Contributions by the MARQUIS OF EXETER, WILLIAM SENIOR, G. CHRISTOPHER DAVIS, etc. With 7 Plates and numerous Illustrations of Tackle, etc. Crown 8vo., 10s. 6d.

FOOTBALL. By MONTAGUE SHEARMAN, W. J. OAKLEY, G. O. SMITH, FRANK MITCHELL, etc. With 19 Plates and 35 Illustrations in the Text. Cr. 8vo., 10s. 6d.

GOLF. By HORACE G. HUTCHINSON. With Contributions by the Rt. Hon. A. J. BALFOUR, M.P., Sir WALTER SIMPSON, Bart., ANDREW LANG, etc. With 32 Plates and 57 Illustrations in the Text. Cr. 8vo., 10s. 6d.

HUNTING. By His Grace the DUKE OF BEAUFORT, K.G., and MOWBRAY MORRIS. With Contributions by the EARL OF SUFFOLK AND BERKSHIRE, Rev. E. W. L. DAVIES, G. H. LONGMAN, etc. With 5 Plates and 54 Illustrations in the Text. Cr. 8vo., 10s. 6d.

MOUNTAINEERING. By C. T. DENT. With Contributions by Sir W. M. CONWAY, D. W. FRESHFIELD, C. E. MATTHEWS, etc. With 13 Plates and 95 Illustrations in the Text. Cr. 8vo., 10s. 6d.

POETRY OF SPORT (THE).— Selected by HEDLEY PEEK. With a Chapter on Classical Allusions to Sport by ANDREW LANG, and a Special Preface to the BADMINTON LIBRARY by A. E. T. WATSON. With 32 Plates and 74 Illustrations in the Text. Crown 8vo., 10s. 6d.

RACING AND STEEPLE-CHASING. By the EARL OF SUFFOLK AND BERKSHIRE, W. G. CRAVEN, the Hon. F. LAWLEY, ARTHUR COVENTRY, and A. E. T. WATSON. With Frontispiece and 56 Illustrations in the Text. Crown 8vo., 10s. 6d.

RIDING AND POLO. By Captain ROBERT WEIR, J. MORAY BROWN, T. F. DALE, THE DUKE OF BEAUFORT, THE EARL OF SUFFOLK AND BERKSHIRE, etc. With 18 Plates and 41 Illustrations in the Text. Crown 8vo., 10s. 6d.

ROWING. By R. P. P. ROWE and C. M. PITMAN. With Chapters on Steering by C. P. SEROCOLD and F. C. BEGG; Metropolitan Rowing by S. LE BLANC SMITH; and on PUNTING by P. W. SQUIRE. With 75 Illustrations. Crown 8vo., 10s. 6d.

SEA FISHING. By JOHN BICKERDYKE, Sir H. W. GORE-BOOTH, ALFREE C. HARMSWORTH, and W. SENIOR. With 22 Full-page Plates and 175 Illustrations in the Text. Crown 8vo., 10s. 6d.

SHOOTING.
Vol. I. FIELD AND COVERT. By LORD WALSINGHAM and Sir RALPH PAYNE-GALLWEY, Bart. With Contributions by the Hon. GERALD LASCELLES and A. J. STUART-WORTLEY. With 11 Plates and 94 Illusts. in the Text. Cr. 8vo., 10s. 6d.
Vol. II. MOOR AND MARSH. By LORD WALSINGHAM and Sir RALPH PAYNE-GALLWEY, Bart. With Contributions by LORD LOVAT and Lord CHARLES LENNOX KERR. With 8 Plates and 57 Illustrations in the Text. Crown 8vo., 10s. 6d.

SKATING, CURLING, TOBOGANING. By J. M. HEATHCOTE, C. G. TEBBUTT, T. MAXWELL WITHAM, Rev. JOHN KERR, ORMOND HAKE, HENRY A. BUCK, etc. With 12 Plates and 272 Illustrations in the Text. Crown 8vo., 10s. 6d.

SWIMMING. By ARCHIBALD SINCLAIR and WILLIAM HENRY, Hon. Secs. of the Life-Saving Society. With 13 Plates and 106 Illustrations in the Text. Cr. 8vo., 10s. 6d.

TENNIS, LAWN TENNIS, RACKETS AND FIVES. By J. M. and C. G. HEATHCOTE, E. O. PLEYDELL-BOUVERIE, and A. C. AINGER. With Contributions by the Hon. A. LYTTELTON, W. C. MARSHALL, Miss L. DOD, etc. With 12 Plates and 67 Illustrations in the Text. Cr. 8vo., 10s. 6d.

YACHTING.
Vol. I. CRUISING, CONSTRUCTION OF YACHTS, YACHT RACING RULES, FITTING-OUT, etc. By Sir EDWARD SULLIVAN, Bart., THE EARL OF PEMBROKE, LORD BRASSEY, K.C.B., C. E. SETH-SMITH, C.B., G. L. WATSON, R. T. PRITCHETT, E. F. KNIGHT, etc. With 21 Plates and 93 Illustrations in the Text. Crown 8vo., 10s. 6d.
Vol. II. YACHT CLUBS, YACHTING IN AMERICA AND THE COLONIES, YACHT RACING, etc. By R. T. PRITCHETT, THE MARQUIS OF DUFFERIN AND AVA, K.P., THE EARL OF ONSLOW, JAMES McFERRAN. etc. With 35 Plates and 160 Illustrations in the Text. Crown 8vo., 10s. 6d.

Sport and Pastime—*continued.*
FUR, FEATHER, AND FIN SERIES.
Edited by A. E. T. WATSON.

Crown 8vo., price 5s. each Volume, cloth.

** *The Volumes are also issued half-bound in Leather, with gilt top.   The price can be had from all Booksellers.*

THE PARTRIDGE. Natural History, by the Rev. H. A. MACPHERSON; Shooting, by A. J. STUART-WORTLEY; Cookery, by GEORGE SAINTSBURY. With 11 Illustrations and various Diagrams in the Text. Crown 8vo., 5s.

THE GROUSE. Natural History, by the Rev. H. A. MACPHERSON; Shooting, by A. J. STUART-WORTLEY; Cookery, by GEORGE SAINTSBURY. With 13 Illustrations and various Diagrams in the Text. Crown 8vo., 5s.

THE PHEASANT. Natural History, by the Rev. H. A. MACPHERSON; Shooting, by A. J. STUART-WORTLEY; Cookery, by ALEXANDER INNES SHAND. With 10 Illustrations and various Diagrams. Crown 8vo., 5s.

THE HARE. Natural History, by the Rev. H. A. MACPHERSON; Shooting, by the Hon. GERALD LASCELLES; Coursing, by CHARLES RICHARDSON; Hunting, by J. S. GIBBONS and G. H. LONGMAN; Cookery, by Col. KENNEY HERBERT. With 9 Illustrations. Crown 8vo., 5s.

RED DEER.—Natural History, by the Rev. H. A. MACPHERSON; Deer Stalking, by CAMERON OF LOCHIEL; Stag Hunting, by Viscount EBRINGTON; Cookery, by ALEXANDER INNES SHAND. With 10 Illustrations. Crown 8vo., 5s.

THE SALMON. By the Hon. A. E. GATHORNE-HARDY. With Chapters on the Law of Salmon Fishing by CLAUD DOUGLAS PENNANT; Cookery, by ALEXANDER INNES SHAND. With 8 Illustrations. Cr. 8vo., 5s.

THE TROUT. By the MARQUESS OF GRANBY. With Chapters on the Breeding of Trout by Col. H. CUSTANCE; and Cookery, by ALEXANDER INNES SHAND. With 12 Illustrations. Crown 8vo., 5s.

THE RABBIT. By JAMES EDMUND HARTING. With a Chapter on Cookery by ALEXANDER INNES SHAND. With 10 Illustrations. Crown 8vo., 5s.

WILDFOWL. By the Hon. JOHN SCOTT MONTAGU, etc. With Illustrations, etc.   [In preparation.

André.—COLONEL BOGEY'S SKETCH-BOOK. Comprising an Eccentric Collection of Scribbles and Scratches found in disused Lockers and swept up in the Pavilion, together with sundry After-Dinner Sayings of the Colonel. By R. ANDRÉ, West Herts Golf Club. Oblong 4to., 2s. 6d.

Blackburne.— MR. BLACKBURNE'S GAMES AT CHESS. Selected, Annotated and Arranged by Himself. Edited, with a Biographical Sketch and a brief History of Blindfold Chess, by P. ANDERSON GRAHAM. 8vo., 7s. 6d. net.

DEAD SHOT (THE): or, Sportsman's Complete Guide. Being a Treatise on the Use of the Gun, with Rudimentary and Finishing Lessons in the Art of Shooting Game of all kinds. Also Game-driving, Wildfowl and Pigeon-shooting, Dog-breaking, etc. By MARKSMAN. With numerous Illustrations. Crown 8vo., 10s. 6d.

Ellis.—CHESS SPARKS; or, Short and Bright Games of Chess. Collected and Arranged by J. H. ELLIS, M.A. 8vo., 4s. 6d.

Folkard.—THE WILD-FOWLER: A Treatise on Fowling, Ancient and Modern, descriptive also of Decoys and Flight-ponds, Wild-fowl Shooting, Gunning-punts, Shooting-yachts, etc. Also Fowling in the Fens and in Foreign Countries, Rock-fowling, etc., etc., by H. C. FOLKARD. With 13 Engravings on Steel, and several Woodcuts. 8vo., 12s. 6d.

Ford.—THE THEORY AND PRACTICE OF ARCHERY. By HORACE FORD. New Edition, thoroughly Revised and Re-written by W. BUTT, M.A. With a Preface by C. J. LONGMAN, M.A. 8vo., 14s.

Francis.—A BOOK ON ANGLING: or, Treatise on the Art of Fishing in every Branch; including full Illustrated List of Salmon Flies. By FRANCIS FRANCIS. With Portrait and Coloured Plates. Crown 8vo., 15s.

Sport and Pastime—*continued.*

Gibson.—*TOBOGGANING ON CROOKED RUNS.* By the Hon. HARRY GIBSON. With Contributions by F. DE B. STRICKLAND and 'LADY-TOBOGANNER'. With 40 Illustrations. Crown 8vo., 6s

Graham.—*COUNTRY PASTIMES FOR BOYS.* By P. ANDERSON GRAHAM. With 252 Illustrations from Drawings and Photographs. Crown 8vo., 3s. 6d.

Hutchinson.—*THE BOOK OF GOLF AND GOLFERS.* By HORACE G. HUTCHINSON. With Contributions by Miss AMY PASCOE, H. H. HILTON, J. H. TAYLOR, H. J. WHIGHAM, and Messrs. SUTTON & SONS. With 71 Portraits, etc. Medium 8vo., 18s. net.

Lang.—*ANGLING SKETCHES.* By ANDREW LANG. With 20 Illustrations. Crown 8vo., 3s. 6d.

Lillie.—*CROQUET:* its History, Rules and Secrets. By ARTHUR LILLIE, Champion, Grand National Croquet Club, 1872; Winner of the 'All-Comers' Championship,' Maidstone, 1896. With 4 Full-page Illustrations by LUCIEN DAVIS, 15 Illustrations in the Text, and 27 Diagrams. Crown 8vo., 6s.

Longman.—*CHESS OPENINGS.* By FREDERICK W. LONGMAN. Fcp. 8vo., 2s. 6d.

Madden.—*THE DIARY OF MASTER WILLIAM SILENCE:* a Study of Shakespeare and of Elizabethan Sport. By the Right Hon. D. H. MADDEN, Vice-Chancellor of the University of Dublin. 8vo., 16s.

Maskelyne.—*SHARPS AND FLATS:* a Complete Revelation of the Secrets of Cheating at Games of Chance and Skill. By JOHN NEVIL MASKELYNE, of the Egyptian Hall. With 62 Illustrations. Crown 8vo., 6s.

Moffat.—*CRICKETY CRICKET:* Rhymes and Parodies. By DOUGLAS MOFFAT, with Frontispiece by Sir FRANK LOCKWOOD, Q.C., M.P., and 53 Illustrations by the Author. Crown 8vo., 2s. 6d.

Park.—*THE GAME OF GOLF.* By WILLIAM PARK, Jun., Champion Golfer, 1887-89. With 17 Plates and 26 Illustrations in the Text. Crown 8vo., 7s. 6d.

Payne-Gallwey (Sir RALPH, Bart.).

LETTERS TO YOUNG SHOOTERS (First Series). On the Choice and use of a Gun. With 41 Illustrations. Crown 8vo., 7s. 6d.

LETTERS TO YOUNG SHOOTERS (Second Series). On the Production, Preservation, and Killing of Game. With Directions in Shooting Wood-Pigeons and Breaking-in Retrievers. With Portrait and 103 Illustrations. Crown 8vo., 12s. 6d.

LETTERS TO YOUNG SHOOTERS. (Third Series.) Comprising a Short Natural History of the Wildfowl that are Rare or Common to the British Islands, with complete directions in Shooting Wildfowl on the Coast and Inland. With 200 Illustrations. Crown 8vo., 18s.

Pole—*THE THEORY OF THE MODERN SCIENTIFIC GAME OF WHIST.* By WILLIAM POLE, F.R.S. Fcp. 8vo., 2s. 6d.

Proctor.—*HOW TO PLAY WHIST: WITH THE LAWS AND ETIQUETTE OF WHIST.* By RICHARD A. PROCTOR. Crown 8vo., 3s. 6d.

Ribblesdale.—*THE QUEEN'S HOUNDS AND STAG-HUNTING RECOLLECTIONS.* By Lord RIBBLESDALE, Master of the Buckhounds, 1892-95. With Introductory Chapter on the Hereditary Mastership by E. BURROWS. With 24 Plates and 35 Illustrations in the Text. 8vo., 25s.

Ronalds.—*THE FLY-FISHER'S ENTOMOLOGY.* By ALFRED RONALDS. With 20 coloured Plates. 8vo., 14s.

Watson.—*RACING AND 'CHASING:* a Collection of Sporting Stories. By ALFRED E. T. WATSON, Editor of the 'Badminton Magazine'. With 16 Plates and 36 Illustrations in the Text. Crown 8vo., 7s. 6d.

Wilcocks.—*THE SEA FISHERMAN:* Comprising the Chief Methods of Hook and Line Fishing in the British and other Seas, and Remarks on Nets, Boats, and Boating. By J. C. WILCOCKS. Illustrated. Cr. 8vo., 6s.

Mental, Moral, and Political Philosophy.

LOGIC, RHETORIC, PSYCHOLOGY, &c.

Abbott.—*THE ELEMENTS OF LOGIC.*
By T. K. ABBOTT, B.D. 12mo., 3s.

Aristotle.
THE ETHICS: Greek Text, Illustrated
with Essay and Notes. By Sir ALEXAN-
DER GRANT, Bart. 2 vols. 8vo., 32s.

*AN INTRODUCTION TO ARISTOTLE'S
ETHICS.* Books I.-IV. (Book X. c. vi.-ix.
in an Appendix). With a continuous
Analysis and Notes. By the Rev. E.
MOORE, D.D. Crown 8vo. 10s. 6d.

Bacon (FRANCIS).
COMPLETE WORKS. Edited by R. L.
ELLIS, JAMES SPEDDING and D. D.
HEATH. 7 vols. 8vo., £3 13s. 6d.

LETTERS AND LIFE, including all his
occasional Works. Edited by JAMES
SPEDDING. 7 vols. 8vo., £4 4s.

THE ESSAYS: with Annotations. By
RICHARD WHATELY, D.D. 8vo., 10s. 6d.

THE ESSAYS: with Notes. By F.
STORR and C. H. GIBSON. Cr. 8vo, 3s. 6d.

THE ESSAYS: with Introduction,
Notes, and Index. By E. A. ABBOTT, D.D.
2 Vols. Fcp. 8vo., 6s. The Text and Index
only, without Introduction and Notes, in
One Volume. Fcp. 8vo., 2s. 6d.

Bain (ALEXANDER).
MENTAL SCIENCE. Cr. 8vo., 6s. 6d.
MORAL SCIENCE. Cr. 8vo., 4s. 6d.
*The two works as above can be had in one
volume, price* 10s. 6d.

SENSES AND THE INTELLECT. 8vo., 15s.
EMOTIONS AND THE WILL. 8vo., 15s.
LOGIC, DEDUCTIVE AND INDUCTIVE.
Part I. 4s. Part II. 6s. 6d.
PRACTICAL ESSAYS. Cr. 8vo., 2s.

Bray.—*THE PHILOSOPHY OF NECES-
SITY:* or, Law in Mind as in Matter. By
CHARLES BRAY. Crown 8vo., 5s.

Crozier (JOHN BEATTIE).
CIVILISATION AND PROGRESS: being
the Outlines of a New System of Political,
Religious and Social Philosophy. 8vo.,14s.

*HISTORY OF INTELLECTUAL DE-
VELOPMENT:* on the Lines of Modern
Evolution.
Vol. I. Greek and Hindoo Thought ; Græco-
Roman Paganism ; Judaism ; and Christi-
anity down to the Closing of the Schools
of Athens by Justinian, 529 A.D. 8vo., 14s.

Davidson.—*THE LOGIC OF DEFINI-
TION,* Explained and Applied. By WILLIAM
L. DAVIDSON, M.A. Crown 8vo., 6s.

Green (THOMAS HILL.).—THE WORKS
OF. Edited by R. L. NETTLESHIP.
Vols. I. and II. Philosophical Works. 8vo.,
16s. each.
Vol. III. Miscellanies. With Index to the
three Volumes, and Memoir. 8vo., 21s.

*LECTURES ON THE PRINCIPLES OF
POLITICAL OBLIGATION.* With Preface
by BERNARD BOSANQUET. 8vo., 5s.

Hodgson (SHADWORTH H.)
TIME AND SPACE: A Metaphysical
Essay. 8vo., 16s.
THE THEORY OF PRACTICE: an
Ethical Inquiry. 2 vols. 8vo., 24s.
THE PHILOSOPHY OF REFLECTION.
2 vols. 8vo., 21s.
THE METAPHYSIC OF EXPERIENCE.
Book I. General Analysis of Experience ;
Book II. Positive Science ; Book III.
Analysis of Conscious Action ; Book IV.
The Real Universe. 4 vols. 8vo., 36s. net.

Hume.—*THE PHILOSOPHICAL WORKS
OF DAVID HUME.* Edited by T. H. GREEN
and T. H. GROSE. 4 vols. 8vo., 28s. Or
separately, ESSAYS. 2 vols. 14s. TREATISE
OF HUMAN NATURE. 2 vols. 14s.

James.—*THE WILL TO BELIEVE,* and
Other Essays in Popular Philosophy. By
WILLIAM JAMES, M.D., LL.D., etc. Crown
8vo., 7s. 6d.

Justinian.—*THE INSTITUTES OF
JUSTINIAN:* Latin Text, chiefly that of
Huschke, with English Introduction, Trans-
lation, Notes, and Summary. By THOMAS
C. SANDARS, M.A. 8vo., 18s.

Kant (IMMANUEL).
*CRITIQUE OF PRACTICAL REASON,
AND OTHER WORKS ON THE THEORY OF
ETHICS.* Translated by T. K. ABBOTT,
B.D. With Memoir. 8vo., 12s. 6d.

*FUNDAMENTAL PRINCIPLES OF THE
METAPHYSIC OF ETHICS.* Translated by
T. K. ABBOTT, B.D. Crown 8vo, 3s.

*INTRODUCTION TO LOGIC, AND HIS
ESSAY ON THE MISTAKEN SUBTILTY OF
THE FOUR FIGURES..* Translated by T.
K. ABBOTT. 8vo., 6s.

Killick.—*HANDBOOK TO MILL'S
SYSTEM OF LOGIC.* By Rev. A. H.
KILLICK, M.A. Crown 8vo., 3s. 6d.

Mental, Moral and Political Philosophy—*continued.*
LOGIC, RHETORIC, PSYCHOLOGY, &c.

Ladd (GEORGE TRUMBULL).

A THEORY OF REALITY: an Essay in Metaphysical System upon the Basis of Human Cognitive Experience. 8vo., 18s.

ELEMENTS OF PHYSIOLOGICAL PSYCHOLOGY. 8vo., 21s.

OUTLINES OF DESCRIPTIVE PSYCHOLOGY: a Text-Book of Mental Science for Colleges and Normal Schools. 8vo., 12s.

OUTLINES OF PHYSIOLOGICAL PSYCHOLOGY. 8vo., 12s.

PRIMER OF PSYCHOLOGY. Cr. 8vo., 5s. 6d.

Lecky.—*THE MAP OF LIFE:* Conduct and Character. By WILLIAM EDWARD HARTPOLE LECKY. 8vo., 10s. 6d.

Lutoslawski.—*THE ORIGIN AND GROWTH OF PLATO'S LOGIC.* With an Account of Plato's Style and of the Chronology of his Writings. By WINCENTY LUTOSLAWSKI. 8vo., 21s.

Max Müller (F.).

THE SCIENCE OF THOUGHT. 8vo., 21s.

THE SIX SYSTEMS OF INDIAN PHILOSOPHY. 8vo., 18s.

Mill.—*ANALYSIS OF THE PHENOMENA OF THE HUMAN MIND.* By JAMES MILL. 2 vols. 8vo., 28s.

Mill (JOHN STUART).

A SYSTEM OF LOGIC. Cr. 8vo., 3s. 6d.

ON LIBERTY. Crown 8vo., 1s. 4d.

CONSIDERATIONS ON REPRESENTATIVE GOVERNMENT. Crown 8vo., 2s.

UTILITARIANISM. 8vo., 2s. 6d.

EXAMINATION OF SIR WILLIAM HAMILTON'S PHILOSOPHY. 8vo., 16s.

NATURE, THE UTILITY OF RELIGION, AND THEISM. Three Essays. 8vo., 5s.

Monck. — *AN INTRODUCTION TO LOGIC.* By WILLIAM HENRY S. MONCK, M.A. Crown 8vo., 5s.

Romanes.—*MIND AND MOTION AND MONISM.* By GEORGE JOHN ROMANES, LL.D., F.R.S. Cr. 8vo., 4s. 6d.

Stock.—*LECTURES IN THE LYCEUM;* or, Aristotle's Ethics for English Readers. Edited by ST. GEORGE STOCK. Crown 8vo., 7s. 6d.

Sully (JAMES).

THE HUMAN MIND: a Text-book of Psychology. 2 vols. 8vo., 21s.

OUTLINES OF PSYCHOLOGY. Crown 8vo., 9s.

THE TEACHER'S HANDBOOK OF PSYCHOLOGY. Crown 8vo., 6s. 6d.

STUDIES OF CHILDHOOD. 8vo., 10s. 6d.

CHILDREN'S WAYS: being Selections from the Author's 'Studies of Childhood'. With 25 Illustrations. Crown 8vo., 4s. 6d.

Sutherland. — *THE ORIGIN AND GROWTH OF THE MORAL INSTINCT.* By ALEXANDER SUTHERLAND, M.A. 2 vols. 8vo., 28s.

Swinburne. — *PICTURE LOGIC:* an Attempt to Popularise the Science of Reasoning. By ALFRED JAMES SWINBURNE, M.A. With 23 Woodcuts. Cr. 8vo., 2s. 6d.

Webb.—*THE VEIL OF ISIS:* a Series of Essays on Idealism. By THOMAS E. WEBB, LL.D., Q.C. 8vo., 10s. 6d.

Weber.—*HISTORY OF PHILOSOPHY.* By ALFRED WEBER, Professor in the University of Strasburg. Translated by FRANK THILLY, Ph.D. 8vo., 16s.

Whately (ARCHBISHOP).

BACON'S ESSAYS. With Annotations. 8vo., 10s. 6d.

ELEMENTS OF LOGIC. Cr. 8vo., 4s. 6d.

ELEMENTS OF RHETORIC. Cr. 8vo., 4s. 6d.

Zeller (Dr. EDWARD).

THE STOICS, EPICUREANS, AND SCEPTICS. Translated by the Rev. O. J. REICHEL, M.A. Crown 8vo., 15s.

OUTLINES OF THE HISTORY OF GREEK PHILOSOPHY. Translated by SARAH F. ALLEYNE and EVELYN ABBOTT, M.A., LL.D. Crown 8vo., 10s. 6d.

PLATO AND THE OLDER ACADEMY. Translated by SARAH F. ALLEYNE and ALFRED GOODWIN, B.A. Crown 8vo., 18s.

SOCRATES AND THE SOCRATIC SCHOOLS. Translated by the Rev. O. J. REICHEL, M.A. Crown 8vo., 10s. 6d.

ARISTOTLE AND THE EARLIER PERIPATETICS. Translated by B. F. C. COSTELLOE, M.A., and J. H. MUIRHEAD, M.A. 2 vols. Crown 8vo., 24s.

Mental, Moral, and Political Philosophy—*continued*.

MANUALS OF CATHOLIC PHILOSOPHY.
(Stonyhurst Series.)

A MANUAL OF POLITICAL ECONOMY. By C. S. DEVAS, M.A. Crown 8vo., 6s. 6d.

FIRST PRINCIPLES OF KNOWLEDGE. By JOHN RICKABY, S.J. Crown 8vo., 5s.

GENERAL METAPHYSICS. By JOHN RICKABY, S.J. Crown 8vo., 5s.

LOGIC. By RICHARD F. CLARKE, S.J. Crown 8vo., 5s.

MORAL PHILOSOPHY (ETHICS AND NATURAL LAW). By JOSEPH RICKABY, S.J. Crown 8vo., 5s.

NATURAL THEOLOGY. By BERNARD BOEDDER, S.J. Crown 8vo., 6s. 6d.

PSYCHOLOGY. By MICHAEL MAHER, S.J. Crown 8vo., 6s. 6d.

History and Science of Language, &c.

Davidson.—*LEADING AND IMPORTANT ENGLISH WORDS:* Explained and Exemplified.   By WILLIAM L. DAVIDSON, M.A. Fcp. 8vo., 3s. 6d.

Farrar.—*LANGUAGE AND LANGUAGES:* By F. W. FARRAR, D.D., Dean of Canterbury.   Crown 8vo., 6s.

Graham. — *ENGLISH SYNONYMS,* Classified and Explained : with Practical Exercises. By G. F. GRAHAM. Fcp. 8vo., 6s.

Max Muller (F.).

THE SCIENCE OF LANGUAGE.—Founded on Lectures delivered at the Royal Institution in 1861 and 1863. 2 vols. Crown 8vo., 10s.

BIOGRAPHIES OF WORDS, AND THE HOME OF THE ARYAS. Crown 8vo., 5s.

Roget.—*THESAURUS OF ENGLISH WORDS AND PHRASES.* Classified and Arranged so as to Facilitate the Expression of Ideas and assist in Literary Composition. By PETER MARK ROGET, M.D., F.R.S. With full Index. Crown 8vo., 10s. 6d.

Whately.—*ENGLISH SYNONYMS.* By E. JANE WHATELY. Fcp. 8vo., 3s.

Political Economy and Economics.

Ashley.—*ENGLISH ECONOMIC HISTORY AND THEORY.* By W. J. ASHLEY, M.A. Cr. 8vo., Part I., 5s. Part II., 10s. 6d.

Bagehot.—*ECONOMIC STUDIES.* By WALTER BAGEHOT. Crown 8vo., 3s. 6d.

Brassey.— *PAPERS AND ADDRESSES ON WORK AND WAGES.* By Lord BRASSEY. Edited by J. POTTER, and with Introduction by GEORGE HOWELL, M.P. Crown 8vo., 5s.

Channing.— *THE TRUTH ABOUT AGRICULTURAL DEPRESSION:* an Economic Study of the Evidence of the Royal Commission. By FRANCIS ALLSTON CHANNING, M.P., one of the Commission. Crown 8vo., 6s.

Devas.—*A MANUAL OF POLITICAL ECONOMY.* By C. S. DEVAS, M.A. Cr. 8vo., 6s. 6d. (*Manuals of Catholic Philosophy.*)

Jordan.—*THE STANDARD OF VALUE.* By WILLIAM LEIGHTON JORDAN. Cr. 8vo., 6s.

Leslie.—*ESSAYS ON POLITICAL ECONOMY.* By T. E. CLIFFE LESLIE, Hon. LL.D., Dubl. 8vo, 10s. 6d.

Macleod (HENRY DUNNING).

ECONOMICS FOR BEGINNERS. Crown 8vo., 2s.

THE ELEMENTS OF ECONOMICS. 2 vols. Crown 8vo., 3s. 6d. each.

BIMETALISM. 8vo., 5s. net.

THE ELEMENTS OF BANKING. Cr. 8vo., 3s. 6d.

THE THEORY AND PRACTICE OF BANKING. Vol. I. 8vo., 12s. Vol. II. 14s.

THE THEORY OF CREDIT. 8vo. In 1 Vol., 30s. net; or separately, Vol. I., 10s. net. Vol. II., Part I., 10s. net. Vol. II., Part II., 10s. net.

Mill.—*POLITICAL ECONOMY.* By JOHN STUART MILL.
Popular Edition. Crown 8vo., 3s. 6d.
Library Edition. 2 vols. 8vo., 30s.

Political Economy and Economics—*continued.*

Mulhall.—*INDUSTRIES AND WEALTH OF NATIONS.* By MICHAEL G. MULHALL, F.S.S. With 32 Diagrams. Cr. 8vo., 8s. 6d.

Stephens.—*HIGHER LIFE FOR WORKING PEOPLE:* its Hindrances Discussed. An attempt to solve some pressing Social Problems, without injustice to Capital or Labour. By W. WALKER STEPHENS. Cr. 8vo., 3s. 6d.

Symes.—*POLITICAL ECONOMY.* With a Supplementary Chapter on Socialism. By J. E. SYMES, M.A. Crown 8vo., 2s. 6d.

Toynbee.—*LECTURES ON THE INDUSTRIAL REVOLUTION OF THE 18TH CENTURY IN ENGLAND.* By ARNOLD TOYNBEE. With a Memoir of the Author by BENJAMIN JOWETT, D.D. 8vo., 10s. 6d.

Webb (SIDNEY and BEATRICE).

THE HISTORY OF TRADE UNIONISM. With Map and full Bibliography of the Subject. 8vo., 18s.

INDUSTRIAL DEMOCRACY: a Study in Trade Unionism. 2 vols. 8vo., 25s. net.

PROBLEMS OF MODERN INDUSTRY: Essays. 8vo., 7s. 6d.

Wright.—*OUTLINE OF PRACTICAL SOCIOLOGY.* With Special Reference to American Conditions. By CARROLL D. WRIGHT, LL.D. With 12 Maps and Diagrams. Crown 8vo., 9s.

STUDIES IN ECONOMICS AND POLITICAL SCIENCE.

Issued under the auspices of the London School of Economics and Political Science.

GERMAN SOCIAL DEMOCRACY. By BERTRAND RUSSELL, B.A. With an Appendix on Social Democracy and the Woman Question in Germany by ALYS RUSSELL, B.A. Crown 8vo., 3s. 6d.

THE REFERENDUM IN SWITZERLAND. By SIMON DEPLOIGE, Advocate. Translated by C. P. TREVELYAN, M.P. Edited, with Notes, Introduction and Appendices, by LILIAN TOMN. Crown 8vo., 7s. 6d.

THE HISTORY OF LOCAL RATES IN ENGLAND: Five Lectures. By EDWIN CANNAN, M.A. Crown 8vo., 2s. 6d.

LOCAL VARIATIONS IN WAGES. By F. W. LAWRENCE, M.A., Fellow of Trinity College, Cambridge. Medium 4to., 8s. 6d.

THE ECONOMIC POLICY OF COLBERT. By A. J. SARGENT, B.A., Senior Hulme Exhibitioner of Brasenose College, Oxford. Crown 8vo., 2s. 6d.

SELECT DOCUMENTS ILLUSTRATING THE HISTORY OF TRADE UNIONISM.
1. The Tailoring Trade. Edited by W. F. GALTON. With a Preface by SIDNEY WEBB, LL.B. Crown 8vo., 5s.

Evolution, Anthropology, &c.

Clodd (EDWARD).

THE STORY OF CREATION: a Plain Account of Evolution. With 77 Illustrations. Crown 8vo., 3s. 6d.

A PRIMER OF EVOLUTION: being a Popular Abridged Edition of 'The Story of Creation'. With Illustrations. Fcp. 8vo., 1s. 6d.

Lang (ANDREW).

CUSTOM AND MYTH: Studies of Early Usage and Belief. With 15 Illustrations. Crown 8vo., 3s. 6d.

MYTH, RITUAL, AND RELIGION. 2 vols. Crown 8vo., 7s.

Lubbock.—*THE ORIGIN OF CIVILISATION, and the Primitive Condition of Man.* By Sir J. LUBBOCK, Bart., M.P. With 5 Plates and 20 Illustrations. 8vo., 18s.

Romanes (GEORGE JOHN).

DARWIN, AND AFTER DARWIN: an Exposition of the Darwinian Theory, and a Discussion on Post-Darwinian Questions.

Part I. THE DARWINIAN THEORY. With Portrait of Darwin and 125 Illustrations. Crown 8vo., 10s. 6d.

Part II. POST-DARWINIAN QUESTIONS: Heredity and Utility. With Portrait of the Author and 5 Illustrations. Cr. 8vo., 10s. 6d.

Part III. Post-Darwinian Questions: Isolation and Physiological Selection. Crown 8vo., 5s.

AN EXAMINATION OF WEISMANN-ISM. Crown 8vo., 6s.

ESSAYS. Edited by C. LLOYD MORGAN, Principal of University College, Bristol. Crown 8vo., 6s.

Classical Literature, Translations, &c.

Abbott.—*HELLENICA.* A Collection of Essays on Greek Poetry, Philosophy, History, and Religion. Edited by EVELYN ABBOTT, M.A., LL.D. Crown 8vo., 7s. 6d.

Æschylus.—*EUMENIDES OF ÆSCHYLUS.* With Metrical English Translation. By J. F. DAVIES. 8vo., 7s.

Aristophanes. — *THE ACHARNIANS OF ARISTOPHANES,* translated into English Verse. By R. Y. TYRRELL. Crown 8vo., 1s.

Aristotle.—*YOUTH AND OLD AGE, LIFE AND DEATH, AND RESPIRATION.* Translated, with Introduction and Notes, by W. OGLE, M.A., M.D. 8vo., 7s. 6d.

Becker (W. A.), Translated by the Rev. F. METCALFE, B.D.

GALLUS: or, Roman Scenes in the Time of Augustus. With Notes and Excursuses. With 26 Illustrations. Post 8vo., 3s. 6d.

CHARICLES: or, Illustrations of the Private Life of the Ancient Greeks. With Notes and Excursuses. With 26 Illustrations. Post 8vo., 3s. 6d.

Butler—*THE AUTHORESS OF THE ODYSSEY, WHERE AND WHEN SHE WROTE, WHO SHE WAS, THE USE SHE MADE OF THE ILIAD, AND HOW THE POEM GREW UNDER HER HANDS.* By SAMUEL BUTLER, Author of 'Erewhon,' etc. With Illustrations and 4 Maps. 8vo., 10s. 6d.

Cicero.—*CICERO'S CORRESPONDENCE.* By R. Y. TYRRELL. Vols. I., II., III., 8vo., each 12s. Vol. IV., 15s. Vol. V., 14s. Vol. VI., 12s.

Homer.

THE ILIAD OF HOMER. Rendered into English Prose for the use of those who cannot read the original. By SAMUEL BUTLER, Author of 'Erewhon,' etc. Crown 8vo., 7s. 6d.

THE ODYSSEY OF HOMER. Done into English Verse. By WILLIAM MORRIS. Crown 8vo., 6s.

Horace.—*THE WORKS OF HORACE, RENDERED INTO ENGLISH PROSE.* With Life, Introduction and Notes. By WILLIAM COUTTS, M.A. Crown 8vo., 5s. net.

Lang.—*HOMER AND THE EPIC.* By ANDREW LANG. Crown 8vo., 9s. net.

Lucan.—*THE PHARSALIA OF LUCAN.* Translated into Blank Verse. By Sir EDWARD RIDLEY. 8vo., 14s.

Mackail.—*SELECT EPIGRAMS FROM THE GREEK ANTHOLOGY.* By J. W. MACKAIL. Edited with a Revised Text, Introduction, Translation, and Notes. 8vo., 16s.

Rich.—*A DICTIONARY OF ROMAN AND GREEK ANTIQUITIES.* By A. RICH, B.A. With 2000 Woodcuts. Crown 8vo., 7s. 6d.

Sophocles.—Translated into English Verse. By ROBERT WHITELAW, M.A., Assistant Master in Rugby School. Cr. 8vo., 8s. 6d.

Tyrrell. — *DUBLIN TRANSLATIONS INTO GREEK AND LATIN VERSE.* Edited by R. Y. TYRRELL. 8vo., 6s.

Virgil.

THE ÆNEID OF VIRGIL. Translated into English Verse by JOHN CONINGTON. Crown 8vo., 6s.

THE POEMS OF VIRGIL. Translated into English Prose by JOHN CONINGTON. Crown 8vo., 6s.

THE ÆNEIDS OF VIRGIL. Done into English Verse. By WILLIAM MORRIS. Crown 8vo., 6s.

THE ÆNEID OF VIRGIL, freely translated into English Blank Verse. By W. J. THORNHILL. Crown 8vo., 7s. 6d.

THE ÆNEID OF VIRGIL. Translated into English Verse by JAMES RHOADES. Books I.-VI. Crown 8vo., 5s. Books VII.-XII. Crown 8vo., 5s.

THE ECLOGUES AND GEORGICS OF VIRGIL. Translated into English Prose by J. W. MACKAIL, Fellow of Balliol College, Oxford. 16mo., 5s.

Wilkins.—*THE GROWTH OF THE HOMERIC POEMS.* By G. WILKINS. 8vo., 6s.

Poetry and the Drama,

Armstrong (G. F. SAVAGE).

POEMS : Lyrical and Dramatic. Fcp. 8vo., 6s.

KING SAUL. (The Tragedy of Israel, Part I.) Fcp. 8vo., 5s.

KING DAVID. (The Tragedy of Israel, Part II.) Fcp. 8vo., 6s.

KING SOLOMON. (The Tragedy of Israel, Part III.) Fcp. 8vo., 6s.

UGONE : a Tragedy. Fcp. 8vo., 6s.

A GARLAND FROM GREECE : Poems. Fcp. 8vo., 7s. 6d.

STORIES OF WICKLOW : Poems. Fcp. 8vo., 7s. 6d.

MEPHISTOPHELES IN BROADCLOTH : a Satire. Fcp. 8vo., 4s.

ONE IN THE INFINITE : a Poem. Crown 8vo., 7s. 6d.

Armstrong.—*THE POETICAL WORKS OF EDMUND J. ARMSTRONG.* Fcp. 8vo., 5s.

Arnold.—*THE LIGHT OF THE WORLD :* or, The Great Consummation. By Sir EDWIN ARNOLD. With 14 Illustrations after HOLMAN HUNT. Crown 8vo., 6s.

Barraud. — *THE LAY OF THE KNIGHTS.* By the Rev. C. W. BARRAUD, S.J., Author of ' St. Thomas of Canterbury, and other Poems '. Crown 8vo., 4s.

Bell (MRS. HUGH).

CHAMBER COMEDIES : a Collection of Plays and Monologues for the Drawing Room. Crown 8vo., 6s.

FAIRY TALE PLAYS, AND HOW TO ACT THEM. With 91 Diagrams and 52 Illustrations. Crown 8vo., 3s. 6d.

Coleridge.—*SELECTIONS FROM.* With Introduction by ANDREW LANG. With 18 Illustrations by PATTEN WILSON. Crown 8vo., 3s. 6d.

Goethe.

THE FIRST PART OF THE TRAGEDY OF FAUST IN ENGLISH. By THOS. E. WEBB, LL.D., sometime Fellow of Trinity College ; Professor of Moral Philosophy in the University of Dublin, etc. New and Cheaper Edition, with *THE DEATH OF FAUST,* from the Second Part. Crown 8vo., 6s.

Gore-Booth.—*POEMS.* By EVA GORE-BOOTH. Fcp. 8vo., 5s.

Ingelow (JEAN).

POETICAL WORKS. Complete in One Volume. Crown 8vo., 7s. 6d.

LYRICAL AND OTHER POEMS. Selected from the Writings of JEAN INGELOW. Fcp. 8vo., 2s. 6d. cloth plain, 3s. cloth gilt.

Lang (ANDREW).

GRASS OF PARNASSUS. Fcp. 8vo., 2s. 6d. net.

THE BLUE POETRY BOOK. Edited by ANDREW LANG. With 100 Illustrations. Crown 8vo., 6s.

Layard and Corder.—*SONGS IN MANY MOODS.* By NINA F. LAYARD ; *THE WANDERING ALBATROSS,* etc. By ANNIE CORDER. In One Volume. Crown 8vo., 5s.

Lecky.—*POEMS.* By the Right Hon. W. E. H. LECKY. Fcp. 8vo., 5s.

Lytton (THE EARL OF), (OWEN MEREDITH).

THE WANDERER. Cr. 8vo., 10s. 6d.

LUCILE. Crown 8vo., 10s. 6d.

SELECTED POEMS. Cr. 8vo., 10s. 6d.

Macaulay.—*LAYS OF ANCIENT ROME, WITH ' IVRY' AND ' THE ARMADA '.* By Lord MACAULAY.
Illustrated by G. SCHARF. Fcp. 4to., 10s. 6d.
———————————— Bijou Edition. 18mo., 2s. 6d. gilt top.
———————————— Popular Edition. Fcp. 4to., 6d. sewed, 1s. cloth.
Illustrated by J. R. WEGUELIN. Crown 8vo., 3s. 6d.
Annotated Edition. Fcp. 8vo., 1s. sewed, 1s. 6d. cloth.

Poetry and the Drama—*continued*.

MacDonald (GEORGE, LL.D.).

A BOOK OF STRIFE, IN THE FORM OF THE DIARY OF AN OLD SOUL: Poems. 18mo., 6s.

RAMPOLLI: GROWTHS FROM A LONG-PLANTED ROOT: being Translations, New and Old (mainly in verse), chiefly from the German; along with 'A Year's Diary of an Old Soul'. Crown 8vo., 6s.

Moffat.—*CRICKETY CRICKET:* Rhymes and Parodies. By DOUGLAS MOFFAT. With Frontispiece by Sir FRANK LOCKWOOD, Q.C., M.P., and 53 Illustrations by the Author. Crown 8vo, 2s. 6d.

Moon.—*POEMS OF LOVE AND HOME*, etc. By GEORGE WASHINGTON MOON, Hon. F.R.S.L., Author of 'Elijah,' etc. 16mo., 2s. 6d.

Morris (WILLIAM).

POETICAL WORKS—LIBRARY EDITION. Complete in Eleven Volumes. Crown 8vo., price 6s. each.

THE EARTHLY PARADISE. 4 vols. 6s. each.

THE LIFE AND DEATH OF JASON. 6s.

THE DEFENCE OF GUENEVERE, and other Poems. 6s.

THE STORY OF SIGURD THE VOLSUNG, AND THE FALL OF THE NIBLUNGS. 6s.

LOVE IS ENOUGH; or, the Freeing of Pharamond: A Morality; and *POEMS BY THE WAY.* 6s.

THE ODYSSEY OF HOMER. Done into English Verse. 6s.

THE ÆNEIDS OF VIRGIL. Done into English Verse. 6s.

THE TALE OF BEOWULF, SOMETIME KING OF THE FOLK OF THE WEDERGEATS. Translated by WILLIAM MORRIS and A. J. WYATT. Crown 8vo., 6s.

Certain of the POETICAL WORKS may also be had in the following Editions :—

THE EARTHLY PARADISE.

Popular Edition. 5 vols. 12mo., 25s.; or 5s. each, sold separately.

The same in Ten Parts, 25s.; or 2s. 6d. each, sold separately.

Cheap Edition. in 1 vol. Crown 8vo., 7s. 6d.

POEMS BY THE WAY. Square crown 8vo., 6s.

. For Mr. William Morris's Prose Works, see pp. 22 and 31.

Nesbit.—*LAYS AND LEGENDS.* By E. NESBIT (Mrs. HUBERT BLAND). First Series. Crown 8vo., 3s. 6d. Second Series. With Portrait. Crown 8vo , 5s.

Riley (JAMES WHITCOMB).

OLD FASHIONED ROSES: Poems. 12mo., 5s.

RUBÁIYÁT OF DOC SIFERS. With 43 Illustrations by C. M RELYEA. Crown 8vo.

THE GOLDEN YEAR. From the Verse and Prose of JAMES WHITCOMB RILEY. Compiled by CLARA E. LAUGHLIN. Fcp. 8vo., 5s.

Romanes.—*A SELECTION FROM THE POEMS OF GEORGE JOHN ROMANES, M.A., LL.D., F.R.S.* With an Introduction by T. HERBERT WARREN, President of Magdalen College, Oxford. Crown 8vo., 4s. 6d.

Russell.—*SONNETS ON THE SONNET:* an Anthology. Compiled by the Rev. MATTHEW RUSSELL, S.J. Crown 8vo., 3s. 6d.

Samuels.—*SHADOWS, AND OTHER POEMS.* By E. SAMUELS. With 7 Illustrations by W. FITZGERALD, M.A. Crown 8vo., 3s. 6d.

Shakespeare.

BOWDLER'S FAMILY SHAKESPEARE. With 36 Woodcuts. 1 vol. 8vo., 14s. Or in 6 vols. Fcp. 8vo., 21s.

SHAKESPEARE'S SONNETS. Reconsidered, and in part Rearranged, with Introductory Chapters and a Reprint of the Original 1609 Edition, by SAMUEL BUTLER, Author of 'Erewhon,' 'Life and Habit,' 'The Authoress of the Odyssey,' 'Life and Letters of Dr. Samuel Butler,' etc. 8vo. [*Nearly ready.*

THE SHAKESPEARE BIRTHDAY BOOK. By MARY F. DUNBAR. 32mo., 1s. 6d.

Wagner.—*THE NIBELUNGEN RING.* Done into English Verse by REGINALD RANKIN, B.A. of the Inner Temple, Barrister-at-Law. Vol. I. Rhinegold and Valkyrie.

Wordsworth. — *SELECTED POEMS.* By ANDREW LANG. With Photogravure Frontispiece of Rydal Mount. With 16 Illustrations and numerous Initial Letters. By ALFRED PARSONS, A.R.A. Crown 8vo., gilt edges, 3s. 6d.

Wordsworth and Coleridge.—*A DESCRIPTION OF THE WORDSWORTH AND COLERIDGE MANUSCRIPTS IN THE POSSESSION OF MR. T. NORTON LONGMAN.* Edited, with Notes, by W. HALE WHITE. With 3 Facsimile Reproductions. 4to., 10s. 6d.

Fiction, Humour, &c.

Anstey.—*VOCES POPULI.* Reprinted from 'Punch'. By F. ANSTEY, Author of 'Vice Versâ'. First Series. With 20 Illustrations by J. BERNARD PARTRIDGE. Crown 8vo., 3s. 6d.

Beaconsfield (THE EARL OF). *NOVELS AND TALES.* Complete in 11 vols. Crown 8vo., 1s. 6d. each.

Vivian Grey.
The Young Duke, etc.
Alroy, Ixion, etc.
Contarini Fleming, etc.
Tancred.

Sybil.
Henrietta Temple.
Venetia.
Coningsby.
Lothair.
Endymion.

Birt.—*CASTLE CZVARGAS:* a Romance. Being a Plain Story of the Romantic Adventures of Two Brothers, Told by the Younger of Them. Edited by ARCHIBALD BIRT. Crown 8vo., 6s.

'Chola.'—*A NEW DIVINITY, AND OTHER STORIES OF HINDU LIFE.* By 'CHOLA'. Crown 8vo., 2s. 6d.

Diderot. — *RAMEAU'S NEPHEW:* a Translation from Diderot's Autographic Text. By SYLVIA MARGARET HILL. Crown 8vo., 3s. 6d.

Dougall.—*BEGGARS ALL.* By L. DOUGALL. Crown 8vo., 3s. 6d.

Doyle (A. CONAN).
MICAH CLARKE: A Tale of Monmouth's Rebellion. With 10 Illustrations. Cr. 8vo., 3s. 6d.
THE CAPTAIN OF THE POLESTAR, and other Tales. Cr. 8vo., 3s. 6d.
THE REFUGEES: A Tale of the Huguenots. With 25 Illustrations. Cr. 8vo., 3s. 6d.
THE STARK MUNRO LETTERS. Cr. 8vo, 3s. 6d.

Farrar (F. W., DEAN OF CANTERBURY).
DARKNESS AND DAWN: or, Scenes in the Days of Nero. An Historic Tale. Cr. 8vo., 7s. 6d.
GATHERING CLOUDS: a Tale of the Days of St. Chrysostom. Cr. 8vo., 7s. 6d.

Fowler (EDITH H.).
THE YOUNG PRETENDERS. A Story of Child Life. With 12 Illustrations by Sir PHILIP BURNE-JONES, Bart. Crown 8vo., 6s.
THE PROFESSOR'S CHILDREN. With 24 Illustrations by ETHEL KATE BURGESS. Crown 8vo., 6s.

Francis.— *YEOMAN FLEETWOOD.* By M. E. FRANCIS, Author of 'In a North-country Village,' etc. Crown 8vo., 6s.

Froude.—*THE TWO CHIEFS OF DUNBOY:* an Irish Romance of the Last Century. By JAMES A. FROUDE. Cr. 8vo., 3s. 6d.

Gurdon.—*MEMORIES AND FANCIES:* Suffolk Tales and other Stories; Fairy Legends; Poems; Miscellaneous Articles. By the late LADY CAMILLA GURDON, Author of 'Suffolk Folk-Lore'. Crown 8vo., 5s.

Haggard (H. RIDER).
SWALLOW: a Tale of the Great Trek. With 8 Illustrations. Crown 8vo., 6s.
DR. THERNE. Crown 8vo., 3s. 6d.
HEART OF THE WORLD. With 15 Illustrations. Crown 8vo., 3s. 6d.
JOAN HASTE. With 20 Illustrations. Crown 8vo., 3s. 6d.
THE PEOPLE OF THE MIST. With 16 Illustrations. Crown 8vo., 3s. 6d.
MONTEZUMA'S DAUGHTER. With 24 Illustrations. Crown 8vo., 3s. 6d.
SHE. With 32 Illustrations. Crown 8vo., 3s. 6d.
ALLAN QUATERMAIN. With 31 Illustrations. Crown 8vo., 3s. 6d.
MAIWA'S REVENGE. Cr. 8vo., 1s. 6d.
COLONEL QUARITCH, V.C. With Frontispiece and Vignette. Cr. 8vo., 3s. 6d.
CLEOPATRA. With 29 Illustrations. Crown 8vo., 3s. 6d.
BEATRICE. With Frontispiece and Vignette. Cr. 8vo., 3s. 6d.
ERIC BRIGHTEYES. With 51 Illustrations. Crown 8vo., 3s. 6d.
NADA THE LILY. With 23 Illustrations. Crown 8vo., 3s. 6d.
ALLAN'S WIFE. With 34 Illustrations. Crown 8vo., 3s. 6d.
THE WITCH'S HEAD. With 16 Illustrations. Crown 8vo., 3s. 6d.
MR. MEESON'S WILL. With 16 Illustrations. Crown 8vo., 3s. 6d.
DAWN. With 16 Illustrations. Cr. 8vo., 3s. 6d.

Haggard and Lang.—*THE WORLD'S DESIRE.* By H. RIDER HAGGARD and ANDREW LANG. With 27 Illustrations. Crown 8vo., 3s. 6d.

Fiction, Humour, &c.—*continued.*

Harte.—*IN THE CARQUINEZ WOODS.* By BRET HARTE. Crown 8vo., 3s. 6d.

Hope.—*THE HEART OF PRINCESS OSRA.* By ANTHONY HOPE. With 9 Illustrations. Crown 8vo., 6s.

Jerome.—*SKETCHES IN LAVENDER: BLUE AND GREEN.* By JEROME K. JEROME. Crown 8vo., 3s. 6d.

Joyce.—*OLD CELTIC ROMANCES.* Twelve of the most beautiful of the Ancient Irish Romantic Tales. Translated from the Gaelic. By P. W. JOYCE, LL.D. Crown 8vo., 3s. 6d.

Lang.—*A MONK OF FIFE;* a Story of the Days of Joan of Arc. By ANDREW LANG. With 13 Illustrations by SELWYN IMAGE. Crown 8vo., 3s. 6d.

Levett-Yeats (S.).

THE CHEVALIER D'AURIAC. Crown 8vo., 3s. 6d.

THE HEART OF DENISE, and other Tales. Crown 8vo., 6s.

Lyall (EDNA).

THE AUTOBIOGRAPHY OF A SLANDER. Fcp. 8vo., 1s., sewed.
Presentation Edition. With 20 Illustrations by LANCELOT SPEED. Crown 8vo., 2s. 6d. net.

THE AUTOBIOGRAPHY OF A TRUTH. Fcp. 8vo., 1s., sewed; 1s. 6d., cloth.

DOREEN. The Story of a Singer. Crown 8vo., 6s.

WAYFARING MEN. Crown 8vo., 6s.

HOPE THE HERMIT: a Romance of Borrowdale. Crown 8vo., 6s.

Max Müller. — *DEUTSCHE LIEBE (GERMAN LOVE):* Fragments from the Papers of an Alien. Collected by F. MAX MÜLLER. Translated from the German by G. A. M. Crown 8vo., 5s.

Melville (G. J. WHYTE).

The Gladiators.	Holmby House.
The Interpreter.	Kate Coventry.
Good for Nothing.	Digby Grand.
The Queen's Maries.	General Bounce.

Crown 8vo., 1s. 6d. each.

Merriman.—*FLOTSAM:* A Story of the Indian Mutiny. By HENRY SETON MERRIMAN. Crown 8vo., 3s. 6d.

Morris (WILLIAM).

THE SUNDERING FLOOD. Cr. 8vo., 7s. 6d.

THE WATER OF THE WONDROUS ISLES. Crown 8vo., 7s. 6d.

THE WELL AT THE WORLD'S END. 2 vols. 8vo., 28s.

THE STORY OF THE GLITTERING PLAIN, which has been also called The Land of the Living Men, or The Acre of the Undying. Square post 8vo., 5s. net.

THE ROOTS OF THE MOUNTAINS, wherein is told somewhat of the Lives of the Men of Burgdale, their Friends, their Neighbours, their Foemen, and their Fellows-in-Arms. Written in Prose and Verse. Square crown 8vo., 8s.

A TALE OF THE HOUSE OF THE WOLFINGS, and all the Kindreds of the Mark. Written in Prose and Verse. Square crown 8vo., 6s.

A DREAM OF JOHN BALL, AND A KING'S LESSON. 12mo., 1s. 6d.

NEWS FROM NOWHERE; or, An Epoch of Rest. Being some Chapters from an Utopian Romance. Post 8vo., 1s. 6d.

. For Mr. William Morris's Poetical Works, see p. 20.

Newman (CARDINAL).

LOSS AND GAIN: The Story of a Convert. Crown 8vo. Cabinet Edition, 6s.; Popular Edition, 3s. 6d.

CALLISTA: A Tale of the Third Century. Crown 8vo. Cabinet Edition, 6s.; Popular Edition, 3s. 6d.

Phillipps-Wolley.—*SNAP;* a Legend of the Lone Mountain. By C. PHILLIPPS-WOLLEY. With 13 Illustrations. Crown 8vo., 3s. 6d.

Raymond (WALTER).

TWO MEN O' MENDIP. Cr. 8vo., 6s.

NO SOUL ABOVE MONEY. Cr. 8vo., 6s.

Reader.—*PRIESTESS AND QUEEN:* a Tale of the White Race of Mexico; being the Adventures of Ignigene and her Twenty-six Fair Maidens. By EMILY E. READER. Illustrated by EMILY K. READER. Crown 8vo., 6s.

Fiction, Humour, &c.—*continued.*

Sewell (ELIZABETH M.).

A Glimpse of the World.	Amy Herbert
Laneton Parsonage.	Cleve Hall.
Margaret Percival.	Gertrude.
Katharine Ashton.	Home Life.
The Earl's Daughter.	After Life.
The Experience of Life.	Ursula. Ivors.

Cr. 8vo., 1s. 6d. each cloth plain. 2s. 6d. each cloth extra, gilt edges.

Somerville and Ross.—*SOME EX-PERIENCES OF AN IRISH R.M.* By E. Œ. SOMERVILLE and MARTIN ROSS. With 31 Illustrations by E. Œ. SOMERVILLE. Crown 8vo., 6s.

Stebbing. — *PROBABLE TALES.* Edited by WILLIAM STEBBING. Crown 8vo., 4s. 6d.

Stevenson (ROBERT LOUIS).

THE STRANGE CASE OF DR. JEKYLL AND MR. HYDE. Fcp. 8vo., 1s. sewed. 1s. 6d. cloth.

THE STRANGE CASE OF DR. JEKYLL AND MR. HYDE; WITH OTHER FABLES. Crown 8vo., 3s. 6d.

MORE NEW ARABIAN NIGHTS—THE DYNAMITER. By ROBERT LOUIS STEVENSON and FANNY VAN DE GRIFT STEVENSON. Crown 8vo., 3s. 6d.

THE WRONG BOX. By ROBERT LOUIS STEVENSON and LLOYD OSBOURNE. Crown 8vo., 3s. 6d.

Suttner.—*LAY DOWN YOUR ARMS* (*Die Waffen Nieder*): The Autobiography of Martha von Tilling. By BERTHA VON SUTTNER. Translated by T. HOLMES. Cr. 8vo., 1s. 6d.

Taylor. — *EARLY ITALIAN LOVE-STORIES.* Taken from the Originals by UNA TAYLOR. With 13 Illustrations by HENRY J. FORD. Crown 4to., 15s. net.

Trollope (ANTHONY).

THE WARDEN. Cr. 8vo., 1s. 6d.

BARCHESTER TOWERS. Cr. 8vo., 1s. 6d.

Walford (L. B.).

THE INTRUDERS. Crown 8vo., 6s.

LEDDY MARGET. Crown 8vo., 2s. 6d.

IVA KILDARE: a Matrimonial Problem. Crown 8vo., 6s.

MR. SMITH: a Part of his Life. Crown 8vo., 2s. 6d.

Walford (L. B.)—*continued.*

THE BABY'S GRANDMOTHER. Cr. 8vo., 2s. 6d.

COUSINS. Crown 8vo., 2s. 6d.

TROUBLESOME DAUGHTERS. Cr. 8vo., 2s. 6d.

PAULINE. Crown 8vo., 2s. 6d.

DICK NETHERBY. Cr. 8vo., 2s. 6d.

THE HISTORY OF A WEEK. Cr. 8vo. 2s. 6d.

A STIFF-NECKED GENERATION. Cr. 8vo. 2s. 6d.

NAN, and other Stories. Cr. 8vo., 2s. 6d.

THE MISCHIEF OF MONICA. Cr. 8vo., 2s. 6d.

THE ONE GOOD GUEST. Cr. 8vo. 2s. 6d.

'*PLOUGHED,*' and other Stories. Crown 8vo., 2s. 6d.

THE MATCHMAKER. Cr. 8vo., 2s. 6d.

Ward. *—ONE POOR SCRUPLE.* By Mrs. WILFRID WARD. Crown 8vo., 6s.

Watson.—*RACING AND CHASING:* a Collection of Sporting Stories. By ALFRED E. T. WATSON, Editor of the 'Badminton Magazine'. With 16 Plates and 36 Illustrations in the Text. Crown 8vo., 7s. 6d.

Weyman (STANLEY).

THE HOUSE OF THE WOLF. With Frontispiece and Vignette. Crown 8vo., 3s. 6d.

A GENTLEMAN OF FRANCE. With Frontispiece and Vignette. Cr. 8vo., 6s.

THE RED COCKADE. With Frontispiece and Vignette. Crown 8vo., 6s.

SHREWSBURY. With 24 Illustrations by CLAUDE A. SHEPPERSON. Cr. 8vo., 6s.

Popular Science (Natural History, &c.).

Beddard. — *THE STRUCTURE AND CLASSIFICATION OF BIRDS.* By FRANK E. BEDDARD, M.A., F.R.S., Prosector and Vice-Secretary of the Zoological Society of London. With 252 Illustrations. 8vo., 21s. net.

Butler. — *OUR HOUSEHOLD INSECTS.* An Account of the Insect-Pests found in Dwelling-Houses. By EDWARD A. BUTLER, B.A., B.Sc. (Lond.). With 113 Illustrations. Crown 8vo., 3s. 6d.

Furneaux (W.).

THE OUTDOOR WORLD; or The Young Collector's Handbook. With 18 Plates (16 of which are coloured), and 549 Illustrations in the Text. Crown 8vo., 7s. 6d.

BUTTERFLIES AND MOTHS (British). With 12 coloured Plates and 241 Illustrations in the Text. Crown 8vo., 7s. 6d.

LIFE IN PONDS AND STREAMS. With 8 coloured Plates and 331 Illustrations in the Text. Crown 8vo., 7s. 6d.

Hartwig (DR. GEORGE).

THE SEA AND ITS LIVING WONDERS. With 12 Plates and 303 Woodcuts. 8vo., 7s. net.

THE TROPICAL WORLD. With 8 Plates and 172 Woodcuts. 8vo., 7s. net.

THE POLAR WORLD. With 3 Maps, 8 Plates and 85 Woodcuts. 8vo., 7s. net.

THE SUBTERRANEAN WORLD. With 3 Maps and 80 Woodcuts. 8vo., 7s. net.

THE AERIAL WORLD. With Map, 8 Plates and 60 Woodcuts. 8vo., 7s. net.

HEROES OF THE POLAR WORLD. With 19 Illustrations. Cr. 8vo., 2s.

WONDERS OF THE TROPICAL FORESTS. With 40 Illustrations. Cr. 8vo., 2s.

WORKERS UNDER THE GROUND. With 29 Illustrations. Cr. 8vo., 2s.

MARVELS OVER OUR HEADS. With 29 Illustrations. Cr. 8vo., 2s.

SEA MONSTERS AND SEA BIRDS. With 75 Illustrations. Cr. 8vo., 2s. 6d.

DENIZENS OF THE DEEP. With 117 Illustrations. Cr. 8vo., 2s. 6d.

Hartwig (DR. GEORGE)—*continued.*

VOLCANOES AND EARTHQUAKES. With 30 Illustrations. Cr. 8vo., 2s. 6d.

WILD ANIMALS OF THE TROPICS. With 66 Illustrations. Cr. 8vo., 3s. 6d.

Helmholtz. — *POPULAR LECTURES ON SCIENTIFIC SUBJECTS.* By HERMANN VON HELMHOLTZ. With 68 Woodcuts. 2 vols. Cr. 8vo., 3s. 6d. each.

Hudson (W. H.).

BRITISH BIRDS. With a Chapter on Structure and Classification by FRANK E. BEDDARD, F.R.S. With 16 Plates (8 of which are Coloured), and over 100 Illustrations in the Text. Cr. 8vo., 7s. 6d.

BIRDS IN LONDON. With 17 Plates and 15 Illustrations in the Text, by BRYAN HOOK, A. D. McCORMICK, and from Photographs from Nature, by R. B. LODGE. 8vo., 12s.

Proctor (RICHARD A.).

LIGHT SCIENCE FOR LEISURE HOURS. Familiar Essays on Scientific Subjects. 3 vols. Cr. 8vo., 5s. each. Vol. I., Cheap Edition. Crown 8vo., 3s. 6d.

ROUGH WAYS MADE SMOOTH. Familiar Essays on Scientific Subjects. Crown 8vo., 3s. 6d.

PLEASANT WAYS IN SCIENCE. Crown 8vo., 3s. 6d.

NATURE STUDIES. By R. A. PROCTOR, GRANT ALLEN, A. WILSON, T. FOSTER and E. CLODD. Crown 8vo., 3s. 6d.

LEISURE READINGS. By R. A. PROCTOR, E. CLODD, A. WILSON, T. FOSTER and A. C. RANYARD. Cr. 8vo., 3s. 6d.

*** *For Mr. Proctor's other books see pp. 13, 28 and 31, and Messrs. Longmans & Co.'s Catalogue of Scientific Works.*

Stanley. — *A FAMILIAR HISTORY OF BIRDS.* By E. STANLEY, D.D., formerly Bishop of Norwich. With 160 Illustrations. Cr. 8vo., 3s. 6d.

Popular Science (Natural History, &c.)—*continued*.

Wood (REV. J. G.).

HOMES WITHOUT HANDS: A Description of the Habitations of Animals, classed according to the Principle of Construction. With 140 Illustrations. 8vo., 7s. net.

INSECTS AT HOME : A Popular Account of British Insects, their Structure, Habits and Transformations. With 700 Illustrations. 8vo., 7s. net.

OUT OF DOORS; a Selection of Original Articles on Practical Natural History. With 11 Illustrations. Cr. 8vo., 3s. 6d.

STRANGE DWELLINGS: a Description of the Habitations of Animals, abridged from 'Homes without Hands'. With 60 Illustrations. Cr. 8vo., 3s. 6d.

Wood (REV. J. G.)—*continued*.

PETLAND REVISITED. With 33 Illustrations. Cr. 8vo., 3s. 6d.

BIRD LIFE OF THE BIBLE. With 32 Illustrations. Cr. 8vo., 3s. 6d.

WONDERFUL NESTS. With 30 Illustrations. Cr. 8vo., 3s. 6d.

HOMES UNDER THE GROUND. With 28 Illustrations. Cr. 8vo., 3s. 6d.

WILD ANIMALS OF THE BIBLE. With 29 Illustrations. Cr. 8vo., 3s. 6d.

DOMESTIC ANIMALS OF THE BIBLE. With 23 Illustrations. Cr. 8vo., 3s. 6d.

THE BRANCH BUILDERS. With 28 Illustrations. Cr. 8vo., 2s. 6d.

SOCIAL HABITATIONS AND PARASITIC NESTS. With 18 Illustrations. Cr. 8vo., 2s.

Works of Reference.

Gwilt.—*AN ENCYCLOPÆDIA OF ARCHITECTURE.* By JOSEPH GWILT, F.S.A. Illustrated with more than 1100 Engravings on Wood. Revised (1888), with Alterations and Considerable Additions by WYATT PAPWORTH. 8vo, £2 12s. 6d.

Maunder (Samuel).

BIOGRAPHICAL TREASURY. With Supplement brought down to 1889. By Rev. JAMES WOOD. Fcp. 8vo., 6s.

TREASURY OF GEOGRAPHY, Physical, Historical, Descriptive, and Political. With 7 Maps and 16 Plates. Fcp. 8vo., 6s.

THE TREASURY OF BIBLE KNOWLEDGE. By the Rev. J. AYRE, M.A. With 5 Maps, 15 Plates, and 300 Woodcuts. Fcp. 8vo., 6s.

TREASURY OF KNOWLEDGE AND LIBRARY OF REFERENCE. Fcp. 8vo., 6s.

HISTORICAL TREASURY. Fcp. 8vo, 6s.

Maunder (Samuel)—*continued*.

SCIENTIFIC AND LITERARY TREASURY. Fcp. 8vo., 6s.

THE TREASURY OF BOTANY. Edited by J. LINDLEY, F.R.S., and T. MOORE, F.L.S. With 274 Woodcuts and 20 Steel Plates. 2 vols. Fcp. 8vo., 12s.

Roget. — *THESAURUS OF ENGLISH WORDS AND PHRASES.* Classified and Arranged so as to Facilitate the Expression of Ideas and assist in Literary Composition. By PETER MARK ROGET, M.D., F.R.S. Recomposed throughout, enlarged and improved, partly from the Author's Notes, and with a full Index, by the Author's Son. JOHN LEWIS ROGET. Crown 8vo., 10s. 6d.

Willich.—*POPULAR TABLES* for giving information for ascertaining the value of Lifehold, Leasehold, and Church Property, the Public Funds, etc. By CHARLES M. WILLICH. Edited by H. BENCE JONES. Crown 8vo., 10s. 6d.

Children's Books.

Buckland.—*TWO LITTLE RUNAWAYS.*
Adapted from the French of LOUIS DES-
NOYERS. By JAMES BUCKLAND. With 110
Illustrations by CECIL ALDIN. Cr. 8vo., 6s.

Crake (Rev. A. D.).
EDWY THE FAIR ; or, The First
Chronicle of Æscendune. Cr. 8vo., 2s. 6d.

ALFGAR THE DANE ; or, The Second
Chronicle of Æscendune. Cr. 8vo. 2s. 6d.

THE RIVAL HEIRS : being the Third
and Last Chronicle of Æscendune. Cr.
8vo., 2s. 6d.

THE HOUSE OF WALDERNE. A Tale
of the Cloister and the Forest in the Days
of the Barons' Wars. Crown 8vo., 2s. 6d.

BRIAN FITZ-COUNT. A Story of
Wallingford Castle and Dorchester
Abbey. Cr. 8vo., 2s. 6d.

Henty (G.A.).—EDITED BY.
YULE LOGS : A Story-Book for Boys.
With 61 Illustrations. Crown 8vo., 6s.

YULE TIDE YARNS. With 45 Illustrations. Crown 8vo., 6s.

Lang (ANDREW).—EDITED BY.
THE BLUE FAIRY BOOK. With 138
Illustrations. Crown 8vo., 5s.

THE RED FAIRY BOOK. With 100
Illustrations. Crown 8vo., 6s.

THE GREEN FAIRY BOOK. With 99
Illustrations. Crown 8vo., 6s.

THE YELLOW FAIRY BOOK. With
104 Illustrations. Crown 8vo., 6s.

THE PINK FAIRY BOOK. With 67
Illustrations. Crown 8vo., 6s.

THE BLUE POETRY BOOK. With 100
Illustrations. Crown 8vo., 6s.

THE BLUE POETRY BOOK. School
Edition, without Illustrations. Fcp. 8vo.,
2s. 6d.

THE TRUE STORY BOOK. With 66
Illustrations. Crown 8vo., 6s.

THE RED TRUE STORY BOOK. With
100 Illustrations. Crown 8vo., 6s.

THE ANIMAL STORY BOOK. With
67 Illustrations. Crown 8vo., 6s.

THE RED BOOK OF ANIMAL STORIES.
With 65 Illustrations. Crown 8vo., 6s.

*THE ARABIAN NIGHTS ENTERTAIN-
MENTS.* With 66 Illustrations. Cr. 8vo., 6s.

Meade (L. T.).
DADDY'S BOY. With 8 Illustrations.
Crown 8vo., 3s. 6d.

DEB AND THE DUCHESS. With 7
Illustrations. Crown 8vo., 3s. 6d.

THE BERESFORD PRIZE. With 7
Illustrations. Crown 8vo., 3s. 6d.

THE HOUSE OF SURPRISES. With 6
Illustrations. Crown 8vo. 3s. 6d.

Praeger (ROSAMOND).
*THE ADVENTURES OF THE THREE
BOLD BABES: HECTOR, HONORIA AND
ALISANDER.* A Story in Pictures. With
24 Coloured Plates and 24 Outline Pic-
tures. Oblong 4to., 3s. 6d.

*THE FURTHER DOINGS OF THE
THREE BOLD BABIES.* With 24 Coloured
Pictures and 24 Outline Pictures. Oblong
4to., 3s. 6d.

Stevenson.—*A CHILD'S GARDEN OF
VERSES.* By ROBERT LOUIS STEVENSON.
Fcp. 8vo., 5s.

Upton (FLORENCE K. AND BERTHA).
*THE ADVENTURES OF TWO DUTCH
DOLLS AND A 'GOLLIWOGG'.* With 31
Coloured Plates and numerous Illustra-
tions in the Text. Oblong 4to., 6s.

THE GOLLIWOGG'S BICYCLE CLUB.
With 31 Coloured Plates and numerous
Illustrations in the Text. Oblong 4to.,
6s.

THE GOLLIWOGG AT THE SEASIDE.
With 31 Coloured Plates and numerous
Illustrations in the Text. Oblong 4to., 6s.

THE GOLLIWOGG IN WAR. With
Coloured Plates and numerous Illustrations in the Text. Oblong 4to., 6s.

THE VEGE-MEN'S REVENGE. With
31 Coloured Plates and numerous Illustrations in the Text. Oblong 4to., 6s.

The Silver Library.

CROWN 8vo.   3s. 6d. EACH VOLUME.

Arnold's (Sir Edwin) Seas and Lands. With 71 Illustrations. 3s. 6d.

Bagehot's (W.) Biographical Studies. 3s. 6d.

Bagehot's (W.) Economic Studies. 3s. 6d.

Bagehot's (W.) Literary Studies. With Portrait. 3 vols. 3s. 6d. each.

Baker's (Sir S. W.) Eight Years in Ceylon. With 6 Illustrations. 3s. 6d.

Baker's (Sir S. W.) Rifle and Hound in Ceylon. With 6 Illustrations. 3s. 6d.

Baring-Gould's (Rev. S.) Curious Myths of the Middle Ages. 3s. 6d.

Baring-Gould's (Rev. S.) Origin and Development of Religious Belief. 2 vols. 3s. 6d. each.

Becker's (W. A.) Gallus: or, Roman Scenes in the Time of Augustus. With 26 Illus. 3s. 6d.

Becker's (W. A.) Charicles: or, Illustrations of the Private Life of the Ancient Greeks. With 26 Illustrations. 3s. 6d.

Bent's (J. T.) The Ruined Cities of Mashonaland. With 117 Illustrations. 3s. 6d.

Bratsey's (Lady) A Voyage in the 'Sunbeam'. With 66 Illustrations. 3s. 6d.

Churchill's (W. S.) The Story of the Malakand Field Force, 1897. With 6 Maps and Plans. 3s. 6d.

Clodd's (E.) Story of Creation: a Plain Account of Evolution. With 77 Illustrations. 3s. 6d.

Conybeare (Rev. W. J.) and Howson's (Very Rev. J. S.) Life and Epistles of St. Paul. With 46 Illustrations. 3s. 6d.

Dougall's (L.) Beggars All: a Novel. 3s. 6d.

Doyle's (A. Conan) Micah Clarke. A Tale of Monmouth's Rebellion. With 10 Illusts. 3s. 6d.

Doyle's (A. Conan) The Captain of the Polestar, and other Tales. 3s. 6d.

Doyle's (A. Conan) The Refugees: A Tale of the Huguenots. With 25 Illustrations. 3s. 6d.

Doyle's (A. Conan) The Stark Munro Letters. 3s. 6d.

Froude's (J. A.) The History of England, from the Fall of Wolsey to the Defeat of the Spanish Armada. 12 vols. 3s. 6d. each.

Froude's (J. A.) The English in Ireland. 3 vols. 10s. 6d.

Froude's (J. A.) The Divorce of Catherine of Aragon. 3s. 6d.

Froude's (J. A.) The Spanish Story of the Armada, and other Essays. 3s. 6d.

Froude's (J. A.) Short Studies on Great Subjects. 4 vols. 3s. 6d. each.

Froude's (J. A.) Oceana, or England and Her Colonies. With 9 Illustrations. 3s. 6d.

Froude's (J. A.) The Council of Trent. 3s. 6d.

Froude's (J. A.) The Life and Letters of Erasmus. 3s. 6d.

Froude's (J. A.) Thomas Carlyle: a History of his Life.

1795-1835. 2 vols. 7s.   1834-1881. 2 vols. 7s.

Froude's (J. A.) Cæsar: a Sketch. 3s. 6d.

Froude's (J. A.) The Two Chiefs of Dunboy: an Irish Romance of the Last Century. 3s. 6d.

Gleig's (Rev. G. R.) Life of the Duke of Wellington. With Portrait. 3s. 6d.

Greville's (C. C. F.) Journal of the Reigns of King George IV., King William IV., and Queen Victoria. 8 vols. 3s. 6d. each.

Haggard's (H. R.) She: A History of Adventure. With 32 Illustrations. 3s. 6d.

Haggard's (H. R.) Allan Quatermain. With 20 Illustrations. 3s. 6d.

Haggard's (H. R.) Colonel Quaritch, V.C.: a Tale of Country Life. With Frontispiece and Vignette. 3s. 6d.

Haggard's (H. R.) Cleopatra. With 29 Illustrations. 3s. 6d.

Haggard's (H. R.) Eric Brighteyes. With 51 Illustrations. 3s. 6d.

Haggard's (H. R.) Beatrice. With Frontispiece and Vignette. 3s. 6d.

Haggard's (H. R.) Allan's Wife. With 34 Illustrations. 3s. 6d.

Haggard (H. R.) Heart of the World. With 15 Illustrations. 3s. 6d.

Haggard's (H. R.) Montezuma's Daughter. With 25 Illustrations. 3s. 6d.

Haggard's (H. R.) The Witch's Head. With 16 Illustrations. 3s. 6d.

Haggard's (H. R.) Mr. Meeson's Will. With 16 Illustrations. 3s. 6d.

Haggard's (H. R.) Nada the Lily. With 23 Illustrations. 3s. 6d.

Haggard's (H. R.) Dawn. With 16 Illusts. 3s. 6d.

Haggard's (H. R.) The People of the Mist. With 16 Illustrations. 3s. 6d.

Haggard's (H. R.) Joan Haste. With 20 Illustrations. 3s. 6d.

Haggard (H. R.) and Lang's (A.) The World's Desire. With 27 Illustrations. 3s. 6d.

Harte's (Bret) In the Carquinez Woods and other Stories. 3s. 6d.

Helmholtz's (Hermann von) Popular Lectures on Scientific Subjects. With 68 Illustrations. 2 vols. 3s. 6d. each.

Hornung's (E. W.) The Unbidden Guest. 3s. 6d.

Howitt's (W.) Visits to Remarkable Places. With 80 Illustrations. 3s. 6d.

Jefferies' (R.) The Story of My Heart: My Autobiography. With Portrait. 3s. 6d.

Jefferies' (R.) Field and Hedgerow. With Portrait. 3s. 6d.

Jefferies' (R.) Red Deer. With 17 Illusts. 3s. 6d.

Jefferies' (R.) Wood Magic: a Fable. With Frontispiece and Vignette by E. V. B. 3s. 6d.

Jefferies (R.) The Toilers of the Field. With Portrait from the Bust in Salisbury Cathedral. 3s. 6d.

Kaye (Sir J.) and Malleson's (Colonel) History of the Indian Mutiny of 1857-8. 6 vols. 3s. 6d. each.

Knight's (E. F.) The Cruise of the 'Alerte': the Narrative of a Search for Treasure on the Desert Island of Trinidad. With 2 Maps and 23 Illustrations. 3s. 6d.

Knight's (E. F.) Where Three Empires Meet: a Narrative of Recent Travel in Kashmir, Western Tibet, Baltistan, Gilgit. With a Map and 54 Illustrations. 3s. 6d.

Knight's (E. F.) The 'Falcon' on the Baltic: a Coasting Voyage from Hammersmith to Copenhagen in a Three-Ton Yacht. With Map and 11 Illustrations. 3s. 6d.

Köstlin's (J.) Life of Luther. With 62 Illustrations and 4 Facsimiles of MSS. 3s. 6d.

Lang's (A.) Angling Sketches. With 20 Illustrations. 3s. 6d.

Lang's (A.) Custom and Myth: Studies of Early Usage and Belief. 3s. 6d.

Lang's (A.) Cock Lane and Common-Sense. 3s. 6d.

Lang's (A.) The Book of Dreams and Ghosts. 3s. 6d.

The Silver Library—*continued.*

Lang's (A.) A Monk of Fife: a Story of the Days of Joan of Arc. With 13 Illusts. 3s. 6d.

Lang's (A.) Myth, Ritual, and Religion. 2 vols. 7s.

Lees (J. A.) and Clutterbuck's (W. J.) B. C. 1887, A Ramble in British Columbia. With Maps and 75 Illustrations. 3s. 6d.

Levett-Yeats' (S.) The Chevalier D'Auriac. 3s. 6d.

Macaulay's (Lord) Complete Works. 'Albany' Edition. With 12 Portraits. 12 vols. 3s. 6d. each.

Macaulay's (Lord) Essays and Lays of Ancient Rome, etc. With Portrait and 4 Illustrations to the 'Lays'. 3s. 6d.

Macleod's (H. D.) Elements of Banking. 3s. 6d.

Marbot's (Baron de) Memoirs. Translated. 2 vols. 7s.

Marshman's (J. C.) Memoirs of Sir Henry Havelock. 3s. 6d.

Merivale's (Dean) History of the Romans under the Empire. 8 vols. 3s. 6d. each.

Merriman's (H. S.) Flotsam: A Tale of the Indian Mutiny. 3s. 6d.

Mill's (J. S.) Political Economy. 3s. 6d.

Mill's (J. S.) System of Logic. 3s. 6d.

Milner's (Geo.) Country Pleasures: the Chronicle of a Year chiefly in a Garden. 3s. 6d.

Nansen's (F.) The First Crossing of Greenland. With 142 Illustrations and a Map. 3s. 6d.

Phillipps-Wolley's (C.) Snap: a Legend of the Lone Mountain With 13 Illustrations. 3s. 6d.

Proctor's (R. A.) The Orbs Around Us. 3s. 6d.

Proctor's (R. A.) The Expanse of Heaven. 3s. 6d.

Proctor's (R. A.) Light Science for Leisure Hours. First Series. 3s. 6d.

Proctor's (R. A.) The Moon. 3s. 6d.

Proctor's (R. A.) Other Worlds than Ours. 3s. 6d.

Proctor's (R. A.) Our Place among Infinities: a Series of Essays contrasting our Little Abode in Space and Time with the Infinities around us. 3s. 6d.

Proctor's (R. A.) Other Suns than Ours. 3s. 6d.

Proctor's (R. A.) Rough Ways made Smooth. 3s. 6d.

Proctor's (R. A.) Pleasant Ways in Science. 3s. 6d.

Proctor's (R. A.) Myths and Marvels of Astronomy. 3s. 6d.

Proctor's (R. A.) Nature Studies. 3s. 6d.

Proctor's (R. A.) Leisure Readings. By R. A. Proctor, Edward Clodd, Andrew Wilson, Thomas Foster, and A. C. Ranyard. With Illustrations. 3s. 6d.

Rossetti's (Maria F.) A Shadow of Dante. 3s. 6d.

Smith's (R. Bosworth) Carthage and the Carthaginians. With Maps, Plans, etc. 3s. 6d.

Stanley's (Bishop) Familiar History of Birds. With 160 Illustrations. 3s. 6d.

Stephen's (L.) The Playground of Europe (The Alps). With 4 Illustrations. 3s. 6d.

Stevenson's (R. L.) The Strange Case of Dr. Jekyll and Mr. Hyde; with other Fables. 3s. 6d.

Stevenson (R. L.) and Osbourne's (Ll.) The Wrong Box. 3s. 6d.

Stevenson (Robert Louis) and Stevenson's (Fanny van de Grift) More New Arabian Nights.—The Dynamiter. 3s. 6d.

Trevelyan's (Sir G. O.) The Early History of Charles James Fox. 3s. 6d.

Weyman's (Stanley J.) The House of the Wolf: a Romance. 3s. 6d.

Wood's (Rev. J. G.) Petland Revisited. With 33 Illustrations. 3s. 6d.

Wood's (Rev. J. G.) Strange Dwellings. With 60 Illustrations. 3s. 6d.

Wood's (Rev. J. G.) Out of Doors. With 11 Illustrations. 3s. 6d.

Cookery, Domestic Management, &c.

Acton. — *Modern Cookery.* By Eliza Acton. With 150 Woodcuts. Fcp. 8vo., 4s. 6d.

Ashby.—*Health in the Nursery.* By Henry Ashby, M.D., F.R.C.P., Physician to the Manchester Children's Hospital, and Lecturer on the Diseases of Children at the Owens College. With 25 Illustrations. Crown 8vo., 3s. 6d.

Buckton.—*Comfort and Cleanliness:* The Servant and Mistress Question. By Mrs. Catherine M. Buckton. With 14 Illustrations. Crown 8vo., 2s.

Bull (Thomas, M.D.).

Hints to Mothers on the Management of their Health during the Period of Pregnancy. Fcp. 8vo., 1s. 6d.

The Maternal Management of Children in Health and Disease. Fcp. 8vo., 1s. 6d.

De Salis (Mrs.).

Cakes and Confections à la Mode. Fcp. 8vo., 1s. 6d.

De Salis (Mrs.).—*continued.*

Dogs: A Manual for Amateurs. Fcp. 8vo., 1s. 6d.

Dressed Game and Poultry à la Mode. Fcp. 8vo., 1s. 6d.

Dressed Vegetables à la Mode. Fcp. 8vo., 1s 6d.

Drinks à la Mode. Fcp. 8vo., 1s. 6d.

Entrées à la Mode. Fcp. 8vo., 1s. 6d.

Floral Decorations. Fcp. 8vo., 1s. 6d.

Gardening à la Mode. Fcp. 8vo. Part I., Vegetables, 1s. 6d. Part II., Fruits, 1s. 6d.

National Viands à la Mode. Fcp. 8vo., 1s. 6d.

New-laid Eggs. Fcp. 8vo., 1s. 6d.

Oysters à la Mode. Fcp. 8vo., 1s. 6d.

Soups and Dressed Fish à la Mode. Fcp. 8vo., 1s. 6d.

Cookery, Domestic Management, &c.—*continued.*

De Salis (MRS.)—*continued.*

SAVOURIES À LA MODE. Fcp. 8vo., 1s. 6d.

PUDDINGS AND PASTRY À LA MODE. Fcp. 8vo., 1s. 6d.

SWEETS AND SUPPER DISHES À LA MODE. Fcp. 8vo., 1s. 6d.

TEMPTING DISHES FOR SMALL INCOMES. Fcp. 8vo., 1s. 6d.

WRINKLES AND NOTIONS FOR EVERY HOUSEHOLD. Crown 8vo., 1s. 6d.

Lear.—MAIGRE COOKERY. By H. L. SIDNEY LEAR. 16mo., 2s.

Mann.—MANUAL OF THE PRINCIPLES OF PRACTICAL COOKERY. By E. E. MANN. Crown 8vo. 1s.

Poole.—COOKERY FOR THE DIABETIC. By W. H. and Mrs. POOLE. With Preface by Dr. PAVY. Fcp. 8vo., 2s. 6d.

Walker (JANE H.).

A BOOK FOR EVERY WOMAN. Part I., The Management of Children in Health and out of Health. Crown 8vo., 2s. 6d.

Part II. Woman in Health and out of Health. Crown 8vo., 2s. 6d.

A HANDBOOK FOR MOTHERS : being Simple Hints to Women on the Management of their Health during Pregnancy and Confinement, together with Plain Directions as to the Care of Infants. Crown 8vo., 2s. 6d.

Miscellaneous and Critical Works.

Armstrong.—ESSAYS AND SKETCHES. By EDMUND J. ARMSTRONG. Fcp. 8vo., 5s.

Bagehot.—LITERARY STUDIES. By WALTER BAGEHOT. With Portrait. 3 vols. Crown 8vo., 3s. 6d. each.

Baring-Gould.— CURIOUS MYTHS OF THE MIDDLE AGES. By Rev. S. BARING-GOULD. Crown 8vo., 3s. 6d.

Baynes. — SHAKESPEARE STUDIES, and other Essays. By the late THOMAS SPENCER BAYNES, LL.B., LL.D. With a Biographical Preface by Professor LEWIS CAMPBELL. Crown 8vo., 7s. 6d.

Boyd (A. K. H.) ('A.K.H.B.').

And see MISCELLANEOUS THEOLOGICAL WORKS, p. 32.

AUTUMN HOLIDAYS OF A COUNTRY PARSON. Crown 8vo., 3s. 6d.

COMMONPLACE PHILOSOPHER. Cr. 8vo., 3s. 6d.

CRITICAL ESSAYS OF A COUNTRY PARSON. Crown 8vo., 3s. 6d.

EAST COAST DAYS AND MEMORIES. Crown 8vo., 3s. 6d.

LANDSCAPES, CHURCHES, AND MORALITIES. Crown 8vo., 3s. 6d.

LEISURE HOURS IN TOWN. Crown 8vo., 3s. 6d.

LESSONS OF MIDDLE AGE. Crown 8vo., 3s. 6d.

OUR LITTLE LIFE. Two Series. Crown 8vo., 3s. 6d. each.

OUR HOMELY COMEDY : AND TRAGEDY. Crown 8vo., 3s. 6d.

RECREATIONS OF A COUNTRY PARSON. Three Series. Crown 8vo., 3s. 6d. each.

Butler (SAMUEL).

EREWHON. Crown 8vo., 5s.

THE FAIR HAVEN. A Work in Defence of the Miraculous Element in our Lord's Ministry. Cr. 8vo., 7s. 6d.

LIFE AND HABIT. An Essay after a Completer View of Evolution. Cr. 8vo., 7s. 6d.

EVOLUTION, OLD AND NEW. Cr. 8vo., 10s. 6d.

ALPS AND SANCTUARIES OF PIEDMONT AND CANTON TICINO. Illustrated. Pott 4to., 10s. 6d.

LUCK, OR CUNNING, AS THE MAIN MEANS OF ORGANIC MODIFICATION ? Cr. 8vo., 7s. 6d.

EX VOTO. An Account of the Sacro Monte or New Jerusalem at Varallo-Sesia. Crown 8vo. 10s. 6d.

SELECTIONS FROM WORKS, with Remarks on Mr. G. J. Romanes' 'Mental Evolution in Animals,' and a Psalm of Montreal. Crown 8vo., 7s. 6d.

THE AUTHORESS OF THE ODYSSEY, WHERE AND WHEN SHE WROTE, WHO SHE WAS, THE USE SHE MADE OF THE ILIAD, AND HOW THE POEM GREW UNDER HER HANDS. With 14 Illustrations. 8vo., 10s. 6d.

THE ILIAD OF HOMER. Rendered into English Prose for the use of those who cannot read the original. Crown 8vo., 7s. 6d.

SHAKESPEARE'S SONNETS. Reconsidered, and in part Rearranged, with Introductory Chapters and a Reprint of the Original 1609 Edition. 8vo.

Miscellaneous and Critical Works—*continued.*

Calder.—*ACCIDENT IN FACTORIES :* its Distribution, Causation, Compensation, and Prevention. A Practical Guide to the Law and to the Safe-Guarding, Safe-Working, and Safe-Construction of Factory Machinery, Plant, and Premises. With 20 Tables and 124 Illustrations. By JOHN CALDER.

CHARITIES REGISTER, THE ANNUAL, AND DIGEST: being a Classified Register of Charities in or available in the Metropolis. With an Introduction by C. S. LOCH, Secretary to the Council of the Charity Organisation Society, London. 8vo., 4s.

Comparetti. — *THE TRADITIONAL POETRY OF THE FINNS.* By DOMENICO COMPARETTI. Translated by ISABELLA M. ANDERTON. With Introduction by ANDREW LANG. 8vo., 16s.

Evans.—*THE ANCIENT STONE IMPLEMENTS, WEAPONS AND ORNAMENTS OF GREAT BRITAIN.* By Sir JOHN EVANS, K.C.B., D.C.L., LL.D., F.R.S., etc. With 537 Illustrations. Medium 8vo., 28s.

Haggard. — *A FARMER'S YEAR:* being 'his Commonplace Book for 1898'. By H. RIDER HAGGARD. With 36 Illustrations by G. LEON LITTLE. Crown 8vo., 7s. 6d. net.

Hamlin.—*A TEXT-BOOK OF THE HISTORY OF ARCHITECTURE.* By A. D. F. HAMLIN, A.M. With 229 Illustrations. Crown 8vo., 7s. 6d.

Haweis.—*MUSIC AND MORALS.* By the Rev. H. R. HAWEIS. With Portrait of the Author, and numerous Illustrations, Facsimiles, and Diagrams. Cr. 8vo., 7s. 6d.

Hodgson.—*OUTCAST ESSAYS AND VERSE TRANSLATIONS.* By SHADWORTH H. HODGSON, LL.D. Crown 8vo., 8s. 6d.

Hoenig. — *INQUIRIES CONCERNING THE TACTICS OF THE FUTURE.* Fourth Edition, 1894, of the 'Two Brigades'. By FRITZ HOENIG. With 1 Sketch in the Text and 5 Maps. Translated by Captain H. M. BOWER. 8vo., 15s. net.

Hullah.—*THE HISTORY OF MODERN MUSIC.* By JOHN HULLAH. 8vo., 8s. 6d.

Jefferies (RICHARD).
FIELD AND HEDGEROW: With Portrait. Crown 8vo., 3s. 6d.
THE STORY OF MY HEART: my Autobiography. With Portrait and New Preface by C. J. LONGMAN. Cr. 8vo., 3s. 6d.

Jefferies (RICHARD)—*continued.*
RED DEER. With 17 Illustrations. Crown 8vo., 3s. 6d.
THE TOILERS OF THE FIELD. With Portrait from the Bust in Salisbury Cathedral. Crown 8vo., 3s. 6d.
WOOD MAGIC : a Fable. With Frontispiece and Vignette by E. V. B. Crown 8vo., 3s. 6d.

Jekyll.—*WOOD AND GARDEN:* Notes and Thoughts, Practical and Critical, of a Working Amateur. By GERTRUDE JEKYLL. With 71 Illustrations from Photographs by the Author. 8vo., 10s. 6d. net.

Johnson.—*THE PATENTEE'S MANUAL:* a Treatise on the Law and Practice of Letters Patent. By J. & J. H. JOHNSON, Patent Agents, etc. 8vo., 10s. 6d.

Joyce.—*THE ORIGIN AND HISTORY OF IRISH NAMES OF PLACES.* By P. W. JOYCE, LL.D. 2 vols. Crown 8vo., 5s. each.

Kingsley.—*A HISTORY OF FRENCH ART,* 1100-1899. By ROSE G. KINGSLEY. 8vo., 12s. 6d. net.

Lang (ANDREW).
LETTERS TO DEAD AUTHORS. Fcp. 8vo., 2s. 6d. net.
BOOKS AND BOOKMEN. With 2 Coloured Plates and 17 Illustrations. Fcp. 8vo., 2s. 6d. net.
OLD FRIENDS. Fcp. 8vo., 2s. 6d. net.
LETTERS ON LITERATURE. Fcp. 8vo., 2s. 6d. net.
ESSAYS IN LITTLE. With Portrait of the Author. Crown 8vo., 2s. 6d.
COCK LANE AND COMMON-SENSE. Crown 8vo., 3s. 6d.
THE BOOK OF DREAMS AND GHOSTS. Crown 8vo., 3s. 6d.

Macfarren. — *LECTURES ON HARMONY.* By Sir GEORGE A. MACFARREN. 8vo., 12s.

Marquand and Frothingham.—*A TEXT-BOOK OF THE HISTORY OF SCULPTURE.* By ALLAN MARQUAND, Ph.D., and ARTHUR L. FROTHINGHAM, Junr., Ph.D., Professors of Archæology and the History of Art in Princetown University. With 113 Illustrations. Crown 8vo., 6s.

Miscellaneous and Critical Works—*continued*.

Max Müller (The Right Hon. F.).

INDIA: WHAT CAN IT TEACH US? Crown 8vo., 5s.

CHIPS FROM A GERMAN WORKSHOP.
Vol. I. Recent Essays and Addresses. Crown 8vo., 5s.
Vol. II. Biographical Essays. Crown 8vo., 5s.
Vol. III. Essays on Language and Literature. Crown 8vo., 5s.
Vol. IV. Essays on Mythology and Folk Lore. Crown 8vo., 5s.

CONTRIBUTIONS TO THE SCIENCE OF MYTHOLOGY. 2 vols. 8vo., 32s.

Milner.—*COUNTRY PLEASURES:* the Chronicle of a Year chiefly in a Garden. By GEORGE MILNER. Crown 8vo., 3s. 6d.

Morris (WILLIAM).

SIGNS OF CHANGE. Seven Lectures delivered on various Occasions. Post 8vo., 4s. 6d.

HOPES AND FEARS FOR ART. Five Lectures delivered in Birmingham, London, etc., in 1878-1881. Cr 8vo., 4s. 6d.

AN ADDRESS DELIVERED AT THE DISTRIBUTION OF PRIZES TO STUDENTS OF THE BIRMINGHAM MUNICIPAL SCHOOL OF ART ON 21ST FEBRUARY, 1894. 8vo., 2s. 6d. net.

ART AND THE BEAUTY OF THE EARTH: a Lecture delivered at Burslem Town Hall, on October 13, 1881. 8vo., 2s. 6d. net.

SOME HINTS ON PATTERN-DESIGNING: a Lecture delivered at the Working Men's College, London, on 10th December, 1881. 8vo., 2s. 6d. net.

ARTS AND CRAFTS ESSAYS. By Members of the Arts and Crafts Exhibition Society. With a Preface by WILLIAM MORRIS. Crown 8vo., 2s. 6d. net.

Pollock.—*JANE AUSTEN:* her Contemporaries and Herself. An Essay in Criticism. By WALTER HERRIES POLLOCK. Crown 8vo.

Poore (GEORGE VIVIAN), M.D., F.R.C.P.

ESSAYS ON RURAL HYGIENE. With 13 Illustrations. Crown 8vo., 6s. 6d.

THE DWELLING HOUSE. With 36 Illustrations. Crown 8vo., 3s. 6d.

Richmond.—*BOYHOOD:* a Plea for Continuity in Education. By ENNIS RICHMOND. Crown 8vo., 2s. 6d.

Richter.—*LECTURES ON THE NATIONAL GALLERY.* By J. P. RICHTER. With 20 Plates and 7 Illustrations in the Text. Crown 4to., 9s.

Rossetti.—*A SHADOW OF DANTE:* being an Essay towards studying Himself, his World and his Pilgrimage. By MARIA FRANCESCA ROSSETTI. With Frontispiece by DANTE GABRIEL ROSSETTI. Crown 8vo., 3s. 6d.

Shadwell.—*THE LONDON WATER SUPPLY.* By ARTHUR SHADWELL, M.B. Oxon., Member of the Royal College of Physicians. Crown 8vo., 5s.

Soulsby (LUCY H. M.).

STRAY THOUGHTS ON READING. Small 8vo., 2s. 6d. net.

STRAY THOUGHTS FOR GIRLS. 16mo., 1s. 6d. net.

STRAY THOUGHTS FOR MOTHERS AND TEACHERS. Fcp. 8vo., 2s. 6d. net.

STRAY THOUGHTS FOR INVALIDS. 16mo., 2s. net.

Southey.—*THE CORRESPONDENCE OF ROBERT SOUTHEY WITH CAROLINE BOWLES.* Edited, with an Introduction, by EDWARD DOWDEN, LL.D. 8vo., 14s.

Stevens.—*ON THE STOWAGE OF SHIPS AND THEIR CARGOES.* With Information regarding Freights, Charter-Parties, etc. By ROBERT WHITE STEVENS, Associate-Member of the Institute of Naval Architects. 8vo., 21s.

Turner and Sutherland.—*THE DEVELOPMENT OF AUSTRALIAN LITERATURE.* By HENRY GYLES TURNER and ALEXANDER SUTHERLAND. With Portraits and Illustrations. Crown 8vo., 5s.

Van Dyke.—*A TEXT-BOOK ON THE HISTORY OF PAINTING.* By JOHN C. VAN DYKE, Professor of the History of Art in Rutgers College. U.S. With 110 Illustrations. Crown 8vo, 6s.

Warwick.—*PROGRESS IN WOMEN'S EDUCATION IN THE BRITISH EMPIRE:* being the Report of Conferences and a Congress held in connection with the Educational Section, Victorian Era Exhibition. Edited by the COUNTESS OF WARWICK. Cr. 8vo. 6s.

White.—*AN EXAMINATION OF THE CHARGE OF APOSTASY AGAINST WORDSWORTH.* By W. HALE WHITE, Editor of the 'Description of the Wordsworth and Coleridge MSS. in the Possession of Mr. T. Norton Longman'. Crown 8vo., 3s. 6d.

Willard.—*HISTORY OF MODERN ITALIAN ART.* By ASHTON ROLLINS WILLARD. With Photogravure Frontispiece and 28 Full-page Illustrations. 8vo., 18s. net.

Miscellaneous Theological Works.

. *For Church of England and Roman Catholic Works see* MESSRS. LONGMANS & Co.'s *Special Catalogues.*

Balfour. — *THE FOUNDATIONS OF RELIEF:* being Notes Introductory to the Study of Theology. By the Right Hon. ARTHUR J. BALFOUR, M.P. 8vo., 12s. 6d.

Boyd (A. K. H.) ('A.K.H.B.').

COUNSEL AND COMFORT FROM A CITY PULPIT. Crown 8vo., 3s. 6d.

SUNDAY AFTERNOONS IN THE PARISH CHURCH OF A SCOTTISH UNIVERSITY CITY. Crown 8vo., 3s. 6d.

CHANGED ASPECTS OF UNCHANGED TRUTHS. Crown 8vo., 3s. 6d.

GRAVER THOUGHTS OF A COUNTRY PARSON. Three Series. Crown 8vo., 3s. 6d. each.

PRESENT DAY THOUGHTS. Crown 8vo., 3s. 6d.

SEASIDE MUSINGS. Cr. 8vo., 3s. 6d.

'*TO MEET THE DAY*' through the Christian Year: being a Text of Scripture, with an Original Meditation and a Short Selection in Verse for Every Day. Crown 8vo., 4s. 6d.

Campbell. — *RELIGION IN GREEK LITERATURE.* By the Rev. LEWIS CAMPBELL, M.A., LL.D., Emeritus Professor of Greek, University of St. Andrews. 8vo., 15s.

Davidson. — *THEISM,* as Grounded in Human Nature, Historically and Critically Handled. Being the Burnett Lectures for 1892 and 1893, delivered at Aberdeen. By W. L. DAVIDSON, M.A., LL.D. 8vo., 15s.

Gibson. — *THE ABBÉ DE LAMENNAIS. AND THE LIBERAL CATHOLIC MOVEMENT IN FRANCE.* By the Hon. W. GIBSON. With Portrait. 8vo., 12s. 6d.

Lang (ANDREW).

THE MAKING OF RELIGION. 8vo., 12s.

MODERN MYTHOLOGY: a Reply to Professor Max Müller. 8vo., 9s.

MacDonald (GEORGE).

UNSPOKEN SERMONS. Three Series. Crown 8vo., 3s. 6d. each.

THE MIRACLES OF OUR LORD. Crown 8vo., 3s. 6d.
5000/10/99.

Martineau (JAMES).

HOURS OF THOUGHT ON SACRED THINGS: Sermons, 2 vols. Crown 8vo., 3s. 6d. each.

ENDEAVOURS AFTER THE CHRISTIAN LIFE. Discourses. Crown 8vo., 7s. 6d.

THE SEAT OF AUTHORITY IN RELIGION. 8vo., 14s.

ESSAYS, REVIEWS, AND ADDRESSES. 4 Vols. Crown 8vo., 7s. 6d. each.

HOME PRAYERS, with *TWO SERVICES* for Public Worship. Crown 8vo., 3s. 6d.

Max Müller (F.).

THE SIX SYSTEMS OF INDIAN PHILOSOPHY. 8vo., 18s.

CONTRIBUTIONS TO THE SCIENCE OF MYTHOLOGY. 2 vols. 8vo., 32s.

THE ORIGIN AND GROWTH OF RELIGION, as illustrated by the Religions of India. The Hibbert Lectures, delivered at the Chapter House, Westminster Abbey, in 1878. Crown 8vo., 5s.

INTRODUCTION TO THE SCIENCE OF RELIGION: Four Lectures delivered at the Royal Institution. Crown 8vo., 5s.

NATURAL RELIGION. The Gifford Lectures, delivered before the University of Glasgow in 1888. Crown 8vo., 5s.

PHYSICAL RELIGION. The Gifford Lectures, delivered before the University of Glasgow in 1890. Crown 8vo., 5s.

ANTHROPOLOGICAL RELIGION. The Gifford Lectures, delivered before the University of Glasgow in 1891. Cr. 8vo., 5s.

THEOSOPHY, OR PSYCHOLOGICAL RELIGION. The Gifford Lectures, delivered before the University of Glasgow in 1892. Crown 8vo., 5s.

THREE LECTURES ON THE VEDÂNTA PHILOSOPHY, delivered at the Royal Institution in March, 1894. 8vo., 5s.

RAMAKRISHNA: HIS LIFE AND SAYINGS. Crown 8vo., 5s.

Romanes. — *THOUGHTS ON RELIGION.* By GEORGE J. ROMANES, LL.D., F.R.S. Crown 8vo., 4s. 6d.

Vivekananda. — *YOGA PHILOSOPHY:* Lectures delivered in New York, Winter of 1895-96, by the SWAMI VIVEKANANDA, on Raja Yoga ; or, Conquering the Internal Nature ; also Patanjali's Yoga Aphorisms, with Commentaries. Crown 8vo., 3s. 6d.

Williamson. — *THE GREAT LAW:* A Study of Religious Origins and of the Unity underlying them. By WILLIAM WILLIAMSON. 8vo., 14s.